LOW PROFILE

Recent Titles by Nick Oldham from Severn House

BACKLASH
SUBSTANTIAL THREAT
DEAD HEAT
BIG CITY JACKS
PSYCHO ALLEY
CRITICAL THREAT
CRUNCH TIME
THE NOTHING JOB
SEIZURE
HIDDEN WITNESS
FACING JUSTICE
INSTINCT
FIGHTING FOR THE DEAD
BAD TIDINGS
JUDGEMENT CALL
LOW PROFILE

LOW PROFILE

A Detective Superintendent Henry Christie Novel

Nick Oldham

This first world edition published 2014
in Great Britain and the USA by
SEVERN HOUSE PUBLISHERS LTD of
19 Cedar Road, Sutton, Surrey, England, SM2 5DA.

British Library Cataloguing in Publication Data

Oldham, Nick, 1956- author.
  Low profile. – (A Henry Christie novel)
  1. Christie, Henry (Fictitious character)–Fiction.
  2. Murder–Investigation–Fiction. 3. Police–England–
  Blackpool–Fiction. 4. Detective and mystery stories.
  I. Title II. Series
  823.9'2-dc23

ISBN-13: 978-07278-8390-2 (cased)

All Severn House titles are printed on acid-free paper.

Severn House Publishers support the Forest Stewardship Council™ [FSC™],
the leading international forest certification organisation. All our titles that
are printed on FSC certified paper carry the FSC logo.

Typeset by Palimpsest Book Production Ltd.,
Falkirk, Stirlingshire, Scotland.
Printed and bound in Great Britain by
TJ International, Padstow, Cornwall.

This one is for Philip Joseph Oldham

ONE

Hawke smiled warmly at the woman.

She returned the smile hesitantly and he could see from the look in her eyes that it was slowly dawning on her he might not be the person he claimed to be. But he kept his smile warm and genuine and said, 'Yes, please, I'd love a cup of tea. I'll bet you have Earl Grey, don't you?'

She nodded.

'Just a drop of milk, though,' he said, touching his thumb and forefinger together to emphasize the tiny amount required.

'OK.' She stood up and crossed to the door of the living room, glancing his way.

He watched her, still smiling. He knew he would have to follow her into the kitchen to stop her making the call. But he didn't rise or give any indication of his intent because he wanted her to go through the motions of putting the kettle on, setting up the tea pot and cups – and then picking up the phone.

Because that moment was one of the pleasures of Hawke's work. The moment they picked up the phone to make *the call* and he would appear silently by their shoulder to reach out and peel the phone gently from their grasp whilst they were halfway through dialling the number which, if they had connected, would only have served to confirm what they had begun to suspect: that Hawke was not here for a legitimate reason.

As she closed the door, Hawke's smile dropped instantly from his face and was replaced by a happy smirk. This was exactly the kind of killing he revelled in.

One of those that built up nicely, stage by stage. A continuum of terror. First, as the witness slowly began to realize things were not just quite right. That the person who had entered their home – with their permission, it had to be said – started to make them feel uncomfortable, then agitated, then angry, then afraid and then terrified.

And then, of course, helpless. The circle would be complete when they also realized they had been promoted from witness to victim.

It could be a long-drawn-out process.

And Hawke loved it. The unfolding drama. The tension. Much more fun than the straightforward executions that were his bread and butter, the gun-to-the-back-of-the-head ones which were over as soon as they had begun. They required little finesse and made him a lot of easy money.

If he had been honest with himself he could have made this killing just like that, but he had opted for the change in MO because the female had answered the door, not his actual target. He had seen the possibility of some fun and switched instantly into ad lib mode.

He could simply have blown the back of her head off using the soft-nosed .38 rounds loaded into his silenced four-inch-barrelled Smith & Wesson Model Ten revolver, with the stubby, bulbous silencer, his rather staid and old-fashioned, but extremely reliable, weapon of choice. Her face would have imploded like a pillow being punched and her skull exploded with the exit of the bullet. She would have been driven backwards down the hallway, most of her brains splattering the wall. He could simply have stepped over her twitching body, dragged her further in, closed the door and waited for the real target to arrive home.

But . . . wouldn't have been an awful lot of pleasure in that.

She was a nice, pretty woman, and it would have been criminal not to have at least some fun with her. Get to know her a little, let her get to know him. Have some connection . . . maybe even flirt a little.

So, on the pretence of being a business partner-to-be of the target and claiming he had a prearranged appointment with him – which did make her frown slightly – he was glib enough to get her to invite him into the house. The presence of the sleek Porsche 911 parked alongside her nippy little Fiat 500 in the driveway helped to smooth matters.

Hawke stood up.

One problem with spending this quality time with an additional victim was, of course, the possibility of leaving a trail of evidence behind him. Fingerprints, DNA, fibres, that sort of thing.

In the leather briefcase he carried – another little bit of fine detail that had helped convince the woman of his genuineness – he had a tightly folded white paper suit which he unravelled and stepped into, then pulled a pair of elasticated slippers over his shoes after which he fitted a hair net – a touch he particularly liked. The billowing paper suit and silly footwear made him look ridiculous enough, but the hair net took the comedic look to a completely new level. At least that was what Hawke thought. It made him almost clown-like, and he certainly appreciated the terror that clowns could induce. If he killed with a machete, the picture would have been complete, like something out of a slasher movie, but he had no wish to hack someone to death, mainly because of the forensic implications of massive blood splatter, which was impossible to control. He knew this because he had once hacked someone to pieces, got blood everywhere. He liked a bit of splatter but not too much.

Next he fitted his latex gloves, snapping them on to his hands like a surgeon.

There was a mirror over the fireplace in which he checked his appearance. He pulled the hood of his paper suit over his head and drew the drawstring tight so that only the basic features of his face could be seen, a circle around his eyes, nose and mouth. Satisfied, he picked the revolver out of his case and walked to the living room door, stepping silently into the hallway, sliding slowly along the parquet flooring like an ice skater, until he was at the kitchen door. He paused, his head cocked to one side, then sidled into the kitchen.

As ever he was right. Two cups by the kettle, a tea pot, the kettle actually burbling away and the woman – he had learned she was called Charlotte, but her friends called her Lottie – standing with her back to him, a mobile phone in her hands, thumbs desperately working the keypad, her concentration absolute.

Making the call.

She had no inkling he was right behind her. Right up to the moment his left hand snaked over her shoulder and slipped the phone from her grip and he said, 'I'll take that please, Lottie,' in a quiet, gentle way.

She contorted away from him, gasping as she took in the vision he had become.

Hawke was still smiling, even though his features were drawn tight by the hood, and outwardly calm, although underneath he was now excited, blood pulsing through his veins, his breathing a little short.

'Shh.' He held his fingertip to his lips.

'What do you want?'

He paused before replying. 'I want you to stay in control of yourself, Lottie,' he said. 'You're not the one I'm interested in, so what we have to do is settle down and wait awhile . . . and maybe I could trouble you for that cup of tea, yeah?'

'You shouldn't be calling me,' she whispered hoarsely into her mobile phone.

'But I need help.'

'What sort of help?' Lisa Christie stepped out on to the balcony of the apartment in Costa Teguise, slid the door closed behind her. 'You know you can't phone me, we're over, finished. I'm getting my life together – properly.'

'I know all that.' The anxiety was audible in the man's voice.

Lisa walked to the balcony rail and looked across the multi-form swimming pool in the centre of the apartment complex. 'I'm not here for you now, you know that.'

'Yes, yes, I know . . . but . . .'

'Well? Why are you phoning?' she demanded.

'I've done something really, really stupid.'

Lisa waited impatiently. She was dressed and changed, ready to go out for the evening, just waiting for her fiancé, Rik Dean, to finish his ablutions and come out smelling of Kouros. She took a sip from the glass of white, chilled wine.

'That doesn't sound like you,' she said, trying to urge him on and get the phone call over with.

And it didn't – it sounded more like her. She was the rash, reckless one, the one who followed her heart, not her head. It certainly did not sound anything like Percy Astley-Barnes, the man she had been seriously involved with for a short period of time the year before. That was until she realized that what she really needed in her life was Rik, the man she had treated so abominably and who had so generously accepted her back into his life when he could so easily have shoved a hand in her face and told her to get lost.

Percy had taken the split in his stride, accepting gracefully that he wasn't the man for Lisa Christie. That didn't mean he wasn't besotted by her, though.

'I made an error of judgement.'

Lisa frowned, trying to work out what she could hear in his voice. Fear?

'And how can I possibly help?' She glanced back through the window into the apartment. Rik was still in the bathroom.

'I don't know,' Percy admitted with a sob.

'Jeez, Percy,' Lisa said, taken aback. If there was one thing Percy didn't do, that was cry. He was a decent, caring man but also a hard-headed businessman and not someone who showed his inner emotions. To hear him sob jarred her.

'I'm in big trouble.'

'What kind of trouble?'

'Criminal trouble.'

Lisa had turned outwards to face the pool again, but spun quickly, guiltily, when the balcony door slid back and the freshly washed, manicured and he-man smelling Rik Dean stepped out with a chilled bottle of San Miguel in his hand. She gave him a helpless look.

'What kind of criminal trouble?' Lisa asked and shrugged at Rik, who scowled and mouthed silently, *Who is it?*

'I can't tell you over the phone,' Percy said.

'You can't tell me face to face, either.'

'Why? I need to see you. You're the only person I can think of.'

'First, I'm with Rik, and your problems are yours now; second – are you in Lanzarote by any chance?'

'Uh – no.'

'Well I am.'

'Shit, *shit.*'

Lisa squinted painfully at Rik and shrugged again, feeling trapped and definitely not wanting to take a phone call from an ex-lover in the presence of her current lover. Rik – who looked like he'd guessed who was on the other end of the link – wasn't likely to be magnanimous about it.

'I thought you could help me,' Percy whispered.

'Me personally?'

'I need some . . . advice . . . no, that's wrong . . . not advice . . .'

'What the hell then?'

'Protection,' he said. 'I've gone and truly fucked up and now I think I'm a dead man.'

The tea was just about perfect. Well, just a little stewed, because the events of the moments after Hawke had taken Lottie's phone had got a little fraught and perhaps the teabag had stood just a little too long in the hot water.

Still, it was pleasant enough, nicely fragrant.

Hawke raised his delicate tea cup to Lottie and took another sip but, thinking ahead, he knew he would have to wash the cup thoroughly because his lips had come into contact with it. Another forensic issue.

He shook his head sadly at her. She had made a sudden dash for the back door, but he had been ready for it, tripped her easily, sweeping her feet from under her, sending her sprawling across the tiled kitchen floor.

It seemed like slow motion to him, a ballet. Placing the gun and phone down on a worktop, then dropping on to her with all his weight above his right knee, driving it hard into her spine at the point halfway between her shoulder blades, knocking every last gasp of breath out of her lungs, then pinning her there whilst, methodically, he eased her arms behind her back and reached for the roll of parcel tape he had brought with him. It was ready prepared to rip off the roll, and in moments she was bound. He flipped her over and stuck another strip across her mouth and then continued to wind tape around her head, then underneath her jaw, ensuring he left a gap below her nostrils. He wanted to keep her alive, not suffocate her, because that was all part of the process.

He had dragged her back into the living room, where he had bound her ankles together before heaving her across the sofa, then going back into the kitchen to retrieve his gun and tea, returning to the lounge and settling himself down.

He was prepared to wait for as long as necessary now.

Her terrified eyes watched him.

'Why's he phoning you?' Rik asked aggressively.

'He said he was in trouble, didn't know who else to call.'

'He's never heard of treble-nine?' Rik's voice rose. 'You know – which service do you require? Or maybe he tried that and asked for "ex-lover, please".'

'Rik! It doesn't sound as simple as phoning the police,' Lisa said.

Rik necked a large swallow of his San Mig, unconvinced.

'Look,' Lisa said softly, 'I made a mistake with what happened, him and me, and we've been through all the sorrys. He's history, darling, I promise you. Now it's just you and me, babe, honestly. This is the first time he's ever called me since we got back together – and that's why I think it's more complicated than him speaking to a nine-nine-nine operator.'

Rik half-burped, banged his chest with his fist and regarded Lisa.

She smiled wanly and cooed, 'Honest, babe, love you.' Then the smile turned wicked. 'Wine and dine me and I'll show you just how much.'

Rik balanced his beer on the balcony rail and turned towards her. A moment later they were in each other's arms, then they staggered back into the apartment where their personal preparation for the night out was smudged and spoiled by lust and bodily fluids.

The lovemaking wasn't a long-drawn-out affair. It was fast, wild and over within minutes when Rik slumped down on to her, snuffling like a truffle pig at her wonderfully smelling, soft neck.

'Did he say what sort of trouble?' he mumbled, now confident his alpha male position had been re-established, although in truth it had never been in doubt.

'No, but he said he was a dead man.' She grabbed Rik's bum with both hands, squeezed, dug her nails in and slammed him into her, forcing a long moan of pleasure from him.

'You know what to do, then,' Rik gasped throatily.

Percy Astley-Barnes sat numbly in the seat of his Aston Martin DB9, his mind blank as he looked at the screen of his iPhone.

'Oh God,' he whispered, closing his eyes, wondering how long it might take to gas himself on the exhaust fumes emitted by the magnificent sports car, if he could find a hose and then attach it to the tail pipe. With the stringent emission regulations now in force, he guessed it would take a long, long time. Not that he even knew where to find a hosepipe, so committing suicide by those means wasn't really an option.

His only remaining option was to flee. Get home – pack – flee.

Detective Superintendent Henry Christie watched the child killer being led away to the cells, then leaned on the custody office desk to combat a wave of exhaustion, combined with nausea, that rolled through him. The exhaustion from the long day of concentrated evidence gathering that Henry had had, followed by a difficult, protracted interview; the nausea from his shoulder in which, not many months before, he had taken a bullet from a deranged criminal he had cornered. The fact that the criminal was a young female did not make the wound any less painful, and though it was technically healed the pain was still there, always pulsing away and occasionally searing through him like ten thousand volts.

He turned to the local detective chief inspector, who was called Woodcock and had been with him throughout the investigation. 'Bloody hell, Henry, you're good,' the DCI complimented him genuinely.

Henry acknowledged the accolade with a modest tilt of his head but admitted, 'He was stuffed whether or not he admitted it. The forensics would have scuppered him.'

'Yeah, but you didn't let it go, and you could've.'

'I never like to chuck away an unopened oyster,' Henry said enigmatically as he signed the custody record, and the DCI chuckled. 'I'll leave it with you from here, Pete,' Henry told him.

Henry strolled out of the custody office into the back yard of Blackpool police station, where he inhaled a long, stuttering breath and massaged his tender shoulder.

It was midnight and Henry needed rest. He had been on the go since six that morning, eighteen hours straight, coffee and fast food his stimulants. His mind was now fuzzy, his body weak. He owned a house on a small estate in the Marton area of Blackpool but now spent most of his time living with his fiancée, Alison, at the Tawny Owl, the pub she owned in Kendleton, a village set far in the northern reaches of the county of Lancashire, at least thirty miles from where he stood. His own house in Blackpool was for sale but it still served as a handy crash-pad for Henry, particularly on days like these.

He really wanted to head up to Kendleton and snuggle up to Alison but wasn't sure he would be able to stop himself from falling asleep at the wheel. Sadly he realized that he would be spending the night alone in a partly furnished house that had once been his marital home, though the memory of that life was slowly starting to diminish. His life had moved on since the tragic death of his wife, Kate, and he knew he had to let go; keep her in a special place in his heart and soul, but wave adios to most of the possessions they once shared. At least the ones that didn't mean anything.

He sighed and shuffled out his mobile phone from his jacket pocket. It had been in silent mode during the interview and the screen showed three missed calls and a text.

One of the calls was from Alison, two from his sister Lisa, and the text was also from Alison. He went to this first, read it with a smile. It was one of those 'Thinking about you, lover' ones. The missed calls from Lisa puzzled him slightly. He knew she was away on holiday with her groom-to-be Rik Dean, who was now a DCI on Lancashire Constabulary's Force Major Investigation Team (FMIT), which Henry headed jointly with two other detective superintendents.

The fact that the pair of them were away was not what puzzled Henry. It was that, over the last few months since their mother had died, Lisa hadn't really spoken to Henry at all. She had been too engrossed in putting her private life with Rik back together after a stupid fling with a local businessman.

But, there and then, after a sixteen hour day, Henry wasn't curious enough to call her back.

His first call, anyway, had to be to Alison. He knew she would still be up in spite of the late hour. Running a country pub with guest rooms meant she was rarely in bed before one a.m. – and usually up again at six. That was a normal day. Her energy levels made Henry's look like he had the genes of a sloth.

Alison answered quickly, knowing it was Henry calling.

'Hello, darling.'

'Hi hon, how's it going?'

'Busy . . . last minute in-rush of locals who then basically refused to leave at closing time – in a nice way – so I smiled a lot, took their money, y'know? And the guest rooms are all fully let tonight, so there'll be a dozen full Englishes to cook tomorrow morning.' Henry smiled as he listened to her voice. 'And how about you?' she asked.

'Oh, y'know . . . nailed a child killer . . . all in a day's work,' he said mock-casually. Then, 'Look, babe . . .'

'You're getting your head down in Blackpool?' she guessed correctly, Henry's tone of voice telegraphing what he was about to say.

'Yeah, sorry. I'll be on this thing again straight away tomorrow.'

'No probs. But if you come back here . . .'

'I know, I know . . . warm bum on offer.'

The call ended after a long-drawn-out lovey-dovey exchange as Henry walked through the dimly lit police car park to his car. As he pointed his remote control lock at his Audi convertible, his mobile rang.

Henry frowned at the phone, considering whether or not to answer it.

Henry knew exactly where Percy Astley-Barnes lived. He knew this because, a couple of years before, Henry had been involved in investigating what is known as a tiger kidnap involving Percy. This is where a criminal gang takes members of a family, or employees of a business, hostage and holds them under threat of death or serious bodily harm whilst another member of the family or head of the business, acting under duress, carries out the instructions of the gang. It was a method the IRA had used on several occasions to acquire funds for their cause.

Henry had become involved with Astley-Barnes when the police received information that a brutal, well-organized gang was going to hold some of the staff who worked in Percy's jewellery shops hostage, whilst Percy himself was going to be forced to act under the gang's instructions.

Fortunately the police lay in wait for the gang and arrested them before they struck. Subsequently they were convicted of virtually all the offences Henry could think of to chuck at them and no staff member, or Percy himself, was ever put in danger. A great result.

Which was why Henry knew where Percy lived.

He had tried to call him, having been given the number by Lisa – who sounded more drunk than concerned – but got no reply. Reluctantly Henry decided to drive out to Percy's house which was on the outskirts of Poulton-le-Fylde, a small, pleasant town about three miles east of Blackpool.

He was only going because Lisa's story sounded slightly odd.

From Henry's interaction with Percy over the tiger kidnap attempt he recalled that, despite his posh sounding double-barrelled name and obvious wealth, Percy came across as a down to earth, level-headed businessman, certainly not prone to making spurious claims about his life being under threat. Unless it was.

Which was why Henry decided to touch base with him.

He drove out of Blackpool, was soon on the road out towards Poulton, until he reached a major junction controlled by a set of traffic lights. By bearing left, he crossed into the very rural Pool Foot Lane where Percy's house was situated in about four acres of high-walled, landscaped gardens sloping all the way down to the banks of the River Wyre. The house was only accessible through remotely controlled security gates operated from the house itself or from Percy's car.

Henry had expected to find the heavy wrought iron gates secured and closed. He stopped on the lane and squinted up through the windscreen of the Audi, seeing they were actually wide open. This, he thought, was unusual. Certainly since the attempted kidnap, and following some very strong crime prevention advice, Percy was now ultra-cautious about security, and leaving the gates yawning wide open was a definite no-no.

He paused for a moment, then drove past the entrance and pulled on to the grass verge. He called Percy's mobile number again. It remained unanswered and clicked on to voicemail, at which point Henry ended the call. He reached over to his glove compartment and found his Maglite torch.

TWO

Hawke placed the silenced muzzle of the .38 gently against Lottie's left temple. Although he had wrapped the parcel tape around her head, leaving only a slit so she could see, he could see the ultimate fear in the eyes and was happy he had reached this end point on his continuum of terror. At least as far as this woman was concerned.

He had thought that at some stage in his life he might try and sell this model – this continuum – to some criminal psychologist. Academics would love it, he believed. Perhaps he himself might become a criminologist in the future, imparting his knowledge from first-hand experience. He'd even thought that he could combine the professions. Remain an executioner and, at the same time, teach. An appealing prospect. That said, he'd probably end up killing his students.

Away from those daydreams, the one thing he felt was important in all this was that when this end point was reached, it should be over quickly. There was no point in dragging it out now. He wasn't that cruel.

Hawke glanced across at the kneeling and bound target who was to witness this, gave him a wink, then pulled the trigger.

The bullet entered her temple, did its damage in a microsecond, then exited, the force of the impact driving the light-framed woman sideways. She died as instantly as it was possible to die, and her blood back-sprayed on to Hawke's paper suit, flecking across him like a modernist painting. He stepped back as though shocked, but laughed as he looked down at himself.

Then, even though he knew she was dead, he made absolutely certain – as a professional killer he always did. He stood astride her like a colossus and fired one more bullet into her already pulped brain.

The target reacted to this horrific scenario, toppling sideways from his kneeling position and, although he too was bound with parcel tape at his wrists and ankles, his head also wrapped in a similar way to Lottie's, he began a desperate wriggle towards the door like a huge python. A terrible but muted sound came from his throat.

Then the killer's feet were in front of him, obstructing his way.

All the target could see from his prone position was the pair of paper shoes and the elasticated hem of the paper suit around Hawke's ankles, and the specks of Lottie's blood on them.

Percy Astley-Barnes stopped moving. He heard the rustle of the paper suit and sensed that the killer had squatted down on his haunches over him.

'You had to see that,' the man's soft voice explained. 'It was necessary for you to see your loved one die so you know just how seriously your threat and your transgression were taken.'

Percy retched with fear and vomited into his mouth, the sickness trapped there, unable to be ejected and finding its only exit up through his nasal passages, out through his nostrils, and flowing backwards down his throat as he desperately swallowed and gagged and choked. Hawke watched from above, a sneer of contempt on his face. Then he realized that his target might actually die from suffocating on his own vomit unless he acted quickly.

That would not do. There was no pleasure in watching such an undignified death, the kind of death an alcoholic might suffer.

Hawke reached down and tore away the strip of tape from Percy's mouth. Percy convulsed and coughed and managed to spit out the chunky sick on to the carpet on which he lay until he reached the point where he was breathing normally again, if raggedly.

'Have I made my point?' Hawke asked.

Percy uttered something completely incomprehensible.

'I'll take that as a yes,' Hawke grinned.

He hauled Percy back on to his knees, steadying and balancing him there. Hawke did not want to shoot Percy whilst his head was on the carpet – at least not the first shot. This was because it was something else Hawke quite liked – the action/reaction of placing a gun against a target's head whilst they were upright, then shooting them. There was, he thought, something almost poetic and balletic in the movement. The tightly squeezed face (why, he thought, did people scrunch up their faces like that? It made not one jot of difference. You could squeeze up, anticipate as much as you wanted, but the result was the same), then the touch of the muzzle to the head, held there for just the tiniest of seconds, then the trigger pull and the discharge, the bullet entering the head, the brains being blown out and the physical reaction of the body.

Pure fucking poetry, he thought.

Over in a jiff, but implanted in his mind for leisurely replay, over and over again.

So, having balanced Percy, Hawke simply did what he was supposed to do – killed him – then stood over the dead body and put another round into him.

Hawke exhaled as he stood in the centre of the living room, pulled off the hood, one dead body either side of him; then he breathed in the reek of blood and cordite in the air as though he was sniffing a flower glade in spring.

He glanced at his handiwork. Job well done, money well earned, he congratulated himself.

Until he suddenly tensed up when he heard the noise.

Henry walked through the open gates and up the fifty metre long driveway, the packed gravel scrunching underneath the soles of his shoes. The house ahead of him, illuminated by discreetly placed ground level lights, was a modernized executive detached property; from the rear Henry knew there were sweeping panoramic views of a wide curve of the River Wyre. He recalled there was even a small jetty where Percy kept a speedboat, though access to the river was dependent on tides.

Three cars were parked on the wide turnaround at the front of the house. He recognized Percy's Aston Martin with the personalized number plates, but not the black Porsche 911 or the brightly coloured Fiat 500. None of the cars seemed to be out of place, just the sort of array Henry would expect to see outside a wealthy person's home in this neck of the woods.

On the face of it, therefore, nothing unusual.

Except for the open gates and the fact that a person who had made a desperate phone call was not now answering his phone.

The instinct acquired over thirty years of being a cop gave Henry a bad feeling about it all. He paused at the back of the Aston Martin, glancing at the registered number, fleetingly thinking about the amount of money the car had cost, plus the number plate. Henry had gone to town with his Audi, but the cost of the Aston dwarfed what Henry had forked out. It took real wealth to run one of these beasts. But these were only passing thoughts, running parallel to everything else going on in his mind.

He walked past the car, placing his hand on the sleek, low bonnet, feeling the heat from the engine, then alongside the Porsche. He flashed his torch beam across its glossy, but slightly ugly and squat, black bodywork. He registered the stick-on sign in the back window indicating the car was actually a rental. He touched the rear bonnet and it was cold, no heat from the rear-engine car.

Then he went past the gaudy Fiat. In a very sexist thought, Henry saw it as a woman's car, and when he saw the pink, dangling, fluffy pair of dice hanging from the rear view mirror, and the eyelashes on the headlights, his stereotype was only reinforced.

He went up the steps to the front door, all frosted glass, which opened into a large vestibule. Henry pushed the door and found it to be open, another little, almost inconsequential factor to add to the growing list of inconsequential factors, which made his nostrils dilate and his senses click up a gear, his tiredness replaced by tension. The front gate open, the front door open, at this time of day.

He swallowed drily, realizing how dehydrated he was from his long day, which had included a lot of coffee but no straight water or juice. And crap food.

He stepped into the intricately tiled vestibule, ten feet to the next, inner door, beyond which was a wide entrance hall, stairs off to the right and access to the reception rooms, dining room and kitchen. He placed his hand on the door knob, turned and pushed it open with a click and a slight creaking sound.

First the noise, then the voice: 'Mr Barnes? Percy? This is the police. Can I come in, please? Mr Barnes, this is the police . . . Detective Superintendent Christie.'

Hawke froze, standing between the bodies of the two people he had just executed. He shot a glance at Percy's body, which gave one last quiver from head to foot. A death jerk.

Hawke's quick calculation: he had fired four of the six rounds in the Smith & Wesson, two remaining in the chamber. He had two speed loaders in the pocket of his paper suit, so twelve more there; he knew he could reload in seconds.

'Mr Barnes,' the cop shouted again. 'I'm concerned about your welfare and I'm entering your house.'

More calculations: one cop? Or many cops?

Either way, Hawke had to find out.

He stepped over Lottie's body and went to the living room door, moving confidently into the hallway, happy that he was ready for whatever was before him.

He almost burst into laughter.

One man, one cop, a dishevelled, tired looking individual, crumpled jacket, trousers and crumpled face to match. The guy looked old, tired and ragged, his skin a weary grey colour, more like he should be in a retirement home than in the cops.

That said, he thought, I probably look more like I should be advertising tyres rather than someone paid to kill people.

Both men straightened up, dramatically tense.

'Drop the gun,' Henry said. 'I'm a police officer.'

Hawke shook his head and gave a short laugh. 'You shouldn't have seen me, you should've arrived five minutes later. I've nothing against cops,' he added in some sort of explanation.

Henry said, 'Put the weapon down.' His voice was calm and authoritative, although inside his heart had instantly started to beat rapidly. His eyes were focused on the gun in the man's hand, not on his face or eyes. He had seen and learned enough in the last ten seconds to know that submission was not on this man's agenda, so why look into his eyes? It was the gun that would be the problem, particularly for a knackered old cop unlucky enough to have stumbled into this scenario on his own. A firearms team might have brokered a different result, maybe. Henry had put everything together now. The forensic suit, the blood splashes on it, meaning the deed had already been done and Henry was too late to save anyone, but just in time to get himself killed. Percy was undoubtedly already dead as, probably, was anyone else in the house, and killing a dumb cop probably wouldn't make too much difference to this man who, by the looks of him, was not the sort of person who got caught.

The revolver came up.

Henry threw himself sideways, whilst in the same movement he launched his Maglite torch as hard as he possibly could at the man, not even sure it would connect. He hit the floor hard and a judder of agony shot through him; he felt the whoosh of the bullet just above his head as the silenced round destroyed a sheet of glass in the door panelling behind him. A second bullet slammed into the wall.

What amazed Henry about the shoulder pain as he hit the floor and rolled was that it was indescribable and almost debilitating, and if he'd had the choice he would have remained where he landed and not moved again until the agony had dissipated.

Unfortunately, being shot at by a gunman didn't give him any time to feel sorry for himself. He had to force himself through it.

He drove himself with an iron will and, ducking behind the staircase where it curved and widened, took the opportunity for one glance.

The gunman had disappeared back into the living room.

Henry did not need any more motivation than that. Holding his shoulder, he sprinted for the door, out through the vestibule on to the front steps, knowing that his only option was to escape and come back with reinforcements, a dead cop being neither use nor ornament to anyone.

He stumbled down the steps on to the gravel, where he lost his footing, tripped and rolled, coming up covered in gravel dust in front of the Fiat. He stayed low, using the cover provided by the cars before veering across the driveway to a row of thick, high rhododendron bushes that lined it. They were taller than him, and dense. He ducked between two, tripping again on a large stone but managing to keep upright, veered right, using the bushes as further cover, and scrambled towards the gates. He did not look back, knowing he had to get off the property and into his car and screech like fuck away.

As he ran he heard a whirring, clanking noise ahead of him – and with dread, realized what this was.

The gates were closing, trapping him in the garden.

Henry crouched low, trying to keep his laboured breathing as silent as possible and at the same time to get a view of the front of Percy's house from behind the bushes. It was still lit by the floodlights angled up from the ground.

Then, with an audible crack of electricity, the exterior lights went out and the house and garden were plunged instantly into almost impenetrable darkness. As there were no street lights on the lane beyond the grounds, there was no ambient lighting other than from the occasional appearance of a bright, virtually full moon from behind clouds scudding across the night sky.

Henry knew what 'lights out' meant.

He had disturbed a killer in the act of murder, a killer who was probably now cursing himself for being so careless as to allow someone else to see his face. And although Henry had only seen it for a very short time, it was imprinted on his mind and he was certain he would be able to ID the man.

Which was bad for Henry.

Because 'gates closed' plus 'lights out' could only mean that a disturbed killer had one more job to do before leaving the scene: hunt down and kill the remaining witness.

It took a few moments for Henry's eyes to adjust to the darkness, but even then it was difficult to see through the gloom, a situation not helped by the fact that in his initial panic to escape he had thrown his torch at the gunman, a reflex action. In retrospect, not a particularly rational act, although if it had hit him it could have been the thing that gave Henry just enough time to dive to one side whilst the man was distracted.

Still, Henry admonished himself, right now, a torch would have been very handy.

He swore, squinting to see, but as the moon went behind a heavy chunk of cloud the blackness was almost total. He fished out his mobile phone and hid the illuminated screen with his hand.

Hawke knew his own carelessness had compromised his task tonight and he had learned a great lesson from this for the future: kill and go. That was his usual MO, it had to be said, but tonight he had fallen into the trap of having too much fun and it had backfired somewhat. Because both his victims had assured him that no one else was expected to arrive at the house, he had allowed himself to dawdle – and, of course, someone had turned up. The Brits called it 'sod's law'.

A fucking cop. One who had ducked and thrown a torch at him that had been better aimed than his own bullets, having struck him right in the centre of his forehead and gouged open his skin in quite a deep, crescent-shaped cut.

A lucky throw which had stunned him temporarily, made him spin back into the living room. It would be the cop's only piece of luck that night.

But by the time he stepped back into the hallway, the cop had gone. Hawke rushed to the front door, saw the man enter the cover of the bushes, obviously heading towards the gates. On the wall by the front door was the control button for them and Hawke slapped his palm down on it and saw them start to close. Then he ducked back into the house, sliding his hand down a rack of light switches just inside the hallway, pitching everything into blackness. He ran through to the living room, wiping his own blood off his forehead with his arm, stepped over Percy's body – no longer twitching – and went to his briefcase, screwed the silencer off the gun for better accuracy and tossed it in the case.

He picked out the other piece of equipment he always carried with him, one of those essential little tools designed to give a killer the edge. He fitted the night vision goggles over his head, clicked them on and adjusted them to fit over his eyes. Suddenly his darkness became green and he could see everything clearly, including the two dead bodies on the floor which still radiated the body heat that the goggles used to work by. He stepped out into the hallway and headed for the front door, out on to the steps.

He was going hunting.

Henry knew he didn't have the physical ability to scale the high walls of the garden or even clamber over the gate. He would probably have impaled himself on the gate's spikes anyway. He also knew that since the kidnap threat the tops of the walls had been threaded with strands of barbed wire, but the cops (that meant Henry) had turned a blind eye to this illegality. This meant Henry was walled in on three sides, and the River Wyre made up the fourth side, a natural barrier that was its own fortification.

He had called nine-nine-nine on his mobile phone and been patched through to a police comms operator at Blackpool. As the connection was being made he moved, still crouching low, to what he thought was better cover behind the trunk of a wide oak tree, whilst still trying to keep an eye on the house.

The depth of the darkness made this difficult and for the first time in his life Henry realized that maybe his eyesight wasn't as sharp as it used to be. In fact, all in all, he was becoming a real old crock.

'Police – how can I help?'

Henry slid down low and quickly explained who and where he was and that he wanted armed patrols to be making their way to Pool Foot Lane urgently . . . but before he had finished the call, he heard the killer call out to him.

'I'll show you mercy if you come out now.'

Henry stopped whispering, ended the call abruptly and shoved his phone back into a pocket to hide the bright screen. He held his breath and hoped they didn't call him back.

'You come out right now; otherwise I'll hunt you down,' the voice threatened.

Henry swallowed but did not move a muscle, knowing he was hidden by the width of the tree.

'Just so you know, I'm wearing night vision goggles, so I will be able to see you.'

Only if you're looking in the right place, Henry thought, because he got the impression that the man's voice was being projected away from where he was hunkered down.

He heard the crunch of a twig in undergrowth some way across to his right, over by the gates. He turned his head slowly, trying to see exactly where the man was. But he could not, although the sound was perhaps only twenty metres away.

If the killer was telling the truth about the goggles it would only be a matter of moments before he turned to face Henry and the heat emanating from his body would be picked up by them. All the man had to do was to move slowly and keep scanning from side to side and he would see Henry sooner rather than later.

Henry prayed he was still looking in the wrong direction.

Another sound, another crack. A little further off, Henry thought.

The man was moving away . . . which didn't really help Henry . . . it just prolonged the agony.

The moon suddenly appeared as the cloud broke, casting a silver light across the trees, and Henry saw the silhouette of the man over by the gates, peering through the bars. He could also make out the shape of the gun dangling in the man's right hand. From its outline, he could see that the silencer had been removed.

Henry looked the other way, towards the river, also lit up by the moon, maybe a hundred metres away, with a boat tied up alongside the small jetty. Percy's speedboat. And it was clear that the river was high and therefore the tide was in.

Henry rose silently into a starting position. He steadied his breathing – again – and counted down from three. On 'one' he sprinted as soundlessly as he could towards the jetty, keeping bent over double, his vision focused, and hoping that the long, wide lawn would not be too slippery because he was wearing totally inappropriate footwear for running, especially across grass. Brown brogues with smooth leather soles were not exactly made for sporting events.

He felt it was going well. Forty metres gone and no sign that the gunman had realized what was going on. The jetty and boat were almost in reach, though he wasn't remotely certain what his plan was when he got there, just had a vague idea that he would leap on to the boat, fire it up and escape in a spectacular churning wake.

The first bullet skimmed by his right ear a microsecond before he heard the crack of the shot and the shockwave burned past his cheek, the knock-on effect being that he slid, tripped and went face down in the manicured grass. Using his momentum he converted this ridiculous fall into a forward roll and emerged still running for his life.

He kept low, zigzagging, hearing the discharge of another bullet but not feeling it either miss him or, more importantly, hit him.

And then he was pounding down the wooden jetty, running alongside the speedboat and leaping into it, causing it to rock precariously on the water. Henry tried to keep his balance, but staggered across the small deck. He tried to stop himself, but completely miscalculated everything and tipped over the rail at the other side, cartwheeling into the icy, murky water of the river, which was ebbing lethargically.

He went under, inhaling a chestful of the gritty, sand-coloured water, floundered and felt his feet touch the river bed, which was soft mud. Using the strength of his arms and upper body, he forced himself back up to the surface, coughing, spluttering and gasping. The water was in his chest, throat and nose. He gagged, sucked in air and then grabbed the rubbing board on the side of the speedboat and, with a gargantuan effort, hauled himself back over the side, dropping breathlessly on the deck, flopping there like a huge starfish.

He cursed, roused himself to move and scrabbled to the mooring

ropes on the port side and yanked them free. Immediately the boat
– like a beast sensing freedom – angled away from the jetty.

Henry glanced back and saw the figure of a man lit by moonlight,
jogging down the sloping lawn, the easy gait of a hunter who knew
his prey was trapped and as good as dead.

Next Henry searched frantically for a starter button or an ignition
key. He had really no idea what he was looking for, but guessed
that steering a boat could not be that much different from driving
a car.

The boat spun lazily in the river.

And the gunman reached the jetty, stopped running and aimed
his gun.

Henry ducked instinctively as the bullet smacked into the side of
the boat. His hands brushed on a plastic case about the size of a
small toolbox.

Another bullet tore into the small boat.

Henry glanced up, saw the man walking with purpose along the
jetty. He looked at the box again, flicked the catches on its side and
flipped up the lid. It contained four flares and a flare gun; Henry
grabbed this and slotted a flare into it.

The boat continued to drift away from the jetty, very slowly, but
now far enough to be sure there was no chance of the gunman
jumping on board, though it was still close enough for him to take
aim and shoot Henry at leisure.

Henry rose on the deck, brought up the flare gun and fired.

Like a heat seeking missile the flare left the muzzle and streaked
the forty or so feet across the water towards the gunman – and into
him before he could duck and avoid it. He screamed and fell backwards, trying to beat out the burning phosphorous flare that had
slammed into him and ignited his clothing. He whirled three hundred
and sixty degrees, fighting the fire, then toppled off the other side
of the jetty. Henry heard the sizzle as he hit the water and the flames
were extinguished.

He lowered the flare gun, only to realize that the speedboat had
been sucked into the sluggish but powerful main current of the river
and was being dragged westwards with the ebb towards the Irish
Sea, about three miles distant. Henry, with no sailing or marine
experience whatsoever, found himself at the helm of a boat he didn't
even know how to start.

THREE

For once, Steve Flynn had some spare change in his pocket and a fairly optimistic view of life in general.

It was coming to the end of a good season. The big game fish had run in plenty, the clients had come every day for the past three months and money had changed hands. Flynn and his crew – the very grouchy Spaniard that was Jose and occasionally Tommy, the teenage son of Flynn's boss – had grafted; some very fine specimens had been hauled up to the boat (then released after being captured on video) and now it was time for a short break in proceedings once this week, the last in September, was over. All three guys were haggard and weary and as much as they loved big game fishing, the trio had had enough of the Atlantic Ocean for the time being.

Jose inspected the fighting chair, rocking it on its hinges, then spat spectacularly over the side of the boat into the marina.

'Needs fixing,' he said. 'Is buggered.'

The thickset Spaniard rattled the chair again to make his point and to attract Flynn's attention.

Flynn, suntanned to a shade that matched teak, was squinting along the quayside, his eyes shaded from the sun by the peak of his battered baseball cap. He sniffed up, frowned and turned to Jose. 'Si,' Flynn said, nodding. He realized the boat, ironically named *Lady Faye2* but usually simply called *Faye*, was due for an overhaul and some TLC. She was as weary as her crew and part of the proposed downtime would include servicing her and sprucing her up for the winter ahead – and repairing the fighting chair, which had taken some real battering recently. 'It'll last until the end of the week,' Flynn said. He wasn't expecting too much 'heavy' business in the next few days, just walk-ons, people who turned up on a whim at the quayside thinking that an exciting trip on a sportfisher was just what was needed, and booked a half or full day charter. Flynn called it the end of season dribble.

That particular day, though, Flynn was expecting two couples who had, yesterday, booked the nine a.m. to three p.m. slot. They had seemed like a nice bunch – not experienced anglers, but Flynn had been looking forward to a pleasant day on the water, showing them the ropes and hopefully hooking them into something worthwhile. There was still a chance of hooking a big marlin, one of the stragglers maybe.

They had seemed keen and paid a deposit, but it was now nine fifteen a.m., they were late and *Faye* was ready to hit the waves. Their tardiness surprised Flynn. He checked his fake Rolex, frowned again and walked across the extending gangplank from the aft of the boat on to the quayside. He went over to the booking kiosk – in reality nothing more than a garden shed with a sliding window – where day-trippers could book their charters.

The lady sitting inside raised her face and smiled warmly at Flynn. Her name was Karen Glass and working at the kiosk was just a temporary measure for her. She was leaving at the end of the week to resume her degree at university in the UK, where she was a mature student taking media studies. She and Flynn had got on well for the last three months and maybe could have taken things further, but Flynn had held back. He didn't want to spoil a good working relationship with the complication of sex and neither did he want anything more than sex, so the two of them circled each other but never closed in for the kill. Besides which, she was his boss's kid sister.

'Hi, Flynnie.'

He grinned at her, part of his mind thinking that she only had a few days left in the heat out here in Gran Canaria, so maybe the circle could be closed without any undue heartache. 'The two couples from yesterday?' he asked.

Karen's eyes lifted to the digital clock on the kiosk wall. 'Oh yeah.'

'You got their number?'

'Here somewhere.' She sifted through the booking forms and found the one.

'Give 'em a bell, eh?'

'Will do, skip.' She saluted him.

Their eyes held for a second longer than absolutely necessary, then she reached for the mobile phone on the counter and started to input the number.

Flynn backed away and stood by the water's edge, waiting and watching, enjoying the morning warmth of the sun before it got too hot. He had been on Gran Canaria, in Puerto Rico, for nearly nine years now and was pretty much immune to the effects of the sun, but he still enjoyed it – with care. His bronzed skin had been slowly nurtured with lots and lots of thick sunblock and not too much direct exposure to the sun's rays. He rarely sunbathed, but living out here meant that a tan was inevitable, especially working on a fishing boat.

Faye was moored on the far side of the Puerto de Escala, so that anyone approaching on foot had to walk all the way around the marina to the boat; this also meant that Flynn could watch anyone heading in his direction.

The morning hadn't got going yet and the quayside was still quiet.

The two other sportfishing boats moored alongside *Faye* were almost ready to set out on their day's fishing, their crews ready, the clients already on board and being shown the equipment. A couple of tourists strolled indolently along the high sea wall, and that was about it.

That was until a Mercedes taxi stopped at the barrier on the opposite side of the marina in front of the small commercial centre. Flynn assumed this was probably his party being dropped off, but only one couple got out and paid the driver, and it wasn't either of the ones who had booked a charter with him, so he relaxed and glanced over to Karen, who held her mobile phone away from her ear and said, 'No answer.'

Flynn nodded. 'They did pay a deposit, didn't they?'

'Five hundred euros.'

He shrugged. That meant they'd be here and if they were late that was their problem and waste of money and Flynn would not give them a discount or extend their time at sea. That was how it went. He crossed back to the kiosk and leaned in. Karen's lips parted as her eyes played over Flynn's face.

'You gonna brew a coffee, then?'

'Might do,' she teased. She had a large cafetière, fresh coffee, a kettle and mugs on a shelf behind her, and her brew was excellent. 'Weak or strong?'

'Definitely strong.'

Flynn saw her swallow, liking the way her throat moved; then she spun on her chair and reached for the kettle behind her. He kept his eyes on her smooth, tanned back, visible almost down to her shoulder blades because of the deep cut of her loose T-shirt collar.

He did this discreetly as she prepared the coffee whilst facing away from him, spooning the coffee grains into the pot. He could smell it already.

'I'm out tonight, if you're interested . . . goodbye drink and all that,' she said, her voice slightly muffled because she was speaking away from him. 'A few mates.'

'Could be tempted,' he said.

'You'd better be,' she said and glanced over her shoulder at him. She had a nice profile and her slightly crooked grin made Flynn shift slightly inside. He leaned his elbows on the counter and watched as she pushed the filter down in the coffee pot, the line of her right bicep tensing.

'Oi!'

The word jarred Flynn. He stood upright and turned slowly to look at its source; it had emanated, he saw, from a man standing some ten feet away from him. He was one half of the couple that Flynn had just seen alighting from the taxi on the other side of the quay, the ones he had briefly thought might have been his missing party.

Flynn looked at him through narrowed eyes. 'Help you?' He had taken an instant dislike to the man and although the female part of the double act, standing a little further away, hadn't spoken yet, Flynn did not like her either.

'This your crate?' The man jerked his thumb at *Faye*.

'Possibly,' Flynn said, feeling the hairs tingle on the nape of his neck as he surveyed the couple.

First the man. Late twenties, early thirties at most. Lean, with dangerous eyes. His face was pock-marked and mean looking and he was dressed in a T-shirt and three-quarter length pants but with totally inappropriate black shoes and ankle socks pulled up his shins, like he had forgotten to pack his flip-flops. His skin was pale and very white and he looked uncomfortable under the sun and for some reason was not wearing a hat to protect his very close-shaved head. None of these features stopped Flynn from pitching him as very definitely a player, but on a fairly low level. A bruiser, a finger breaker, a rent collector. He wasn't large but looked like he could move quickly, and behind the veneer and the dangerous eyes there was a constant hint of threat and challenge – and familiarity.

Flynn thought he recognized some of the facial features but wasn't sure. It had been a long time since he had faced such a man – and, in his time, he had faced many like him.

The woman, much younger, was dressed in a skimpy vest and shorts, and was painfully white. Her dyed blond hair, black roots showing, was scraped harshly back into a bun, revealing a square northern face, bags under the eyes, not especially pretty. Flynn noted the self-inflicted tattoos on her knuckles and arms, ugly attempts gone wrong. She looked uninterested and annoyed.

'You Flynn?' the man asked. He had said six words in total and Flynn had already picked up the northern accent.

'My name is Flynn – and this is my boat,' he responded pleasantly. He had no wish to screw up a good day by being rude to anyone unless it was absolutely necessary.

'Mine for the day,' the man announced.

'I'm afraid she's already chartered. You could come back at three when we return, do a four hour charter.'

'Does it look booked? I can't see any customers, can you? So I'll have it all day, thanks . . . or maybe I haven't made myself clear, mate. The guy that booked it doesn't want it now, but I do.'

Flynn frowned again.

'In other words, I'm chartering the boat for today . . . deposit's been paid, I believe.'

Flynn felt his heart start to pound.

'Met the guy last night, got into conversation and he told me he didn't want the boat today after all, so I gave him his deposit and now you're mine.'

The urge to punch the guy's lights out was suddenly very strong in Flynn, but he remained calm. 'I'm afraid I'll have to confirm that with the customer. You can see my point of view, can't you?'

'Not really.'

'I need him to confirm what you've just told me.'

The man took a step towards Flynn and in that moment Flynn instinctively knew there was going to be trouble here and this man, whoever the hell he was, was going down hard.

'Well, all you've got is my confirmation and that'll just have to do, won't it, Flynn?'

Unfazed, Flynn said, 'Actually, no.'

The expression on the man's face altered fractionally from aggression to wariness and Flynn knew he was someone who wasn't accustomed to the feeling of being challenged, or being denied anything.

'Tell you what,' Flynn said. 'The charter party is late in arriving . . .'

'Because they're not fucking coming,' the other man snarled.

Flynn started again. 'The charter party is late in arriving . . . if they're not here by nine forty-five a.m. and we haven't managed to contact them, then if you're still interested I'll take you out, but you'll have to pay full price for the day upfront, and I'll hold on to the deposit that has already been paid.' He paused for effect, hoping that his conditions would drive the man away. He added, 'So it'll be fifteen hundred euros, cash.'

'You are jokin' me.'

'No I'm not . . . that's how it is. You want to go out, those are my terms. You can try any of the other boats by all means.' Flynn saw that the two sportfishers alongside *Faye* were just about to cast off their lines.

The man stepped back now, clearly infuriated that Flynn had stood up to him, something of an unusual occurrence. Flynn saw a smirk cross the woman's face, like she knew something. Like she knew that Flynn was going to suffer. Like she knew that no one spoke to her man like this and walked away unscathed.

'So that gives you about half an hour,' Flynn said. 'Go get a coffee, maybe, and come back later if you're still interested.'

The man's lips moved as if they were forming a curse, but it remained unspoken. 'We'll be back,' he told Flynn.

Flynn watched the man walk away down the quayside, constantly glancing over his shoulder at Flynn, who pulled down the peak of his cap, folded his arms and rotated his jaw thoughtfully, not liking what he saw but knowing that what the guy had claimed was probably true. He would somehow have met the original charter party last night and by means fair or foul (and Flynn could guess which) had dissuaded them from turning up in the morning and had slotted into their place. Flynn believed this because the man knew enough detail; otherwise why turn up?

But why anyway?

Flynn rolled his neck and shoulders and turned back to Karen, who had witnessed the exchange. She held out a mug of coffee. Flynn took it gratefully.

'What was all that about?'

'Dunno,' he admitted. 'A strange one, but he's bloody wound me up.'

'I can see that. You've gone all tense. You don't have to take him, y'know? Just keep the deposit that's already been paid and put your feet up for the day.'

Flynn mulled it over. 'No, I'll take him if he comes back . . . if he's daft enough to pay fifteen hundred euros then more fool him and we'll just put up with his shit-headedness. But I would like you to keep trying to phone the original party and see if you can find out what's gone on. We can return their deposit if we don't like the story. If they've been leaned on by boyo for some reason, then they should get it back and we'll screw as much cash as possible out of Mr Nasty instead.'

'OK.'

Flynn walked to the end of the quayside with his coffee and stood at the water's edge, staring into the clear sea. Four barracuda zipped quickly past just below the surface, causing a bit of uproar amongst the other, smaller fish in the water, which scattered.

Flynn thought about the man, worked him through his mind, in particular the familiarity he felt about him. What was all that about? Although Flynn had a good memory, he struggled to place him. He was certain it stemmed from a cop thing, but it had been a long time since Flynn had been in the police, and the final year of his service had been a troublesome, unpleasant time, so it was well over nine years since Flynn had been operational, actually coming nose to nose with crims. Nine years was a long time, and if that was subtracted from the age that Flynn estimated the guy to be – say thirty – he would have been twenty or less if Flynn had ever come into contact with him.

Yet Flynn knew he had come across him in some way.

The details eluded his brain cells, but he knew if he dug around in them long enough, they would come up trumps.

A sort of excitement skittered through him. Innately he knew that he should have given the guy short shrift, sent him packing, but his curiosity had been piqued. Even though Flynn could not recall the specifics of the man, he had come across many of his type in the past – tough, albeit second-rate villains, who often worked for first-rate ones – and it was just to satisfy this curiosity that Flynn had decided to see what the guy was really up to. There was one thing for certain: Flynn knew enough about people to be able to say that the guy had probably never set foot on a fishing boat in his life and had no interest in angling.

And Flynn asked himself the question again: why was he here? Flynn sipped the coffee and watched the barracuda darting through the water below, causing mayhem. If nothing else, Flynn looked forward with anticipation to the feel of his fist connecting with the side of the guy's head and rattling the shit out of his brain.

He came back as promised.

Despite constant effort, Karen had been unable to make contact with the original charter, so they had to be written off as a no-show. So other than Flynn telling the guy to get lost – which was his shout as skipper . . . but knowing that fifteen hundred euros was useful money, Flynn really had no choice but to go with the flow.

He slyly watched the couple walk back along the quay from the café they'd been sitting at for the last half hour, whilst he pretended to be busy on the boat.

'Told you I'd come.'

Flynn had been swilling out a bait box. He stood up, smiling, as the fish-blood-stained water dripped from the box. 'That's great.' He pointed to Karen in the kiosk. 'You'll need to pay her, please, and give her your contact details.'

'You really gonna make me pay fifteen hundred euros?' the man asked, his narrowed eyes playing over Flynn's face, looking as though he was trying to place him.

'I've only got your word about the situation, Mr . . . ?' Flynn said, giving him the chance to reveal his name; but he didn't. Flynn went on, 'So as far as I'm concerned, your dealings with the other party may or may not have happened. All I know is that they've paid a deposit and haven't turned up, so they've lost it. Unless the party tell me any different, that deposit is not transferable. They haven't, so it isn't. Fifteen hundred euros – cash, end of,' Flynn stated.

'Your day rate is only a grand,' the man whined.

'Went up this morning, just haven't had a chance to update the website,' Flynn lied badly, hoping to discourage him.

But he nodded. 'If that's how you want to play it.'

'That's the way,' Flynn confirmed. 'Karen will take your booking fee.' He gestured towards the kiosk.

'OK . . . the name's Costain, incidentally . . . Scott Costain.' He watched Flynn's eyes for a moment, waiting for a reaction, got none. 'You can call me Mr Costain.' He flipped the hefty rucksack he had with him over his shoulder and turned away.

Flynn was not sure how he managed to conceal his reaction to the name Costain, the sound of which jarred him. But he did – too many nights playing three card brag in a dingy club in the commercial centre probably helped – and he only allowed his face to register his horror when the couple turned to walk to the booking kiosk.

'Fuck,' he muttered under his breath. 'A Costain.'

'Trouble?' Jose asked. He had witnessed both interactions, the earlier one and this, and knew what was going on. He was lounging at the entrance to the bridge.

Flynn's top lip sneered like Elvis. 'Yeah – but I don't know why.' He didn't look at Jose, continued to swill out the bait box and hose down the deck as he worked through the ramifications of the name and what it meant to him. He began to sort things in his mind, now realizing why he had seemed so familiar. Flynn was positive that he had never met the guy before, but had met several members of his family.

The Costains. A name to conjure with.

Flynn knew he should immediately have marched over to the kiosk, interrupted and told the guy to go, told him that *Faye* had developed a fault or something, but he couldn't bring himself to do the sensible thing because his dormant instincts had been well and truly stirred up and he needed to know why a member of the Costain family was about to board his boat. His sardonic curl of the lip turned into a grim smile.

He tossed the bloody contents of the bait box over the side, causing uproar amongst a shoal of tiny fish as they feasted manically on the traces of blood and flesh of their own kind – then scattered in terror as the four barracuda returned and scythed through them on a killing spree.

*   *   *

'Flynn, can you come here?' Karen called from the booking kiosk. Flynn looked up from the carnage in the water to see Karen at the hatch and the couple, Costain and his so far unnamed lady friend, all looking over at him.

He refitted the lid on the bait box and jumped off the boat, strode to the kiosk. 'What's up?'

Karen looked worried and not a little scared. Flynn's hackles rose again. 'This gentlemen says he doesn't want to go fishing . . .'

'That's right,' Costain cut in. 'Just sightseeing.'

'And that's not all,' Karen cut back in.

'Yeah – ditch the crew. We don't need the greasy dago on board, just you, Flynn. I assume you can handle the boat yourself?'

Flynn's face remained impassive as he logged the racist remark and decided that when he had occasion to punch Costain, he would add an extra one on behalf of Jose, just for good measure.

'It's still fifteen hundred.'

'Never thought it'd be any different.'

Flynn manoeuvred *Faye* out of her mooring and headed out of Puerto Rico, watching the forlorn figure of Jose, standing accusingly at the end of the sea wall, grow ever smaller as Flynn took the boat further away from land, until he was just a pinprick.

Eventually he turned to Costain and said, 'Where do you want to go?'

Costain walked unsteadily across to him and stood by his left shoulder. 'Head east, then when we're out of sight of land, turn back and head north, following but out of sight of the coastline. Sail past Puerto de Mogán and keep going. Think you can do that?'

Flynn glared at him. Costain grinned and said, 'Sightseeing.'

My arse, Flynn thought, and twisted around as Costain's girlfriend rose from the seat she had been occupying, lurched across the deck, hit the rail and puked spectacularly over the side of the boat.

Someone's in for a rough ride, Flynn thought.

FOUR

On a scale of one to ten, one being the least, ten being the most, being adrift on a speedboat over which he had no control was one of the most terrifying experiences Henry Christie had ever had in his life. He would later describe it as nine point nine on the Richter scale.

A swirling eddy knocked Henry off balance and he reeled to one side, grabbing the handrail to stop himself going overboard again as the speedboat, then well and truly caught by the current, did a complete three sixty turnaround. His hands slipped off the chrome rail and he slithered face down on the deck.

Initially he'd thought the river was moving slowly but the boat rocked and spun out into the central channel and he felt it dip and surge as the muddy water seemed to take hold of its belly and throw it westwards in the direction of the coast. It was like being on a conveyor belt.

Henry pulled himself back up to his knees and peered petrified over the side of the boat as the speed increased and the vessel began to hurtle and spin down the river. His terror escalated as he realized he was simply not in control of anything.

'Oh God,' he moaned and crawled across to the cockpit, then heaved himself up on to the seat, his eyes darting through the wheel at the instrument panel. It looked like a car dashboard, but in truth meant nothing to him, although he did work out where the ignition slot was and that it needed a key of some sort to fire it up.

Then the boat thudded into something. Henry was jerked off the chair on to the deck, striking his head on the edge of the wheel as he fell. Underneath him, the boat juddered, scraped something, then stopped momentarily. Then it spun again and shot backwards down the river, rocking dangerously. He guessed it might have hit a sandbank. Then, as the boat moved, it rocked and turned again, faced forwards and was dragged by the receding tide, fast and sleek.

Henry shook his head, feeling it gingerly with his fingertips – nothing broken or cut, though he did feel somewhat woozy. He fought through this sensation and heaved himself back on to the chair behind the wheel. He saw lights either side of the river and tried to work out exactly which point he had reached. He knew the tide was ebbing – fast – and therefore he was Irish Sea bound and if he got that far he would pass the port of Fleetwood on his left and the small town of Knott End-on-Sea on his right (or was that port and starboard?). His grasp of nautical terms was minimal to say the least, his water-borne experience limited to a couple of cross-channel ferries.

He rocked the wheel: it was locked.

The prow of the boat dipped scarily, then ploughed through a wave to emerge upright on the other side of it. Henry clung on to the wheel with one hand and searched his pockets with the other for his phone, which he found, but it refused to turn on.

He tried to clear his head and shivered as a gust of ice-cold wind whipped around him, causing his sodden clothing to mould tightly to his body like an icy coat.

The boat turned a slow forty-five degrees and hit another wave, rocking dangerously. It came through the turbulence, but made Henry get his act together and realize that the boat would probably survive being chucked around and stay upright – he hoped – but if it dipped, swung and tipped and he went overboard he would certainly die from either drowning or hypothermia.

At the very least he was determined not to drown.

In a container next to the chair he found a life jacket which he looped over his head and shoulders and tied in place with tape, noting that his fingers were beginning to go cold and lose their flexibility, the middle joints starting to freeze up.

He glanced around again, trying to work out his location, just as the boat rocked and dipped into a swirling current and rose out of it unscathed.

He recognized where he was. On the left bank were the ICI works, lit up like some sort of science fiction film set. That meant next stop was Fleetwood, then the open sea that was Morecambe Bay, then maybe the Isle of Man.

He tried to stem his rising panic. Not too successfully.

His eyes dropped and came to rest on the flare gun. He slid off the chair and scooped it up, opening the breech like an old-fashioned revolver and pulling out the remnants of the discharged flare, rather like a huge shotgun cartridge, which in essence it was. He looked into the flare box and found a second one, slotted it into place in the chamber and snapped the gun shut. He raised the flare skywards and pulled the trigger. It whooshed out of the barrel, leaving a smoke trail behind, and at a height of maybe a thousand feet it burst into red and orange. Henry watched it hang there for a few moments from his position on his knees until a scraping noise from underneath the boat roused him. Another sandbank, he guessed. The boat skimmed across it and twisted, but did not stop. Henry pulled himself back on to the chair behind the helm, noted his position again, seeing Fleetwood docks and the widening river mouth.

Almost as if the speedboat had seen the same and wanted to go to sea, it surged ahead with the ebb and was drawn quickly past the docks, which Henry stared at in desperation, hopeful someone would spot him. But he didn't see a single figure.

He looked the other way, remembering there was a coastguard station at Knott End, overlooking the estuary. It was unmanned and in darkness and Henry knew that cutbacks in that particular service meant the station was rarely staffed and all emergencies were routed through Liverpool.

Almost like it was showing off, the boat did another complete circle and a bow, then was dragged into a particularly fast current out into the deep central channel used by the car ferries in and out of Fleetwood. The harbour lights became very distant, very quickly.

Henry's terror grew apace as he watched the lights grow dim.

'I'm fucked,' he thought.

In his life he had been in a few situations where he thought he might die, but he had never thought his end would come in Davy Jones's locker.

Henry tried to keep warm, but eventually gave up. The boat drifted quickly into the bay and into even rougher water, rocking perilously and causing spray to come over the side, pelting Henry's face with what felt like buckets full of frozen pebble-dashing, and though he tried there was really no place to hide from the onslaught. The door to the cabin was locked and Henry could not budge it, although it did seem to him that he would be foolish to go under cover even if he could. He knew he needed to be on deck to be aware of what was going on around him . . . but it would have been nice to be able to see what was in there. Maybe waterproof clothing or blankets. But that was not to be. He was at sea in his thin work suit from Marks & Spencer and his best shoes, and that was how it was.

The cold invaded mercilessly, cutting through the material of his suit, through his skin, into his bones.

He was certain he could feel them freezing. His nose was about to drop off and he was sure his fingers had frostbite and would soon be brittle enough to snap off like a Kit Kat.

It surprised him just how cold it was. The end of September was not far away, the very tail end of summer; the weather had been half-decent and he would have expected it to reflect that at sea.

But no.

The chatter of his teeth echoed around his skull as his battle to keep the cold at bay was being lost.

He slithered off the chair and curled up on the deck in a foetal position, that elemental position from the womb that people in desperate situations often turned to. He hugged himself tightly and fought the urge to close his eyes, believing that drifting into sleep would mean death.

He began to drift mentally and hallucinate, suddenly believing there was an overwhelming whump-whump noise above him, then a downdraught, then a strong bright light bathing him in a white glow – until he realized there was a rescue helicopter hovering over him.

He looked up, his mind fuzzy but functioning just enough to wonder if this rescue would feature on TV sometime in the future.

By nine a.m. Henry's body had just about returned to its normal temperature – mostly. His toes were still like little chunks of ice, his nose red raw and constantly dripping, and he refused to relinquish the foil body wrap his rescuers had trussed him up in like a turkey. Underneath he was wearing a surgical gown and a nurse had kindly fitted a Tubigrip bandage over each foot to keep them warm.

He was sitting in a cubicle in the A&E unit at Blackpool Victoria Hospital, feeling exhausted and sorry for himself as well as completely embarrassed by the way things had turned out. His hands encircled a mug of steaming hot, sweet tea and though he was desperate to pee he did not want to move.

The curtain around the cubicle was drawn back, revealing his fiancée, Alison. She had an assortment of clothes folded over her left arm, a pair of trainers in her hand. Following her initial visit to Henry earlier, she had been to his house in Blackpool and found a change of clothing for him.

He gave her a 'sorry for himself' grin.

'Hello again.' She stepped into the cubicle and drew the curtain. 'How are you feeling?'

'That's just it,' he moaned. 'I'm not feeling. I'm a block of ice.' He gave an exaggerated shiver.

'You were lucky.'

'On more than one front . . . at least I'm alive.'

'Yeah, thank God.' Alison lay out his clothing on the bed, then hugged him tightly, making the foil surrounding him crinkle and crackle.

'They're making "get out of here" noises,' Henry told her, 'so I suppose I'd better comply. They've finished with me.'

Alison backed away. He stood up and reluctantly unwrapped himself.

'I'll let you get dressed,' she said and reversed out of the cubicle.

Henry removed the surgical gown, unrolled the Tubigrip socks and got into the clothes Alison had brought for him – underwear, jeans, socks, a T-shirt and a zip-up jacket. He then picked up the large plastic bag his original, sodden clothing had been stuffed into, opened the curtain and revealed himself. His expression said it all.

Alison sighed. 'Despite what you've just been through, you're not coming home, are you?'

'You know me so well.'

She shrugged. It wasn't unexpected. Henry had stumbled on a double murder, a gangland style execution, had almost become a victim of the killer himself, so there was no way he could even contemplate going home, even though he had not now slept in over twenty-four hours.

Once Henry had been formally discharged, Alison drove him in her Suzuki four by four out to Pool Foot Lane. She could not turn into it because it had been sealed off at both ends, so pulled up on Garstang New Road to let Henry get out and walk back to Percy's house. He leaned across and kissed her. For a fleeting moment she was brittle – annoyed that Henry wasn't coming home. Anyone else in their right mind would have – but then she capitulated, melted, turned to him and gave him a passionate kiss on the lips, almost dragging him back into the car. When the kiss ended, they looked into each other's eyes for a moment.

'I love you, Henry.'

'And I love you too, babe.'

'Mm.' Her lips pursed.

'I don't intend to stay here all day,' he said, seeing her expression. 'Just want to catch up on things, see what I didn't see last night, make sure it's all running smoothly. Then I'll collect my car and head back to your place. It's curry night . . . how could I miss that?'

'Rogan josh.'

'My fave . . . see you later.'

They pecked. Henry stepped back on the grass verge as she pulled away, waving, him waving back. Then he turned to make his way to the crime scene, his mind still churning with what had happened over the last eight hours or so.

He had no reason to look up and see or notice the Nissan Note that had been parked up on the forecourt of the petrol station at the nearby junction. No reason to clock it and remember it. No reason to see it drive off the forecourt, shoot through the lights and follow Alison's four by four.

He ducked under the cordon tape and walked down the lane. On his right were fields but on the left were the houses, each one large and detached, all different and some, like Percy Astley-Barnes's, with grounds that spread all the way back to the lazy curve in the River Wyre. It was a small enclave of wealth and peace – but last night someone had brought terror and murder to it.

The whole lane was jam-packed with police cars, marked and unmarked, specialist and general, uniform and detective. Henry's car had been blocked in by these other vehicles and he knew he would have trouble finding the drivers of the offending ones when he wanted to move.

Despite what he'd told Alison, however, he was in no hurry.

He was exhausted, had brushed with death and damn near frozen his bollocks off, but the fact remained he had stumbled into a double murder and let a killer go, so he still had his job to do.

Although he'd been fleeing for his life, he was still very annoyed he had let the bastard go. He just hoped he'd injured him with the flare and maybe dinked him with the Maglite.

At the front gate a uniformed cop was keeping a log of all the comings and goings. Henry dragged out his sodden wallet and slid out his warrant card, which fortunately was laminated and had survived the dunking intact. The officer noted down his name and directed Henry to the back of a Crime Scene Investigator's van where forensic suits and elasticated slip-on shoe covers were being dished out. Basic kit for a serious crime.

He dipped under the crime scene tape and walked up the gravel driveway towards the house, as he had done the night before.

Percy's Aston Martin was still there, as was the Fiat 500 which, he had since learned, belonged to Percy's girlfriend, who was called Charlotte Bowers and, he had also learned, had been shot dead alongside Percy.

The black Porsche was gone. The killer's car. The rental.

Henry paused on the driveway, trying a bit of cognitive recall from the night before, retracing his steps in his mind and wondering if he had seen anything of importance before he reached the point of contact with the killer, after which things were just a bit blurry because all he'd been focused on was saving his own skin, not gathering evidence. He hadn't even known what he'd walked into at that point in the driveway and had only learned for sure what had actually gone on when he was later lying freezing in the hospital, teeth still clattering, bones shaking, and he'd been visited by the night duty detective sergeant. The DS had come, first to check how Henry was, then to brief him about what had happened and, most importantly, to glean any evidence from Henry that might be useful in catching a fleeing assassin.

The sergeant confirmed that this did look like a professional hit, a hypothesis given extra kudos by Henry's description of a killer who was even professional enough to wear a protective forensic suit, someone who didn't want to leave anything behind.

The guy was probably a hired hit man, and at that moment in time Henry knew more about him than anyone else because he had looked him in the eye, at least before concentrating on the gun in his hand. He was definite he could recognize him again and point the accusing finger at him.

And I will, Henry thought grimly. He continued on his walk up to the front door of Percy's house where another uniformed constable hovered, clipboard in hand, recording all arrivals and departures into the actual crime scene. Whilst the officer wrote down his name,

Henry glanced across the garden from the top of the short flight of steps, back to the electronic gates, then over the wide, well-trimmed lawn that dipped to the river, and the tiny jetty where Percy's speedboat had been moored. It wasn't there now but Henry knew an RNLI lifeboat had towed it into the small marina at Fleetwood.

'Sir?'

Henry turned back to the PC, who had stepped aside to allow him into the house. Henry gave him a nod and walked into the crime scene.

In the expansive hallway beyond the vestibule, Henry saw two men in forensic suits talking head to head. One was DCI Woodcock, head of the local CID, who had helped Henry interview the child killer the day before. The other was the Home Office Pathologist, Professor Baines, whom Henry knew well.

Woodcock nodded as Baines explained something to him, listening intently to an expert opinion on something. Then they both glanced sideways and saw Henry watching them. Baines's serious face turned brighter at the sight of Henry. The two men had known each other for too many years and they had lost count of the number of dead bodies across which they'd faced each other.

'Boss,' Woodcock said. Pete Woodcock was definitely in line for a job on FMIT. He was a good, solid detective in his mid-thirties, also a decent leader and decision maker, someone who, Henry guessed, would make a brilliant senior investigating officer (SIO) in due course. Henry liked him and was slowly beckoning him to FMIT.

'Morning, guys,' Henry said, joining them.

'How are you, boss?'

'Cold, embarrassed – but generally shipshape.' He smiled.

'Better cold than dead,' Baines said, 'and on my slab.'

'Good point,' Henry agreed. He gave Baines a pat on the arm and said, 'Glad you're here for this one, mate.' He looked back at Woodcock. 'Where are we up to?'

Henry swallowed as his eyes took in the actual murder scene. The two bodies lying on the plush-carpeted floor of the lounge, not yet moved, still lying in the exact positions in which they'd fallen.

Knowing the forensic and crime scene work had been done without having moved the bodies so far, Henry allowed himself to circle them slowly from a distance of about two metres, taking his time, pausing, crouching, hands in pockets, simply using his eyes and brain while Woodcock told him what they had so far. Which was precious little, and most of it related solely to the scene in front of Henry.

'Blood pattern analysis suggests the female was killed first, then the male,' the DCI was saying. 'Both bound and gagged . . . we think the killer was holding the female hostage until the male arrived home . . . then she was murdered in front of him . . .'

Henry nodded and thought, *she let the killer in.*

'He vomited, as you can see,' Woodcock said.

Henry frowned, looking at the two bodies, trying to re-imagine the sequence of events and work out why or how things had happened in a certain way. Percy had made the frantic call to Lisa. Meanwhile the killer had arrived at the house in the Porsche (good choice of car to allay suspicion), held the female prisoner, waited for Percy to land, which he did, overpowered him and tied him up, then killed them both, woman first. (Was Percy made to see this? Was this getting a message across to him? Henry thought.) It was all fairly easy to work out.

He rubbed his face, looking at the horrific gunshot wounds and the spread of blood underneath and around the bodies. Then he looked at Baines. 'Any observations, Prof?'

'Nothing you haven't already been told or worked out, I suppose. But the victims were both in kneeling positions when they were first shot in the temple. The second shot came when they were on the floor, although I'm pretty certain I'll find that the second shot wasn't necessary to dispatch either victim. The first one did the job.'

Henry's mind became fuzzy all of a sudden and he knew he had to sit down. He perched on an armchair next to a small round table on which was a cup and saucer. He glanced into the cup and saw cold tea covering the bottom of it.

His head cleared.

'A guy who doesn't make mistakes,' he ventured. 'A pro, a murderer, who ensures he stays forensically clean, even down to the fact that he uses a revolver instead of a pistol which chucks shell casings all over the place; they have a tendency to roll into places you can't always recover them from. But he's made a few errors here, not least when I turned up and cocked it up for him. I saw his car, I saw him, I think I hurt him, hopefully, and, best part of all, he didn't wash his tea cup.'

*   *   *

'Where the fuck is this bitch going?' Hawke growled at the wheel of the Nissan Note. The car he was following seemed to be travelling for ever and he was getting annoyed now, wondering if it was worth it . . . though he knew it was.

He had travelled behind the four by four all the way from the point where the woman driver dropped the detective off, then along the A586 through Great Eccleston and St Michael's on Wyre until it hit the A6. She turned left and headed towards Lancaster.

In spite of the raging pain in his chest and upper right arm, Hawke kept to his task.

The four by four drove through Lancaster and straight on to the A683, under the M6 at junction 34 and out into the rural area that was the valley of the River Lune.

'Fuckin' bitch going?' he demanded again, not having a clue as to where he was as they drove through a village called Caton and continued along that 'A' road until eventually bearing right before reaching Hornby, on to very narrow country roads that wound and twisted and were virtually devoid of traffic, making following her without alerting her much harder. He kept a respectable distance, guessing that even if she had seen him behind her, she wouldn't be too concerned. Why would she be? She had no reason to suspect that a hit man was following her.

She drove quickly and confidently along these tight roads which she obviously knew well, cutting and speeding into corners with skill.

Hawke kept her in sight.

Eventually she reached a village signposted as Kendleton, the road plunging down into it. She slowed and turned into the car park of a large old pub called the Tawny Owl, jumped out of her car and walked swiftly in through the front entrance. The place was open for business and as Hawke drove past he saw a sign advertising en suite rooms, breakfasts, morning and afternoon teas and coffees, lunches and dinners.

He swung the car around at the first available turning point and came back into the village, into the pub car park, stopping alongside the four by four.

He was going to go in and say hello.

But first, he needed to re-grease himself.

He slid off his zip-up jacket, unbuttoned his shirt and pulled it down, having to contort his neck in order to be able to look down at his injury. He peeled off the gauze and revealed the ugly, weeping burn on the upper right quarter of his chest, shoulder and bicep where the flare had hit him. Hawke hissed at the pain as he reached for the soothing ointment he had with him and spread it carefully across the wound, gritting his teeth and wincing. He knew he needed proper medical treatment, but that would have to wait until he had done his homework. He replaced the gauze and eased his shirt and jacket back on, then swallowed a handful of extra strong ibuprofen tablets, just to take the edge off the pain. He checked his face in the rear view mirror and snarled at the crescent-shaped cut on his forehead caused by the lucky throw of the torch; fortunately it had now stopped bleeding. Then he was out of the car, walking towards the pub.

He looked at the sign above the door on which the licensee's name was displayed: Alison Marsh. His eyes glanced over the ego-certificates on the wall just inside the entrance. This was a pub-cum-hotel really, advertising half a dozen rooms, and had been awarded various accolades by tourist boards and the local council.

The aroma of frying bacon wafted out, making him feel suddenly hungry.

He had not eaten since his plunge into the river off the jetty and now he was famished. A full English breakfast was just what he needed, so he pushed his way through the revolving door and entered.

To his left, in the dining room, an oldish couple were being served breakfast by a young waitress and as he entered the woman he had just tailed all the way here emerged from the kitchen, fastening on an apron.

She smiled at Hawke. 'Good morning.'

'Hi there . . . saw the sign for breakfasts. Not too late, I hope?'

'Not at all.' She beamed pleasantly. 'Would you like to take a seat in the dining room and I'll bring a menu?'

'Very kindly of ya.'

He went into the dining room and saw there were actually two couples breakfasting. He nodded amicably at them and found a seat at the table by the bow window, overlooking the car park and the village further down the road. The woman came back with the menu.

'Would you like a drink to be going on with?'

'Filter coffee?'

She nodded.

'This is a great place,' he said generously. 'Is it yours?'

'Yes.' She smiled proudly.

He looked at her face, which was very pretty, though there was something slightly out of kilter with it . . . plastic surgery – not much, but there if you looked.

'Wow! Y'run it with your husband?'

She smiled shyly. 'No . . . I don't have one of those . . .'

'Oh gosh, sorry, didn't mean to pry.'

'No, it's not that.'

'Hey – no problem.' He glanced at the menu, then raised his eyes. 'Full English, I reckon . . . rude not to.'

She nodded. 'You're an American.'

'Yeah, just passing through,' he drawled, putting it on thick. 'Checking out the Lake District.'

'Ah well, you're slightly off target.'

'Well,' he corrected himself, 'I know that, but just following my nose, I guess, exploring all around.'

'Don't blame you . . . it may not be the Lakes around here, but it's just as nice . . . where are you staying?'

'Relatives,' he said vaguely.

'Oh, OK.'

'But maybe I should have a night or two here.'

'We have vacancies tonight,' she offered. 'I'll get your coffee and breakfast.'

'Thank you, ma'am.' Hawke watched her go, wondering about her face . . . thinking how much he would like to pound it to a mush, then put a thirty-eight through her skull.

Henry was still at the crime scene, reluctant to leave, reluctant to let anyone touch it or move anything because he knew there was only ever one chance and once the vultures descended – to do their jobs, admittedly – there was never any going back.

The position of the bodies had been recorded by the CSIs on digital cameras and video, as had the whole of the living room and all the approaches to the scene through the house, up the drive, along the lane. When they had eventually been turned over, that moment too was recorded, and the full extent of their head wounds was revealed.

Henry watched dispassionately, but there was a little flutter in his chest as he realized that he could easily have been the third victim here and a crime scene examiner could now be heaving his body over for a better look.

He banished the thought; best not to dwell on it. He looked at DCI Woodcock. 'Let's go for a stroll.'

Hawke had to admit that the full English was excellent, though it was not really the type of food he embraced. After eating he sat back with his second coffee and tried not to think too much about the burning sensation.

'Was that OK for you?'

It was the woman again. He said yes, then, 'So you must be the lady whose name is over the door on that fancy hand-painted sign . . . Alison . . . ?' He pretended not to be quite able to remember her surname.

Alison picked up his plate. 'Marsh . . . yes, that's me.'

'So . . . look, sorry, not to pry, but how come this place is yours? Must be an interestin' story there.' He posed the question in a conversational way.

'It's a long story, but I run it with my stepdaughter, Ginny.'

'You said you didn't have one of those husband things . . .'

'I don't . . . like I said, long story.'

'Hey!' He held up his hands. 'I apologize . . . just curious, and don't mean nothin' by it . . . but I also can't help but notice the rock on "that" finger . . . third finger, left hand . . . engaged?'

'You ask a lot of questions.'

'Us Yanks do . . . inbuilt curiosity.' He grinned, although it was more a grimace than a grin as a shot of pain made him want to crease over.

'I am engaged – you're right,' she said.

'Wow – congratulations.' Hawke held out his hand. Alison, holding his plate with her left hand, shook it with her right. 'Who's the lucky guy?'

'Erm, his name's Henry,' she said, almost shyly.

'Does he work here?'

'No, not yet. He's a police officer . . . hopefully he'll retire soon and then we'll run this place together . . . at least that's the plan.'

'Well, ma'am, you have my very best wishes for the future,' Hawke said magnanimously.

'Thank you, you're very kind.'

Alison collected everything from the table but Hawke's coffee, gave him a sweet smile, then headed back to the kitchen.

Hawke turned to the window, his cold eyes not focusing on the pretty village scene in front of him, his mind collating the information he had just put together by asking a series of very innocent questions. He drank his coffee, left more than enough money on the table for the meal and walked out of the pub.

He had every intention of returning.

FIVE

As instructed, Flynn turned east towards the African mainland once the boat was clear of Puerto Rico; then, when far enough away from the possibility of prying eyes, he spun *Faye* around and headed back, keeping Gran Canaria on his right. He ploughed west through the deep Atlantic, following the lower curve of the southern edge of the island, eventually heading north.

The sea was comparatively smooth, but even so *Faye* crested and dipped through the white caps as she made easy progress. These were the type of sea conditions she revelled in, and Flynn loved being at the helm of a boat he adored. It was a movement, however, that did nothing to alleviate the seasickness that had taken over Costain's girlfriend, who Flynn had learned was called Trish. She hung pitifully over the side, retching horribly on an empty stomach and getting no sympathy from Costain, who seemed unaffected by the motion and stood behind Flynn in the cockpit.

'She might be better in the stateroom,' Flynn suggested over his shoulder. 'She can crash out there in air-conditioned splendour.' He did know, though, that doing this – lying down, eyes closed – often made the condition worse. 'Or failing that she can have a coffee and food. There's some sarnies in the cool box. Sometimes eating actually helps.'

Costain just sniggered.

The girl was left to heave.

They passed Puerto Rico, then, further along the coast, Puerto de Mogán, a more upmarket resort than the now slightly squalid Puerto Rico. Although they were well out of sight of each port, the mountains behind rose grandly, reminding Flynn, as ever, that Gran Canaria was stunningly beautiful.

Beyond Mogán, the coastline became more barren and hostile and less accessible, although there was a series of excellent beaches along this stretch, Lomo Tasarte, but they were difficult to get to other than on foot along some precarious footpaths, or by boat. Costain was consulting a fold-out tourist map of the island he had taken from his rucksack.

Over his shoulder, Flynn said, 'If you're sightseeing, you won't see much of the island from this distance. I need to get in closer.'

'I'm aware of that. Just drive this thing, will you?' He glanced at the map, then Flynn. 'Where are we now?'

Flynn checked his GPS. 'Just about level with Veneguera now.' That was one of the sandy beaches on this stretch of coast.

Costain nodded. 'Keep going and let me know when we get near Punta de las Tetas.'

Flynn said, 'OK.' He set the automatic pilot and stood up from his seat.

'Where the fuck d'you think you're going?'

'To make coffee and to look after my customers. You can keep an eye out for other boats if you want, but the radar will scream like a banshee if we get too close to anyone.'

He shouldered past Costain and crossed the deck to Trish, who had slumped down in a ragged collection of limbs and a lolling head. She glared malevolently at him and growled, 'Fuck this.'

'You might be better inside,' Flynn said. He crouched down next to her. 'At least you can lie down and it's cooler.' He held out his hand and was amazed as an expression of gratitude came over her face; she reached out and grabbed it. He hauled her gently to her wobbly legs and held on to her hand as *Faye* rolled sideways. She staggered a little two-step, so he slid an arm around her waist to steer her across the deck into the stateroom, past Costain who watched darkly and offered no help. Once inside, she flopped gratefully on to the settee and covered her face with her hands, moaning as only a seasickness-stricken person could. Flynn felt sorry for her, being dragged along on this expedition. 'There is chilled water in the fridge and some sandwiches in the cool box,' he told her, but the prospect of food consumption only made her moan even louder, then roll over and bury her face in the cushions.

Flynn came out of the stateroom under Costain's watchful eyes. 'Best place for her is under a tree,' he said.

'Eh?'

'Never mind.' Flynn twisted on to the helm chair and took control of the boat again after having put the kettle on. Checking their position he saw they were sailing parallel to Playa del Cerrillo, about twelve kilometres up the coast from Puerto Rico.

He was suddenly aware of Costain up uncomfortably close behind him. The man's mouth was close to his left ear. A chill slithered down his spine.

'Ever touch that girl again and I'll take umbrage,' Costain breathed. 'Get my meaning?'

Flynn sighed. 'I did what you should have done when I suggested it. Helped a lady in distress.' He used the word 'lady' advisedly.

'I decide what help she gets.'

'And I decide what goes on on my boat. And I decide if we turn back to port or not. Get *my* meaning?' He turned to Costain, who had taken a step away.

They locked on to each other, then Costain's face cracked into a smile. He backed off, hands raised. 'Hey man, only joshing, fuckin' hell!' He was backtracking in every sense.

'Go check on her,' Flynn said, 'then come back on deck and tell me exactly where you want to go and what you want to see.'

Costain's face set hard again, not responding well to other people's orders. He went past Flynn into the stateroom, muttering and slamming the sliding door shut.

The old man's voice was croaky, distant, harsh. 'Where the hell are you?'

Hawke negotiated a tight bend in the road whilst holding the mobile phone to his left ear. 'On my way back.'

'How did it go?' the old man demanded.

'It went. He's dead. Just a bit of a complication.'

'I like the word "dead". I don't like the word "complication".'

'It shouldn't be a problem for you, it's one I have to sort.'

'Make certain of that.'

After hugging the coastline – but not too closely – in a slight north-westerly direction, they rounded the Punta de las Tetas where the island met the sea dramatically in rugged cliffs plummeting into the ocean. Costain emerged from the stateroom and asked Flynn for their current position.

'This is where you wanted to be.' Flynn pointed towards the harsh landscape.

Costain shaded his eyes. The sun was well up into the morning sky now and the heat was beginning to sear. 'The Punta de las Tetas?'

'That's the one. Wanna go in, take some photos or something?'

'Nah, carry on sailing, pal. Up the coast, then tell me when we reach Puerto de la Aldea.'

Flynn sighed. 'OK.' He settled back and decided simply to enjoy the ride. It was quite rare for him to come this far north, as most of his fishing was concentrated in the deep waters south of Puerto Rico.

Costain flopped on the sofa bench in the cockpit and laced his fingers behind his head as he surveyed Flynn critically.

'Do you know who I am?' Costain asked at length.

Flynn did not even glance at him. He took a sip of his coffee, then said, 'Should I?'

Costain shrugged and said, 'Because I know who you are.'

Flynn's mouth dried up instantly. His skin crawled. 'Really – and who am I?'

'A bent cop,' Costain said with a supercilious smirk.

The grounds of the house were being searched by a team of support unit officers; other cops had been dispatched to do a house-to-house in the vicinity, although there were few houses around to knock at; and a couple of police divers were at the small jetty, about to drop in and trawl the area around it.

Henry hoped they would find the remnants of the flare and maybe some of the killer's skin with it.

He walked with DCI Woodcock around the big garden, retracing the steps of his pursuit, reliving it and cursing himself for getting old and past it.

He spent a few moments looking at the height of the garden wall and gates, shaking his head at the thought of not being able to scale them last night, although as he weighed them up he was fairly sure that even in daylight, with a good tail wind, he wouldn't be able to do it . . . which was a slight comfort.

Age, along with the gunshot wound to his shoulder and the general deterioration of his fitness: not a good combination. Maybe five years earlier he could have given it a go, but not now. His career in the cops, the batterings he'd received, the injuries, seemed to be coming home to roost in the decline of his physical abilities.

'You OK, boss?' Woodcock asked him.

'Oh yeah . . . just feel like a knackered old fart these days . . . I just know that I should be pulling pints, not being bloody shot at.' He glanced knowingly at the DCI. 'Retirement is imminent.'

'Surely you're too young yet, sir?' Woodcock quipped.

Henry gave him his best Clint Eastwood stare. 'Brown noser, eh? You'll go far.'

'Who, me? Just an honest viewpoint.'

The two men chuckled. Henry said, 'Let's keep walking.'

Flynn kept altering course fractionally to stay parallel to the coastline until they reached Puerta de la Aldea, the little harbour town tucked under the mountainous cape to the north, almost the very western edge of Gran Canaria.

He eased back the power and announced their position to Costain who was still on the sofa, watching Flynn through slitted eyes.

'OK, you can turn around, let's go back much closer to shore now. I want to see everything from a short distance, especially the beach at GuiGui.' He pronounced it 'Gooey-gooey'. Flynn sneered, but was unable to bring himself to correct Costain. The correct pronunciation was 'Wee-wee', so there wasn't much to choose between the two in terms of hilarity.

'We passed that twenty minutes ago,' Flynn said.

'I know – but we were too far out to see it . . . now I want to see it, OK?'

He spun *Faye* around with more panache than necessary and headed back south. He knew the beach of GuiGui was fine, powdery sand and quite magnificent, but could only be reached on foot or by boat. It was often deserted but he knew some tourists made deals with fishing boats to be dropped off and picked up, and in high summer there were regular boat trips to GuiGui from Puerto Rico. Flynn had done the journey a few times and had always remembered to warn people of the tides in this particular stretch of coastline. They could be fast, high and lethal to the unwary.

Costain rummaged through his rucksack and came out with a pair of powerful looking binoculars. He then sat on the fighting chair, clamped the glasses to his eyes and began surveying the cliffs and bays as Flynn steered *Faye* in closer.

'So what did a million quid feel like?' Costain probed, shouting above the sound of the engines and the splash of the sea.

Flynn sighed, did not respond.

'Bought you this boat, ey?' he said cheekily. 'A life in the sun.'

Flynn's throat began to constrict.

'Oh, sorry,' Costain said. He lowered the glasses and rotated the fighting chair. 'Never proved, was it? Never proved that you and your partner nicked a mill from a drugs baron and then, funnily enough, both left the cops. He fuckin' disappeared, didn't he? But here you are, livin' the life of Riley. Whatchado? Squabble over the money, then kill him? Is he buried up in those mountains – down a deep gully?' Costain teased harshly.

Flynn remained stony silent.

Costain shook his head, amused, and returned to scanning the shoreline with the glasses. The door to the stateroom slid open and Costain's bedraggled girlfriend appeared, leaning against the door jamb. She looked as though she had just woken from a night on the town. Pretty dreadful.

'How are you feeling?' Flynn asked.

'Bit better.'

The boat rose, then rolled on a swell. She held on to the door. Flynn saw her throat rise and fall as she seemed to swallow something that tasted quite unpleasant. She shook her head and retreated quickly backwards, crashing the door closed.

Flynn stealthily slid the throttle open a touch more. He heard the change in the drumbeat of the engine, but Costain did not, nor did he note the very slight increase in speed. Flynn now wanted to spend as little time as possible in the company of this obnoxious man and his puking lady friend, but he had to speed up with subtlety. His curiosity about what Costain was up to had now waned and he didn't care any longer.

He glanced at Costain, who had the binos stuck to his eyes. Flynn gave the throttle another gentle touch, and smiled.

Although the Canary Islands were known for their all-year-round sun and did not really have a tourist off-season as such, there were times when the pace lulled and the tail end of September was one of those times – that gap between high summer and the half-term holidays in mid-October. Gran Canaria was close to its best at this time of year, Flynn thought. Some of the fierce heat had gone out of the sun and it was a time when the more discerning traveller came to the island. The knock-on effect of that was that on week-days there were fewer pleasure and tourist boats plying around the waters, and on that particular morning Flynn had hardly seen any others.

'Bit closer,' Costain urged. They were not far now from GuiGui, at a point north of the beach where the almost perpendicular cliffs hit the sea. Flynn adjusted *Faye*'s nose. 'And fuckin' slow down a bit,' Costain said, pulling the binos from his eyes and scowling at Flynn.

So the bastard had noticed.

Flynn complied, throttled back a notch and put *Faye* about two hundred metres from the cliffs and the dangerous rocks below, maybe half a mile north of the actual beach. Costain joined him in the cockpit, still looking through the binoculars, but forwards this time.

'There!' he said triumphantly.

Flynn frowned. He peered through the windows and in the distance saw a boat he did not recognize, about quarter of a mile away, anchored, or being held steady, quite close to the cliff face and in a fairly precarious spot, Flynn thought. There was activity on board and, even from this distance, Flynn could see that scuba diving equipment was stacked up on deck and someone – a man – was sitting on the side of the boat, kitted up with breathing equipment, two air bottles on his back. He adjusted his face mask, then rolled backwards into the sea.

Flynn pouted. Diving was a passion for many around the islands and a lot of boats took divers out from Puerto Rico, as did Flynn, although he was no great shakes as a diver. He knew the best and safest places to dive around the coast and this wasn't one of them. Not least because of the ferocious way the sea ran here and the danger of jagged rock formations just below the surface that could easily pierce the hull of an unwary craft. And mainly because there was nothing to see down here. Divers liked wrecks and reefs and fish – and safe water – and as far as Flynn knew, this section of sea offered none of those.

Flynn edged *Faye* closer, picking up on Costain's excitement.

'Babe, babe . . . Trish, Trish,' Costain yelled. 'Get your sick arse up here, we've found them.' He kicked the stateroom door to attract her attention.

Flynn's nostrils dilated with anger. 'Oi!' he warned. 'Don't you kick my boat.'

Costain merely scowled at him and fixed the binoculars to his eye sockets.

The stateroom door slid open and Trish materialized looking no better. Pure white, ill. 'What?' she demanded.

Costain pointed. She turned and looked. He whispered in her ear. She became suddenly tense.

'Take us in for a closer look,' Costain ordered Flynn.

'I'm not going in too close. These are dangerous waters.'

'That boat's there, why can't yours be? You got that echo thingy, haven't you?'

'Yes, I have that "echo thingy", but I'm still not going in close. It doesn't make rocks disappear.'

Costain gave him a very pissed off expression. 'As close as you can, OK?'

Resigned, Flynn edged towards the boat. Even closer, he still didn't recognize it.

From about a quarter of a mile away it became obvious that the people on board this boat had clocked *Faye*'s approach. Two men were on deck, looking in their direction, talking and pointing agitatedly.

'Keep going,' Costain said.

Flynn steered towards the boat, which looked a very nice craft. It wasn't a sportfisher but a pleasure cruiser. Flynn recognized the lines as that of a Fairline Targa, probably the Forty-eight model, a good half a million pounds' worth of boat. The name *Destiny* was on her bows.

Flynn throttled back and *Faye* was just crawling along, getting even closer to the other boat.

A third male had joined the other two, looking towards *Faye*, binoculars to his eyes. One of the others began signalling, flapping his hands in a 'go away' gesture.

'Keep going,' Costain said again, his binos clamped to his eyes. Then he pulled them away and whispered something in Trish's ear and she nodded. 'Get in as close as you can. I want to see who's on board,' Costain told Flynn.

From the continuing gestures it was more than evident the people aboard the Fairline did not want *Faye* any closer. One of the men turned and stomped into the cockpit. A moment later, Flynn's radio came to life.

'Calling *Faye2*, calling *Faye2* . . . please answer.'

Flynn picked up his mic. 'Receiving.'

'This is *Destiny* . . . request you back off: private party, many thanks.'

Flynn looked at Costain. 'They're telling us to get lost.'

'Are we in a public place, or not?' Costain retorted. 'Get in close . . . let's look at those fuckers.'

'Repeat,' the voice said over the air, 'pull away, please.'

Flynn said, 'I'm not sure you can make that request. These are open waters and we are not putting you in danger.'

An edge came to the other man's voice. 'Do not, repeat, do not approach.'

'They're not happy teddies,' Flynn said to Costain.

'Fuck 'em. We're allowed. Go in.'

Flynn hung up the microphone and concentrated on manoeuvring *Faye* a little closer. He could easily have gone alongside the Fairline because his echo-sounder was giving him a snapshot of the sea floor which showed plenty of depth and nothing to worry about, but he didn't want to tell Costain this, or push things. For some reason the men aboard the other boat were getting shirty and didn't want anyone else peeking over their shoulders at what they were doing. But whatever they were up to, they were doing it in public, so tough, and now Flynn was intrigued because this was obviously what Costain had come to see.

He took *Faye* closer, maybe one hundred and fifty metres away from the other boat now.

A shout came over the radio: '*Faye2*, please acknowledge. I will not remain polite for very much longer. Turn and go, please.'

Flynn flicked off the radio.

The man who had been making the transmission came out of the cockpit back on deck and then the three men all stood in a row and continued to glare at Flynn's boat.

'Closer,' Costain said.

'OK.' Flynn was quite enjoying annoying people now – until he saw the man who had been on the radio turn back into the cockpit. He came out a moment later and Flynn swore as he swung a rifle up to his shoulder, one with a telescopic sight on it; he drew back the bolt action and slammed a round into place.

Surely not.

The man settled into the rifle and aimed it at *Faye*. A moment later the front screen of Faye's cockpit shattered, there was a rush and zing of air over Flynn's head and a microsecond later came the report of the shot.

'Fuck,' said Flynn, ducking instinctively – too late if the round had struck him. 'Bastard's shooting at us,' he said.

Costain's girlfriend screamed and fell over. Costain himself dropped to his knees and scrambled across the deck to his rucksack, throwing his binos aside.

Flynn held on to the helm and saw the man drawing back the rifle bolt to eject the used shell casing. Flynn slammed *Faye* into reverse and rammed on the power. Her aft sank and her bows rose as the engines roared – but this was a movement she was comfortable with, something Flynn did regularly to assist anglers to haul in their catches.

Another bullet hit *Faye*; this time a side cockpit window exploded and the round whizzed just above Flynn's head.

Costain tipped out the contents of his rucksack and a Russian-made Makarov pistol, a semi-automatic, skittered across the deck; he dived for it and grabbed it. He hauled himself upright on the deck rail and aimed at the Fairline. Before Flynn could scream *no*, Costain started firing wildly at the other boat and all three men aboard ducked, although there was little chance of him hitting anything other than an unlucky seagull – distance and the motion of *Faye* reversing saw to that.

Flynn spun her around and gave her full throttle. She picked up her nose like a Grand National winner and moved quickly and regally forward.

'Twats! Fuckin' twats!' Costain cursed, clinging on to the side rail, looking back at the other boat as Flynn put some real distance between them. The Makarov hung limply by his side.

Trish picked herself up carefully, now more dishevelled than ever.

Grim faced and fuming, Flynn put *Faye* on to autopilot and spun to face Costain, who was ready for the reaction. He was wild-eyed and feral looking now – and the Makarov was aimed at Flynn's belly.

SIX

Henry Christie was beginning to feel cold again, and exhausted. His night-time drenching and near-death experiences were beginning to take their toll and over four hours at the scene of the double murder was enough. He needed to be somewhere warm and cosy, maybe have a long, hot, soapy bath, sit down and fall asleep with a JD for company. He had done as much as was necessary and it was now time to take the bodies to the mortuary at Blackpool Victoria Hospital where they would be stored under lock and key. The pathologist, Baines, who was as busy as ever, would not be able to carry out the post mortems until much later and Henry did not need, or want, to be there for that gruesome task. DCI Woodcock could have that dubious pleasure.

Henry and the DCI were at the front gate of Percy's house, chatting through things as they waited for the arrival of the body removers.

It was a lot of procedural stuff – about setting up a Major Incident Room or MIR, getting the staff sorted, plus some fast-track actions. Henry wanted to get the investigation up and running quickly. There was already someone looking into Percy's background, personal and business, and his recent activity, as well as looking at his girlfriend, Charlotte – or Lottie, as she had preferred to be known – although it looked as if she was collateral damage more than anything: wrong place, wrong time. A detective was trying to trace the origin of the Porsche Henry had seen in the driveway.

But however much Henry wanted to get a hot meal down him after his blessed hot bath, he knew his day wasn't yet over.

One of the many responsibilities of an SIO, and one that Henry took very seriously and never shirked, was taking on the task of personally delivering a death message to the next of kin. Henry always did this in murder cases, first because it was the right thing to do and second because he wanted to see the reactions of the recipient, who might possibly be the killer or know something about what had happened.

He did not think for one moment that Percy's family was behind this, or Charlotte's family, but he needed to know, to see them face to face.

He also needed to speak urgently to his own sister, Lisa, who at that moment seemed to be the last person Percy had spoken to before his death, excluding Lottie and the actual murderer. From a scene search it appeared that the killer had taken Percy's and Lottie's mobile phones with him, so until the service providers had been identified and contacted, it would be impossible to say if Percy had called anyone else in the gap between speaking to Lisa and his death. That line was also being followed up.

Henry also needed his own mobile phone replaced, as it was unusable since its dunking, and headquarters had promised him that a new one with the same number was on the way, being brought across by police motorcyclist.

The two men, Henry and the DCI, raised their heads from their discussion as two hearses crawled regally down Pool Foot Lane.

The body shifters had arrived.

Henry stopped in his tracks. He swallowed something that tasted of petrol: bile. Fear tore all the way through his chest to his groin.

He was looking down the twin side-by-side barrels of a shotgun which were maybe three feet from his nose. Despite the weapon being old and rusting and the barrels looking slightly curved, he truly believed it was still capable of being fired and removing his head.

His eyes moved along the barrel to the shrivelled old man holding the gun.

He could have been a tramp. His white, unwashed hair stuck out at all angles as though he had been electrocuted. The stubble on his face was uneven and unpleasant; his eyebrows sprouted like black caterpillars and nasal hair bushed out like a thicket. His grey eyes, though, were sharp and fierce.

Henry raised his hands slowly, keeping his eyes on the man's right forefinger which was curled around the double trigger. 'Police officer,' he said nervously.

The man sneered contemptuously. 'That's what the last stranger told me – then he robbed me blind.'

Henry could not help but glance past the man at the dilapidated farmhouse behind, which was his home. He also knew that the robbery referred to – more a con, really – had netted two men purporting to be detectives somewhere in the region of one hundred thousand pounds' worth of cut diamonds.

The offenders had arrived at the old man's house with a story that he was urgently needed at Lancaster police station where there were two men who had been arrested following the last theft from the man's home, and he was required to come with the detectives and identify them.

One took him away – all the way to Lancaster – and dumped him in the city centre. The remaining one entered the farmhouse and stole the diamonds.

It was not the sort of crime that Henry investigated, but he knew of it and that no one had ever been arrested for it.

'ID,' the man demanded, shaking the shotgun.

Henry slowly extracted his warrant card, saying, 'We met a while back when I investigated another possible robbery involving your family, when a gang planned to kidnap Percy. I'm Detective Superintendent Christie – remember?' He showed him the warrant card and flashed his best 'please don't shoot me' smile.

The man snatched it with his left hand and peered at it closely, comparing the photograph on it to Henry's actual face. Henry could tell that the man did not recognize him at all.

'Urghh,' he said doubtfully, and handed the card back.

Old Archie Astley-Barnes was a bit of a legend to the cops because he had been conned at least half a dozen times by offenders using a similar ruse: pretending to be police, taking him away from his property and leaving him miles away whilst stealing from his home. Each time it happened, the gangs – none believed to be connected – had become more suave and convincing, but so far none had used actual violence against him. Henry was sure that time would come, because he was easy pickings for thieves in the know. It was estimated he'd had over a million pounds' worth of diamonds stolen from him over the years.

He was also the nominal head of the Astley-Barnes diamond empire – and was Percy's father.

He had made his money from small beginnings, but as he grew older he gradually withdrew from the retail business which Percy had effectively steered for the last twenty years. Old man Archie, however, had not lost his love for diamonds and the wholesale trade and until recently he had kept his hand in though it had become apparent that his mind wasn't what it had been, particularly since the death of his wife, and maybe dementia was setting in.

These were some of the things Henry had learned from his last dealings with the family. It seemed an odd set-up to him, but who was he to judge?

'Could you lower the weapon – please?'

'Where are your so-called colleagues?'

'I'm all alone,' Henry said.

'No partners in crime?'

'Just me.'

He lowered the barrel, seemingly satisfied, then said, 'Do you want to see my rats?'

Flynn backed *Faye* into her mooring at Puerto de Escala, the marina in Puerto Rico, watched by the judgemental eyes of Jose, whose face sagged when he saw the damage to the windows of the boat he cherished as his own.

Flynn tossed him the ropes, then cut the engines and played out the electronic gangplank out to the quayside. Jose tied the ropes and rushed to the plank, but Flynn shot him a gesture that stopped him dead.

'Stay ashore,' Flynn told him.

He turned as Costain opened the stateroom door and beckoned rudely to him. Flynn walked over; Costain said, 'In' and jerked his thumb.

Flynn passed him and went into the stateroom where Trish, having suffered from horrendous seasickness, was now sitting upright, recovering quickly now that the boat was tied to terra firma. Once on land, her recovery would be complete within seconds.

Flynn said, 'What?' to Costain.

'You say fuck all to no one, you got that?'

'My boat has come back into harbour shot to hell . . . people notice tiny details like that.'

'Lie to 'em,' Costain said. 'Just keep your gob shut. If I hear you've been saying anything –' Costain drew his forefinger across his Adam's apple – 'dead man, and I mean it.'

Flynn glared at him, wondering if this was the time to lay that punch on him.

'I'll pay for the damage,' Costain said.

Flynn's mouth closed tight.

'And I want to hire you again tomorrow.'
'You must be—'
'Two thousand euros for the day.'

The rats were in cages in the lounge. Living, breathing creatures of all species. Big ones, fat ones, small ones, very nasty looking ones, all well cared for. Their cages were on the top of an old piano, a sideboard, a bureau, the dining table and coffee table, maybe twelve in total, each with a couple of the creatures inside, scraping away. The whole place stank horribly and was a mess. The settee and armchairs were huge and old with straw-like stuffing sprouting from inside the cushions, as though cultivated. The pictures on the walls were rotting with damp and Henry cringed at this. He knew they were original paintings. Not by young unknowns, but by recognized masters. A Monet, a Picasso and a Constable amongst them. To Henry, they looked as though they were beyond any sort of restoration. It was a criminal act, he thought.

His eyes moved to the bureau; it had a dozen slim drawers in which he knew the old man kept diamonds of all shapes and sizes.

Archie sank into an armchair when Henry broke his sad news.

Deep shock registered in his face as he closed his eyes, shook his head.

'Can I get you anything?' Henry offered, guessing the kitchen would be in as bad a state as the living room.

'No.'

'I'm so sorry,' Henry said.

'Not your fault.'

'But it is my job to catch whoever killed him.'

Archie inhaled deeply, seemingly having aged considerably in the last few minutes.

A rat scratted the bottom of its cage.

'I'm going to need to ask some very searching questions,' Henry said apologetically, 'and I'll need to delve into the business to see if there are any answers or clues there. And into Percy's private life.'

'I don't know much on any of those subjects.'

Henry frowned.

'The business was all Percy's these days. I have nothing to do with it any more, and as for his private life, I don't know anything either.'

'But you are still a diamond merchant?'

'Not in retail. That was Percy's side of the fence. I didn't like the way it was all going, all that TV advertising stuff. I like it neat and personal, and I like wholesale too because that's still one to one. Yeah, Percy ran the shops, I didn't. That said . . .'

Henry always liked it when someone said, 'That said . . .' It was always a good little phrase for a detective . . . but then Archie's eyes misted over. Henry waited for the big reveal. He had been very lucid for a few minutes and Henry worried that possibly his mind was drifting. To keep him on track, he prompted, 'That said, what?'

Archie sighed unsteadily.

'He came asking for help a couple of months ago . . . don't know . . . can't quite think straight.'

'It's OK,' Henry said, seeing the old man was struggling now. 'I do need to have a chat with you sooner rather than later . . . I know your son's death is a major shock . . .'

'What? What do you mean? My son's death? Just who the hell are you?'

Flynn pounded the pavements, taking his usual route, jogging over the cliff-hugging path to the west of Puerto Rico down to the man-made beach at Amadores, where he turned and retraced the run, dropping back down into the port, descending the tight steps to the road – the Doreste y Molina – that ran alongside the beach. He crossed over and, sweating heavily now, ran on to the beach, then sprinted to the water's edge, flicked off his trainers and plunged into the bay, still wearing his running gear. He swam ferociously back and forth for twenty minutes until his limbs were like jelly and he was desperate for a drink. He dragged himself out of the water, collected his trainers and, dripping, walked off the beach and up to the small, semi-detached villa where he lived, just on the perimeter of the town park.

He dumped his footwear on the terrace, entered through the sliding patio doors and went straight under the shower which he ran hot for about ten minutes, then cold for one last blast, emerging refreshed and gasping for food and drink.

And answers.

He dressed in his three-quarter length cut-off jeans, canvas flip-flops and his favourite, but now very tired looking, Keith Richards T-shirt, which had seen much better days.

Then, with a wodge of Scott Costain's money in his back pocket, he headed up to the commercial centre in Puerto Rico with a headful of anger and a feeling that the night ahead could degenerate quite badly.

The lucidity came in bursts from Archie Astley-Barnes. He had a clear memory of some things and no memory at all of others, then no recall of things he had been specific about.

Henry struggled, getting frustrated, because it felt like Archie was toying with him, although he knew this was not the case.

It was like trying to interview a butterfly. Just when he thought he had the man pinned down, he was gone again, and Henry, who had had some experience of dementia in the period leading up to his father's death, realized that Archie needed a home help of some sort at the very least – and some family around him.

He left after an hour, feeling quite emotional, helpless and drained, and was on his new mobile phone straight away, geeing up the officer who was trying to trace Archie's family.

But as tired as he was, Henry still didn't have time to go home and pamper himself for a while yet. There was another death message to deliver.

The Centro Commercial in Puerto Rico had seen much better days. Many of the cheap shops and fast-food restaurants were boarded up, the recession having taken its toll. Now there were days and evenings when it was a bit of a ghost town, although the well run businesses still thrived, even if they were not the cheapest.

Flynn headed initially for one of the Irish bars, the one owned by his boss, Adam Castle, but even that place, normally heaving, was quiet. He wanted somewhere to eat, drink and talk, so he quit the shopping centre and retraced his steps back past his villa to the beach, where a string of restaurants and bars was tucked under the sea wall, overlooked by the promenade. At least he could sit, drink and eat on the beach, even if he couldn't find company. He went into one of the restaurants where he was a regular, found a table literally in the sand and ordered paella for one and a large San Miguel from the tap.

The chairs were big and padded and they swivelled, so he sat back with his drink, waited for his food (twenty minutes) and nibbled some olives while he chewed over his day.

*   *   *

They were a nice family living in a wealthy part of Lytham, one of the huge detached houses within two or three minutes' walking distance of the sea front.

Henry destroyed their lives with a few words.

He watched their world crumble before his eyes, almost wishing he could suck the words back in, reverse away from the house and run.

Mother, father and younger sister – who lived out of town – so mother and father first, then the sister later, if necessary.

No easy way around it. The opening questions, the establishers, the gathering of information, the growing anxiety and puzzlement from the parents. Why was this very senior detective here asking these questions about the whereabouts of their daughter, and who was her boyfriend and what sort of car did she drive? Why was he asking these questions? Henry could see this behind their eyes, the frowns of incomprehension.

'When did you last see your daughter, Charlotte?'

Why the hell did he want to know that?

The mother's hand moving slowly to cover her mouth. The gnawing terror in her eyes.

And then the reveal. The reason for all these questions, on the face of it innocuous, but in the context they were being asked, very, very unpleasant.

The moment when he had to make sure there was no misunderstanding and tell them that their daughter had been brutally murdered.

Not passed away, or gone to a better place, but taken savagely, murdered, dead, gone.

And her boyfriend, too.

Then the terrible shriek from the mother's mouth, the horrendous, unworldly wail that came with the trauma of losing a child, that one dreadful thing that was against the natural course of events. Children should not die before their parents.

Henry stepped back, hovering, allowing the family to have their moment of grief, knowing from experience when to keep his mouth shut tight and when to open it. He had delivered many death messages over the course of his career, the first one when he was only nineteen, barely out of short pants, doing things as a young cop that affected people's lives for ever. The majority of the death messages he delivered in that era of his career as a uniform cop were pretty straightforward, even if they did represent tragedy and sadness to the recipients. Those from hospitals, or from relatives in other parts of the country, or possibly after road deaths, but all he had been was a bearer of bad news.

Those messages he had delivered later in his career, particularly as a senior detective, had been news of suspicious deaths where watching the reaction of the recipients was often crucial to determining their part, if any, in the event.

The instinct gained from those experiences made Henry ninety-nine per cent certain that the grieving family in front of him had nothing to do with their daughter's murder, but he was cynical enough to keep that remaining one per cent back just in case he was wrong. But he was as sure as he could be that he was witnessing a genuine outpouring of grief.

He spent another tough hour with them, by which time he was physically and mentally drained, but had also reached a point where it was natural for him to leave them.

Lottie's father walked out to his car with him, the man's face drawn and etched with deep lines of pain that had not been there when Henry Christie, the Grim Reaper, had knocked.

The two men shook hands.

'I am deeply sorry for your loss,' Henry said: hackneyed words, but the absolute truth.

'I know, I can tell. You are a genuine man and I thank you for your honesty and kindness and patience. It can't have been easy,' Lottie's father said, shaking his head, which was still shrouded in disbelief. 'As you can see, we are a family who wears its heart on its sleeve.'

'Nothing wrong with that,' Henry said. 'I'll come back to you in the morning regarding identification –' Henry had learned that the post mortems had had to be delayed until morning – and he added solemnly, 'I will catch the person responsible.'

'I believe you,' the father said, then went on wistfully, 'You know, we had really high hopes for this relationship. I know Percy was a bit older than Charlotte and he was on the rebound from someone else, but she was also on the rebound from a bad marriage, and I think they were good for each other. She'd been a bit of a wild child – late maturing, I suppose . . .' His mind was a little unfocused. 'But Percy was essentially a good man, I think . . . I can't even begin to imagine why . . . burglary gone wrong is all I can think.'

His voice cracked up and he looked despairingly at Henry, who didn't have the heart to tell him it was no burglary.

But, as much as Henry felt sorry for him, Lottie's dad had started talking about her and Henry's detective instinct suddenly kicked in. He might just say something of interest here, so Henry quickly asked, 'Had Charlotte said anything to you about whether she had fallen out with someone, maybe? Or had she ever mentioned that something was worrying her or Percy at all?'

'No, no, nothing like that. In fact they seemed very happy-go-lucky. Percy had just whisked her away at short notice to the Canaries and back, then over to Florida. They seemed happy and everything was going swimmingly.'

Then he clammed up, losing verbal momentum. His lips tightened, then distorted, and his eyes moistened.

Henry knew the questions would have to wait, though not for long. He patted the man's arm and said goodbye, then zoomed off into the night in his Audi, thinking just how shitty and complicated murder inquiries could be. It was exciting chasing murderers, but the fallout from their crimes was immense. With this one he had the feeling he would have to be on top form. All the hallmarks of a professional hit made it so much more difficult to solve and, even though he had seen the killer, he did not think that would make it much easier.

He floored the accelerator as he hit the motorway.

Flynn had ordered 'blind' paella for one, seafood with all the shells and bones removed before serving, although he much preferred one with all the bits left on because sometimes, especially in company, there was nothing better than dismantling king prawns and crabs' legs, and the taste was much better, but he was not in the mood for that tonight. And he was alone, anyway. It still tasted delicious and the ice-cold San Mig washed it down amazingly. Those things combined with the beach location, the setting sun and some scantily clad ladies who kept eyeing him very obviously had a tranquillizing effect on him.

He pushed his empty plate away and leaned into the folds of the cane-backed chair cushion, took another sip of his beer.

It was at times like this that the island, with its laid back nature, hugged him in its soft arms and made him feel that, although he didn't have much money or a long-term partner-in-love, or even somewhere he could truly call his own, all was right with the world. He really had landed on his feet when he had scuttled here all those years before from his job as a DS on the Drug Squad in Lancashire, under an unjustified cloud, with the spectre of a doomed marriage and not one penny in his pocket from the million quid that had allegedly disappeared during a botched drugs raid on a major dealer's property. On arrival in Gran Canaria, Flynn had thrown himself on the mercy of the people of the island, particularly Adam Castle, owner of several businesses including some charter fishing boats scattered around the Canaries. Castle, who knew Flynn as a holiday guest from previous years, had given him a job on one of his boats and Flynn, through hard work and his intuitive fishing skills, had become a respected skipper, establishing a reputation to be proud of.

He had flitted from property to property, often bedding down in apartments owned by his clients, who were happy to let someone trustworthy live in their properties whilst they were unused, and Flynn paid for gas, electricity and water usage. He had been in his present one for two months but knew the owner was due back on the island for a six week stay and he would have to find somewhere else to rest his head.

The prospect did not worry him. If all else failed, he could crash out on *Faye*, a not altogether displeasing prospect.

He had once found true love on the island but it had ended in tragedy, and though that had been almost four years ago, he wasn't in any rush. All he wanted was a bit of female companionship now and again; he was upfront and honest about that and there were plenty of nice ladies, usually passing through, who were happy to accommodate a short fling, no strings.

All in all he was content. And he hated it when people like Costain appeared and screwed with his peace.

His mind twirled back to his day at sea.

He had denied knowing Costain, but Costain himself hadn't had such qualms and after a period of careful observation had quickly pegged Flynn, which had been an uncomfortable collar-tugging moment for the ex-cop.

Before becoming a detective, Flynn had spent the early years of his Lancashire police service in uniform in Blackpool, and any cop posted to that resort knew the Costains.

They were an extended, complex family who ruled the Shoreside

estate and much of Blackpool in terms of burglary, theft and
intimidation, and any cop who never came across them face to face,
or had to deal with the fallout from their nefarious activities, was
fortunate indeed. Flynn had met them countless times, mainly for
minor things, and recalled them being always uncooperative and
unpleasant.

Flynn had heard various rumours recently that, despite some
major setbacks, the Costains had gone very big and professional
over the last few years and been involved in some very nasty turf
wars with other crime families in the north west of England. Flynn
did not know much more than that and hadn't been especially
inclined to find out.

Being a cop was now a completely different country to him.
News about the Costains only reached him on his infrequent visits
to the UK and had gone in one ear and out the other. His life was
now as skip of a sportfishing boat and he was intent on keeping a
low profile and not rummaging about in the past. He still believed
he had been unfairly hounded out of the job – so being accused
once again of corruption and theft, albeit by pond life like Scott
Costain, rankled him – a man he had never actually met, though it
was always possible that Scott knew him. It was the striking family
resemblance that Flynn had first noticed with Scott, and when he
had told Flynn his name it had only confirmed Flynn's belief. Scott
Costain was well and truly out of the Costain peapod.

Flynn did not like hearing the accusation again. It had been unjust
way back and now, years later, it seemed even more unfair. Flynn
had been branded guilty by association and nothing was ever proved
against him.

Though where his cop partner at the time, a certain Jack Hoyle,
was concerned, it was a completely different story.

'Mmm, Jack Hoyle,' Flynn thought as he stared unfocused across
the beach. His mouth twisted cynically at the thought of the man
he had considered his best friend . . .

Flynn almost jumped out of his skin when a big hand clamped
down on his shoulder. He nearly spilled his beer. He looked up into
Adam Castle's face, his boss, someone to whom he'd had a lot to be
grateful for over the last few years. In return for that first job as crew
on one of Castle's sportfishing boats and a job as a bouncer on the
doors of one of Castle's nightclubs in the commercial centre, Flynn
had never let him down. In fact Flynn had become arguably the best

skipper in the Canaries at that moment, bringing in many repeat bookings, which were the lifeblood of that business. Flynn had also bought a big chunk of *Faye* from his savings and Castle had converted the cash into a forty-nine per cent stake in the boat. Castle had promised the extra two per cent if this year turned out well, which it had every possibility of doing. Castle's stake and interest in the good management of the boat was high and he was entitled to know what was happening.

He sat next to Flynn and ordered two more beers.

Flynn eyed him warily. This was their first chance for a chat since the shooting incident and Flynn would be guessing that Castle wanted reassurance that it wasn't Flynn who was the problem.

At least Castle had the patience to wait for the beers to land before turning full face to Flynn. 'Well?' he said expectantly. Castle owned several well run businesses in the Canaries and hated anything that tarnished his reputation.

Flynn held up a hand and cocked an eyebrow. 'Not down to me,' he assured him.

'There was a gun on board,' Castle said grimly.

'The customer's, not mine. He snuck it on,' Flynn said. There had once been an issue of a hunting rifle that Flynn kept on board – for self-defence, he had argued weakly at the time – but that was now resolved . . . in a way. Flynn went on to explain how the day had panned out and ended up in a firefight across the bows.

Castle considered the story and asked, 'What was he after, this Costain guy?'

'Not sure. Being nosy, on a fact finding mission? Clearly those people on the other boat were diving on something, or there was someone on board whose ID they were trying to hide . . . dunno,' he shrugged. 'Do you know what it could be? Is there a wreck down there, maybe?' Flynn told Castle the exact position of the encounter, where the cliffs plunged deep, straight into the ocean. Castle thought it through but shook his head.

'Nothing comes to mind, but I'll ask around.' He paused. 'You didn't recognize the other boat?'

Flynn said no, but told Castle its name and make.

'OK,' Castle nodded, took a long swig of his beer. 'I'll see if anyone knows anything . . . but in the meantime . . .'

'He's already booked *Faye* for tomorrow. Two thousand euros.'

'Thanks but no thanks. What time is he due?'

'Nine.'

'I'll be there and we can tell him to shove it.'

'OK,' Flynn nodded with a shrug, feeling a slight tinge of disappointment.

With a change in his body language, Castle sat back with his beer. 'Are you going to show your face at Karen's leaving do tonight?'

'I hadn't thought so.'

'She's up at my Irish bar now, then moving on to one of the discos with her mates. I'm sure she would like you to say adios.' Castle leaned forward and gave Flynn a meaningful look. 'If you know what I'm saying.'

The innuendo was startlingly clear. Flynn spluttered, 'But she's your sister!'

'And a grown woman. Divorced. And she likes you a lot and cannot fathom out why you've been keeping her at arms' length.'

Flynn sighed. 'Because she's your sister – and I only want one thing. I don't want to hurt her and piss you off.'

'She can handle herself,' Castle smiled. 'If you ask me, you'd make a great couple and I wouldn't be sad if she decided to stay on the island. I could find her more substantial work if she wanted it.'

'And university? She doesn't want to spend the rest of her life behind a bar or in a booking office . . . she's after a career of some sort, isn't she?'

Castle shrugged. 'It's up to her . . . and you, maybe.'

'You trying to matchmake?'

'No – kick your arse. You're an emotional desert, Flynn; Gill Hartland is gone and that won't change. Time to move on.' Castle finished his beer, winked at Flynn, then left.

Flynn sipped his pensively for a while, mulling Castle's words over.

He was about to rise and make his way up to the commercial centre when he spotted a face he recognized at the bar. Slightly adjusting his trajectory, he went and stood next to the man until he turned and recognized Flynn with a slight look of shock.

Flynn's eyes narrowed. 'How come you didn't show up for the charter this morning?'

The young man frowned and looked annoyed with himself. He was the one who had originally booked *Faye* for the day's fishing for himself, his wife and another couple. These were the ones Flynn was looking forward to taking out, but they had been replaced by the less than charming Scott Costain, who had spun the cock and bull story about the deposit.

'Well, put it this way,' he said to Flynn, 'when a fucking animal turns up and threatens to rape your wife and stick a knife in your ribs if you refuse his offer, then, with all due respect, Steve, you back off – or at least I do. I'm not used to dealing with villains, nor their, frankly, equally scary and evil girlfriends. It was like being confronted by Ian Brady and Myra Hindley, the friggin' Moors murderers.'

Flynn nodded, totally understanding. 'How did he know you had the charter in the first place?'

'He must've heard us talking in the bar we were in last night. We were all really looking forward to it and chatting a bit loud and messing about, I suppose. He muscled in and threatened us all. His girlfriend stood behind him and looked like she ate fava beans and human livers.'

'Did he pay you off?'

'No.' The young man looked crestfallen, having to admit this dent in his pride and courage.

'Which bar were you in?' The man told him. 'You know we tried to contact you this morning?'

'He said we weren't to take any calls from you and if we turned up to complain, he'd drown us. I believed him.'

Flynn's rage began to bubble at the effrontery of Costain, believing he could just waltz in with his insidious threats of violence and get away with it.

'Well, I'm sorry that happened,' Flynn said. He reached into his back pocket and withdrew five neatly folded one hundred euro notes. He handed them to the man. 'This is your deposit back.'

The man's mouth popped open like a grouper fish. 'It's not your fault, it's mine, being a pathetic twat.'

'Take it,' Flynn insisted. 'I've known and dealt with men like Costain all my life and you did the right thing by backing off – honestly. He would have knifed you, trust me. Take the money back.'

'You sure?'

'Oh yes, take it, it's yours . . . and just so you know, I caned him good and proper because I thought his whole story stank.' His eyes twinkled mischievously. 'And I haven't finished with him, either. He caused me too much grief today. How much longer are you on the island for?'

'Four days.'

'Come along to the boat the day after tomorrow, nine o'clock sharp. I'll give you and your party the best day's fishing ever – for free, then we'll all go and get the best paella on the island later.'

The man's eyes bulged. 'Are you certain?'

'Positive. And now I think it's time me and Mr Costain and Cruella de Vil had a heart to heart.'

Fatigue was close to engulfing him, right to his very core. He had thought that he might have wanted a long, hot bath, but found he couldn't be bothered. After he'd eaten the curry of the day, downed a pint, a JD chaser and three paracetamols to ward off the aches he felt were coming, Henry had a hot shower, then crawled into the bed he shared with Alison in the private living accommodation at the rear of the Tawny Owl.

He fell asleep almost instantly.

SEVEN

F lynn strode through the public gardens, past his villa, towards the commercial centre.

The pathway meandering up between the manicured lawns and high palms was quiet, but Flynn did not really notice one way or the other because he was concentrating single-mindedly on his self-imposed quest for vengeance. Just to feel what Scott Costain's skull would be like to punch. When he reached the main road he managed to stop at the end of the walkway as a black Mercedes jerked to a sudden stop right in front of him, impeding his crossing.

Flynn groaned with annoyance but did not pay any attention to the car or even wonder why it had stopped. It was just an obstacle to get around and, instinctively, he began to walk around the back of it.

At which point two things happened simultaneously.

The rear door swung open and a voice somewhere over his left shoulder called, 'Oi, Flynn.'

He twisted to look. Saw two men in dark clothing, neither of whom he recognized, just feet away from him. Then saw the stubby club in the hand of the one on the right arcing towards his head. Flynn ducked, feeling the whizz of air whoosh just an inch away from his ear, but he staggered backwards against the open car door, noting – fleetingly – the dark shape of a man in the back seat of the Merc, at the far side. Fortunately for Flynn, the way in which he had backed against the car door meant he was still facing the two men, one of whom screamed, 'Get the bastard!'

They rushed towards him, the club raised to strike again.

In a parallel thought, Flynn cursed inwardly. His head was muzzy, his reactions slow from three pints of San Miguel and a paella, his thinking skewed because of his concentrated thoughts and the prospect of some sort of physical confrontation with Costain.

He hadn't been mentally prepared to take on two determined attackers who came out of nowhere.

He shook his brain, tried to get into gear, and did the thing that managed to catch the two men off balance.

He dropped his right shoulder and charged between them, keeping his head low. He connected somewhere midway, spinning them around and forcing them off balance. But as the one with the club stumbled sideways he swung the weapon around again as he pivoted away and caught Flynn a glancing blow across the back of his skull like a topspin shot at tennis. It had the desired effect of knocking him off his feet. He went sprawling on to his hands and knees on the footpath.

Quickly recovering their composure after Flynn's surprise fight back, they dived on to him before he could roll up, pinning him to the concrete with their combined weight.

Flynn twisted, fought, squirming and rearing like a bucking bronco, but they straddled him and he couldn't shake them off. One forced his head into the ground, pounding him on the temple with very heavy fists. The other man dragged Flynn's arms around his back. Flynn felt plastic handcuffs going on, drawing his wrists inexorably together.

This served to make him fight harder. With a roar and a rush of strength he rolled over and kicked out wildly.

One of the men howled in agony as Flynn connected. He had

flat-footed him in the groin. The man cradled his smashed testicles and doubled over, sank to his knees, spluttering, 'Oh Jesus, God,' as the pain seared up through his stomach like a skewer.

The other one, armed with the club, swung it hard again at Flynn's head. He saw it coming from the corner of his eye, could not react quickly enough and the heavy stub of lead-filled wood clonked against his head like a mini wrecking ball. For a moment everything went to a juddering blank, decorated by shooting stars, and the next thing Flynn knew for certain was that he was being bundled into the back seat of the Mercedes, thrown heavily into the footwell behind the front seats, his head and shoulders underneath the feet of the man who was already inside. One of his attackers slid in alongside the guy and slammed his feet down on Flynn's rib cage, making him wheeze as the air shot out of his lungs and he wondered if he heard one of his bones crack like a Twiglet.

The other man of the pair who had pounced on him slammed the car door shut and dropped into the front passenger seat, groaning as he sat and readjusted his balls.

The car screeched away from the kerb into the night traffic. The man sitting above Flynn's head stomped his feet repeatedly on to the side of his face like he was pounding some sort of fitness machine. Flynn tried to position his head to lessen the impact, but the blows still came down hard and in the end, pinned down, hardly able to move, his hands tied behind his back, head swimming, he just had to let it all happen. His brain switched off and he closed his eyes without ever expecting to open them again.

At the Tawny Owl, Alison Marsh flopped into bed next to the spread-eagled Henry. She rearranged his limbs gently so she could at least fit in next to her exhausted, half-drowned fiancé.

She snuggled down contentedly, grinning a little as she felt Henry begin to harden.

'Good day, babe?' he murmured into her ear.

She stifled what would have been a long yawn. 'Mmm,' she said dreamily. Her right hand slithered back behind her and she took hold of him in a reverse grip. Somewhere from deep in his throat came a groan.

'Even had an American guy in for breakfast . . . real charmer . . . I now officially run an international business,' she said, let go of Henry and fell asleep.

Henry, who hadn't opened his eyes, said, 'Great,' but then frowned as a thought bounced transiently across his brain. Before he could grab it, dissect it, analyse it, he too was back to sleep. The blood ebbed and he began to snore contentedly in Alison's ear.

Hawke eased his jacket off with care, unbuttoned his shirt and with even more care peeled this garment off slowly, particularly when he extracted his right arm from the sleeve, exposing the burned flesh where the flare had hit him. He gasped as he was forced to tug the last little bit of shirt fabric; it had stuck to the burn, which itself felt as if it was still sizzling. He dropped the shirt on to the floor and looked angrily at his singed flesh.

The burn ran all the way from his right nipple where it spread out in the shape of a fried egg, up his shoulder, across and down his right bicep, then changed into a shape resembling a Chinese dragon – with teeth.

The phosphorus had seared his flesh into a silvery-black colour that shimmered as he twisted his arm and inspected it, his face a crumpled scowl. Some parts of the burn were weeping yellowish green pus that came up through it like olive oil through gauze.

Hawke hissed with pain as he applied a full tube of Savlon antiseptic cream to the wound, jerking when he inadvertently touched it with the neck of the tube.

'Like I said,' the old man was reiterating, watching dispassionately and without sympathy as Hawke treated himself. 'I don't like complications.'

Hawke raised his eyes malignly.

The old man returned the look, unafraid. He then lifted his ragdoll-like paralysed legs one at a time and placed them on the footrest of his motorized wheelchair. Using the joystick, he swung the state of the art chair away from Hawke, almost like he was turning a horse, and accelerated across the wooden floor of the living room to the bar on the rear wall, which had been constructed to his specifications so it was the correct height for him to prepare his own drinks.

He dug some shaved ice out of an icebox and slid it into a long glass, poured in a large measure of whisky and added a blast of soda from a syphon.

'I could do with one of those – neat,' Hawke said.

The old man swilled his drink around, took a sip, ignored Hawke and aimed the wheelchair across the room to the large settee.

Sprawled on it was a young, very slim girl, sleeping. She was fourteen years old and was naked. Hearing the whirring approach of the wheelchair, her oriental eyes shot open. Once these had been beautiful, wide green eyes, the eyes of a child, full of wonder and hope. They were still the eyes of a child, but no longer beautiful. Now they were sunk in their sockets, all fear, exhaustion and resignation. Without hope, without a future. She knew exactly what was expected of her with regard to the evil man, the cripple, in the wheelchair.

She moved slowly on to her back, her dead eyes focused on the ceiling, drew up her knees and parted her legs.

The old man manoeuvred his wheelchair alongside her, a greedy look of lust and scorn on his grey, wrinkled face. He reached out and touched her belly, his thin, gnarled fingers snaking downwards.

'My lovely.' He smiled.

She returned his look with one of abject terror, which made him smile even more as his fingertips extended downwards and she arched herself up to him.

Suddenly he jerked his hand off her stomach, frustrated and annoyed with himself, knowing the only sexual reaction he could have now was within his own head. He despised the fact that he had a beautiful young Asian girl naked on his settee and no amount of touching, probing, licking or biting would ever bring a response from his body.

She gasped a sigh of relief as he jerked the control on his wheelchair and spun away. She hugged herself into a ball, burying her face into the back of the settee.

Hawke had finished plastering himself with the Savlon. He was now at the bar, shirt still off. He threw four Nurofen tablets down his throat and washed them down with the neat whisky he had poured. He had downed over twenty tablets that day. Initially they had taken some of the edge off the constant pulse of pain, but now they were having little effect.

'I need a doctor,' he whined, 'and some decent drugs.'

'I've called my pet GP. He's on his way,' the old man said, staring cynically at Hawke. 'I thought you were a pro.'

'Hey,' he responded, affronted, 'even pros sometimes make

mistakes. The fact a cop showed up –' he shrugged his left shoulder – 'just bad luck.'

He poured more whisky and threw it down his throat.

'Anyways, I'm gonna sort that SOB, cop or no cop. No one gets away with doing this to me.' He glared down at his cream-smeared burn, the pure white Savlon mixing with the oozing green pus, reminding him of oil paint. 'I look like a fuckin' napalmed geek, scarred for life, man, scarred for life. He'll suffer – and so will his bitch of a girlfriend. Henry Christie my ass. Dead Henry.'

'What? Who?' the old man asked sharply. He had not been paying close attention to Hawke's babbling until the name was mentioned. 'What name did you say?'

'Henry Christie.'

'Henry Christie?' the old man said thoughtfully. Then, 'Henry Christie? Are you certain?'

'Oh yeah – dead certain – why?'

'Then you have my blessing. You can kill that man for me right now and rape his girlfriend, then kill her too, in any order you wish. In fact I'll give you good money for it.'

'Why?' Hawke became excited at the prospect of killing someone for pleasure, purely as an act of revenge, *and* getting paid for it. He was already visualizing the scene: both parties tied up, Christie being made to watch the horrific defilement of the lovely Alison, then her death before his own.

'Let's just say he's been a thorn in the side of my family for far too long and this might just be the ideal opportunity to deal with him.'

'Sounds like a good plan.' Hawke looked across the room at the girl on the settee, still curled up tight, her thin bottom towards them, her spine and pelvic bones pushed against her skin.

The old man saw the glance. 'Want her? She's yours,' he told Hawke. 'She's ripe for the punters now.'

'And clean?'

'Clean as a bleached drain,' the old man cackled.

Hawke downed his drink and walked over to her, unzipping his trousers.

EIGHT

t was the fourth hard slap that brought Flynn out of his unconscious state to one of quarter-consciousness. His head lolled, he drooled, then slurped up some sort of thick gloop from the corner of his mouth that tasted foul.

'Wake up . . . c'mon . . .'

There was another stinging slap across his left cheek that fast-cricked his head sideways. His eyes shot open with ferocity and he leapt forward intending to strangle the man who was assaulting him. A reflex, but useless, action. He could not move. His forearms were taped to the arms of a cane chair and someone behind him had clamped their hands down on to his shoulders, preventing him from doing anything silly.

Nevertheless, the man in front of him jerked back in surprise, ensuring he was out of reach.

Flynn's head pounded. He could feel the throb of swellings happening now, the left side of his face, jaw, temple, skull, all pumping agonizingly, the side that he had been stamped on.

'You bastards,' he uttered savagely, but slurring the words through his distorted face. 'Wait till . . .'

'Ah, ah, ah.' Another man stepped in front of him, between Flynn and the original guy, who moved out of Flynn's sight.

This man put his forefinger under Flynn's chin and tilted up his head.

It was at this moment Flynn realized he'd only got one good eye, his right. The other was closed tight, swollen, sore. He swallowed again and this time knew he was tasting a cocktail of his own blood and saliva which clogged the back of his throat.

He attempted to focus on the figure in front of him and also try to start working out where he was, what the hell was going on and, more importantly, how to get out of this mess.

For a moment, as his good eye tried to focus, the man tilting his head remained shimmering and vague . . . the lighting of the location didn't help . . . the room, or wherever he now was, being poorly lit.

After much blinking and head clearing, Flynn's sight began to tighten up. He looked up at the man's face as its contours and features sharpened, like a camera being focused.

Flynn's cut and swollen bottom lip popped open.

'You!' he wheezed.

'Hi, Steve.' The man crouched down in front of Flynn. 'Surprised to see me?'

'Only as surprised as seeing a rat in a drain,' Flynn slurred croakily. 'Jack Hoyle.' He almost laughed.

In his turn, the man – Hoyle – laughed harshly. 'Long time no see.'

Flynn swore at him using the worst word he could imagine, then demanded, 'What's going on?'

'Nice to see you too,' Hoyle said. 'Actually, to be honest, Steve, not nice, but, that said,' he went on in a conversational tone, 'you have a lot to thank me for, mate. If it wasn't for me, you'd be dead and dumped by now. I've kept you alive, me, your former partner in the pursuit of crime. Y'see, these people –' and here Hoyle waggled his finger around the room – 'are not the sort to ask questions. They just kill folk. Occasionally . . . how should I phrase this?' He pretended to think. 'They extract information before putting bullets into brains, but in this case – *your* case – they really have all the info they need, so it's just a case of pulling triggers . . . get my drift?'

Flynn remained uncooperatively silent, his one good eye staring malignly from its socket at Hoyle.

Then he took his eye off Hoyle and tried to make sense of where he was and work out who else was in the room, but they remained out of his line of sight.

Despite the poor lighting, Flynn did notice something – the plastic sheet rolled out across the floor like a carpet.

His eye came back at Hoyle, who went on, 'So, because I know you and we have a history of sorts—'

'Thief,' Flynn blurted.

Hoyle continued as if he had not heard the accusation. 'Because of this—'

'Wife stealer,' Flynn said.

Hoyle clammed up and grinned. 'Let's not go there, Steve,' he said patronizingly.

'You did!'

'And so did the lovely Faye.' Hoyle shook his head sadly. 'Bygones.' He waved his hand dismissively. 'So, as I was saying, because I know you, these nice people have allowed me to ask you one question. If you answer it truthfully and in a way that also makes me believe its veracity, you could live. But if you lie or act like a dick, trust me, Steve, you'll be dead.'

Hoyle's face became deadpan as he regarded Flynn, who glowered back whilst gently and unobtrusively easing and stretching the tape that was wrapped around his wrists, securing him to the chair. Flynn thought it was masking tape, rather than duct or parcel tape, which was good because it was easier to tear.

He moved his backside on the chair, which wasn't the most well-constructed piece of furniture in the world. It felt frail and slightly rickety to Flynn.

'What's the question?' he growled.

'Why were you there today? And what was Scott Costain doing on board?'

Not that he was surprised by this, as it only confirmed his suspicion. There could only be one reason for this abduction – Scott Costain.

'I take it you were on the other boat?'

'I'm asking the questions, Steve – but yes, I was there at the helm.'

'OK,' Flynn said, 'why were you there and why did you shoot at us? Fair question, I believe.'

Hoyle's eyes rolled in their sockets. 'Flynnie, you won't get another chance, mate. These guys will whack you, and the one you bashed in the bollocks wants to slice yours off like sweetmeats and stuff 'em down your throat.' Hoyle leaned forward. 'Last chance saloon, Steve.'

One of the other men moved into Flynn's restricted line of sight – the one whose testicles he had tried to kick up into his throat.

Flynn tilted his head. 'Can you taste your balls, mate?'

The man's face betrayed rage and pain. A gun hung loosely in his hand by his side. He brought it up and held it diagonally across his chest, his eyes ablaze and the message clear.

If Flynn had not known for certain before – and he had, the plastic sheet basically telling him everything – he knew then. In spite of Jack Hoyle's cooing reassurance that he need only speak the truth, it did not really matter what came out of his mouth. He was a dead man.

Flynn flexed his muscles against the masking tape again, trying to work out how many men were in the room.

Two for certain, Hoyle and the guy with upwardly digested balls.

Four men had abducted him – Sore Nuts and one other on the roadside, one in the back of the Mercedes, who could possibly have been Hoyle, and a driver.

That could mean two more were standing silently behind him, guns drawn, all eager to put a bullet in his head.

So it was him – Flynn, strapped to a rickety chair – versus four.

Flynn's mind whirred. Question was, knowing that he was going to die here, wherever 'here' was, did he go down fighting and try to take others with him – such as his ex-partner, who was clearly walking the left-hand path? Answer: yes.

He tested the bindings again. They had loosened slightly, since masking tape has a very slight elasticity to it.

'Well, mate?' Hoyle asked. He was still squatting in front of Flynn and, increasingly confident, he leaned forward even further to get some real eye contact, his face only inches away from Flynn's forehead.

If nothing else, before his death Flynn would be able to deliver a blow to Hoyle that was long overdue.

But Flynn didn't want it to stop there, so his first blow had to be hard, fast, accurate and surprising. It had to count, but it also had to give him advantage. All the luck, speed and strength Flynn could muster had to be mashed into one pot. He had to forget his injuries, his bad head, his closed eye, the fact that he was tied to a chair.

He placed his feet flat on the floor, knowing that the plastic sheet would make all this harder for him because good grip would be vital for the moves he had planned. If he slipped he would look more than stupid. He would probably just topple over and end up with a double tap to the forehead and that would be it. He would be rolled up in the sheet and dumped in the mountains without even having discovered what all this crap was about.

He braced himself.

Then, using the balls of his feet, he rocked the chair backwards slightly to gather some momentum and force, then pitched forward and smashed his forehead as hard as possible into the unprotected bridge of Hoyle's nose. Flynn felt the man's septum crumble. His face imploded as the nose broke.

It hurt Flynn, but it hurt Hoyle even more.

He tumbled backwards with a scream, trying to stop the burst of blood like someone trying to stem the flow of water from a fractured mains pipe.

Much as Flynn would have liked to sit back and admire his handiwork – it was the least he owed Jack for all those years of torture, humiliation and anguish – he didn't have time even to think about it.

He carried on with his momentum, doubling forward on to his feet, the chair effectively stuck on him like a shell on a turtle. He swung the chair around, then propelled himself backwards into Mr Sore Balls, attacking him with the four feet of the chair like a lion tamer. Flynn hoped the man's groin was still throbbing enough to slow down his reactions.

Flynn drove him against the wall with two of the chair legs, one in his chest, the other in his lower belly, and once Flynn knew he had him there, he didn't stop, but pushed even harder, feeling the man's skin give and then split as Flynn forced himself backwards. The points of the feet stabbed through and he screamed as they pierced his chest and stomach and then his internal organs and he fought to pull the chair away, but Flynn pushed harder, forcing the two legs deep into the man's body.

He raised his head and saw there was only one other man in the room, who had watched Flynn's sudden explosive action with astonishment that had made him hesitate just a moment too long. This was the second guy who had taken Flynn off the street, the one armed with the cosh. He fumbled for something in his pocket.

Somewhere in the distance, Flynn heard echoing footsteps, running, shouting, other people coming, drawn by the scream of the man Flynn had stabbed with the chair.

He realized he had to take out this third man quickly, otherwise the game was over, and it would not be an easy task as he was bent double with a chair affixed to his back on to which a man's body was skewered, now a dead weight of about fifteen stone that he was unable to shake off.

The adrenalin that had flushed into his system, overriding his injuries and the sluggishness from his alcohol intake, drove him on. With the chair and man still attached, he pounded in an ungainly way towards the third man like a lumbering but deadly bull and with his head low, tensing the muscles in his neck so much they looked like coils of steel wire. He charged into him, crashing the crown of his head into the man's sternum. He kept his head down and continued to drive the man backwards until he, too, was pinned up against the opposite wall, clawing at Flynn, who reared his head back and crashed his skull into his chest again – though only because the weight on his back prevented him from standing upright and head-butting him. Then, contorting, he twisted and smashed his right knee up into the man's unprotected groin, flattening his second pair of testicles that night.

The man screamed.

So Flynn did it again, harder, then backed off as the man doubled over, incapacitated by the pain. Flynn then twisted and jerked, fighting to dislodge the man from the chair legs. The dead man's arms and legs flailed like a Guy Fawkes dummy, although one made of flesh and blood as opposed to paper and straw. With a sickening audible slurp and a gush of blood from the two massive penetrating wounds, he slithered off and hit the floor untidily. Released from that burden, Flynn smashed the chair hard against the wall in an effort to destroy it.

The chair disintegrated and Flynn's arms came free, although they were still attached by the masking tape to the chair arms, as if they were splints.

Using the chair arm still strapped to his forearm like a bat of some sort, he swung his right forearm against the head of the man he'd just chest-butted and double-kneed, who was still doubled over in agony, clutching his balls – a bit of payback for him earlier clubbing Flynn on the back of the head. The man slid face down on to the plastic sheet.

Spinning back and stepping over the other – dead – man who was lying in a spreading pool of almost black, very oxygenated blood, Flynn went back to Jack Hoyle. He was on his hands and knees, his head flopping between his arms with blood flowing freely from his broken nose, still stunned and disoriented by the head-butt.

Flynn tore the chair arms off, ripping the masking tape with his teeth and pulling it off like removing plaster. He threw them down . . . then another shout from somewhere else in the building told him he had no time for a head to head with his old friend.

Instead he strode up to Hoyle and booted him in the ribs, sending him sprawling across the floor. It was all he had time to do.

He swooped down and picked up the dead man's gun – a semi-automatic pistol of some sort – and went to the door, glancing around and seeing that he was simply in a very bare room without windows, maybe a basement or cellar, he guessed.

He opened the door. Beyond was a fairly wide, long, well-lit hallway or corridor of some sort, two doors to the left, a flight of stairs to the right and dead ahead, at the far end, another door. All the walls were whitewashed and Flynn thought he could well be on the ground floor of a villa. At least he hoped it was the ground floor, whatever type of building it was, because that would make it easier to leave. The stairs on the right gave him the clues he needed.

He twisted out, and tried the first door on his left: locked. Then the next along, also locked. He started walking quickly to the door at the far end, but as he passed the foot of the stairs he saw a man crouching on the landing at the top of them, gun in hand.

Flynn raised the gun he'd seized, not having chance to check it, and pulled the trigger without hesitation, an unaimed shot. The gun fired and the recoil almost broke his wrist. A heavy round, maybe a Magnum load, possibly a .357 load.

Enough to blow a hole clean through the man's chest and hurl him back against the wall, a look of utter surprise on his face. He slithered down the previously pure white wall.

Flynn sprinted on to the door at the end of the corridor, expecting to find it locked, but it was open and he ran through it to find himself outside on a large terrace with a huge infinity swimming pool in front of him; there was a pagoda in one corner, beneath it a table and chairs – fortunately with no one sitting on them. The whole area was lit by under floor floodlights and looked very nice indeed.

He ran across the terrace towards a high wall, ripping off the last remnants of the masking tape. He did not pause to look back as he reached the wall and scaled it, tucking the pistol into his waistband and scrabbling desperately over it. As he reached the top he got a one-eyed glance back at the building he had just left in the instant before tumbling over the other side and hoping it wasn't a twenty foot drop.

It was a large, three storey villa, very classy.

The drop was perhaps six feet on to a footpath. He found himself in a cul-de-sac where there was a cluster of very expensive executive villas, none of which seemed to have any lights on or show any signs of habitation, other than the one he'd just left. The only lighting was from fairly dim street lights along the roadside.

He recognized where he was, remembered once having picked up a charter party from one of the villas.

He crouched as he landed, then ran low, keeping close to the wall for cover and drawing the gun from his waistband. He ran along the cul-de-sac towards the exit and remembered that it was controlled by substantial, remotely controlled metal gates that he knew would be very hard to scale quickly.

That looked as if it would be a problem for him because he did not want to end up caught halfway over like an insect on a zap-trap.

He glanced back.

No one there yet. There would be.

His run slowed whilst he tried to figure this out. He looked up a steep driveway leading to another villa which was all in darkness, but his good eye opened wide. There was a yellow and black sports car parked on this driveway, and the gates were open.

Still crouching low, he ran up the drive alongside the car, now recognizing the sleek shape as that of a Lamborghini. The villa behind was another three storey monstrosity, rising high into the night, and seemingly unoccupied at the moment. The car was a gorgeous piece of engineering and Flynn hesitantly tried the driver's door, wondering if his luck would hold just once.

'Yesss,' he hissed triumphantly as the door opened. And saw the ignition key in the lock. 'Smug rich bastard,' he thought. 'Never expect to get thieved.'

The door cracked and Flynn expected it to open towards him, but it went upwards like a raptor's wing.

He folded himself uncomfortably into the tight driver's seat, his big frame really far too huge for the confines of such a sports car, which was obviously made for midgets. Or tiny rich people.

He pulled the door down, pressed the clutch, slotted the gear stick into neutral and turned the ignition key, dabbing the accelerator gingerly.

The engine came to life with a shrieking roar, then screamed as he tapped the gas pedal again and the twelve cylinders came to life in what seemed to be a very bad temper.

Flynn was now enclosed in what was essentially a bullet on wheels, the like of which he had never driven before, or even sat in . . . 'This night,' he thought, 'just keeps on giving.' He found reverse, released the handbrake, eased up the clutch very gently to find the bite, tapped the accelerator.

Before he knew what was happening the Lamborghini sped backwards down the steep drive at an incredible speed. Flynn hung on to the wheel.

There was a horrible crunching, metallic scraping noise from underneath as the car skimmed the footpath and Flynn realized that taking this very low slung car out was probably best done slowly and carefully.

Not tonight.

He slammed on the brakes just before the car embedded itself in the wall of the villa opposite – and stalled the beast.

Glancing sideways he spotted the dark shapes of two men running towards him, then the muzzle-flash and crack of a shot as one fired a gun. He ducked instinctively and heard the ping of the round glance off the bonnet of the car.

He restarted the engine, ground it into first on the gatefold gear change. Another bullet slammed into the front wing. The men were closing rapidly. Flynn had visions of being shot to death at the wheel of one of the world's greatest supercars, which probably wasn't the worst way to go.

Not tonight.

He released the clutch, yanked the steering wheel down, hit the gas. The car skidded away, the tyres screeching on the asphalt. Almost instantly it was moving at a speed that jarred Flynn's head back against the rest, the power absolutely incredible as the nose lifted and it charged like a black marlin towards the closed metal gates at the end of the road.

Once more, in a parallel thought, Flynn realized he was doing something he had pined to do since he was a lad: screw the backside off a Lambo.

He closed his good eye, gripped the wheel as tight as a rod hooked into a sailfish and floored it.

Less than a second later, with a terrible crunching, tearing noise, the car burst through the wrought iron gates and, although he was not certain, he got the feeling that all four wheels left the ground and the car actually flew.

As it landed on the road beyond the gates, he opened his eye and fought to control the car, knowing that directly opposite was a deep ravine and if he didn't manage to turn, the car would definitely be in mid-air.

Yanking the wheel around, he managed to turn the car right, keep it on the road and race away, fumbling to find the headlight switch.

Flynn knew where he was and where he was going. That he was up in the mountains inland from Puerto Rico and the roads were unlit and treacherous for the unwary – and possibly those with only one eye. The first hairpin bend was approaching and he was doing ninety mph.

Flynn abandoned the Lamborghini near the police station in Puerto Rico. He gave it a rueful backward glance, sorry he had caused so much damage to it, but glad he'd had the chance to drive it, in spite of the circumstances. He dropped the gun into a storm drain after wiping it for prints and hobbled his way painfully up to the commercial centre, which was buzzing with late night revellers, some stag and hen parties stumbling from club to club, the sound of loud music pummelling his ears.

In spite of his appearance he attracted only one or two looks of passing horror, but that was all. A beaten-up person at that time of night in the centre was not an unusual sight.

He went to each bar in turn, walking through, trying to spot his prey: Scott Costain. The man on whom Flynn laid all the blame.

He was eagerly anticipating pinning him up against a wall and interrogating him.

Six bars later he still had not located him and was becoming angrier by the second. In the seventh, he gave up.

Costain would have to wait, because Flynn needed to lick his wounds and think about the not too distant future. He eased his way to the bar, ordered a pint of San Mig with a double Johnny Walker chaser, took his drinks to a deserted booth, sat back, breathed out and sank the whisky in one, feeling the spirit burn its way down his throat into his chest.

Then he drank half the beer, not realizing how dehydrated he was as the adrenalin ebbed out of him and he came down.

As he placed the beer down, he looked up and saw Scott Costain and his girlfriend, Trish, buying drinks.

Flynn moved quickly.

One moment he was seated, next he was behind Costain and dragging him out of the bar by the scruff of the neck. A table went over, two chairs, people stepped out of the way, a few saying 'What the fuck . . .'

By then Flynn had Costain out on the main concourse, keeping him off balance, then into the unlit ginnel by the side of the bar where Flynn spun him and lived the dream. He pushed him up against the wall and punched him in the guts twice. Costain sagged and Flynn let him drop to his knees. Then he side-swiped him with the back of his right hand. The blow lifted Costain off the ground which he hit hard, then started to scramble away from the onslaught – at which moment Trish leapt on to Flynn's back and began strangling, beating and kicking him and screaming dementedly at him.

Flynn spun her round like a helicopter blade, trying to fling her off, unpeeling her forearm from across his throat. But she clung on like a limpet and he could not shake her free.

Then, suddenly, she was hauled off him.

Flynn turned and saw that Karen Glass had pulled Trish off and had her face down on the floor.

He gave her a quick nod of thanks and went for Costain, lifting him bodily by the front of his T-shirt and placing him back against the wall of the bar. Flynn's enraged face was an inch from that of Costain, who struggled desperately.

Flynn dug him once more in the guts and every last ounce of fight whistled out of Costain.

'What,' Flynn demanded, smacking him against the wall, 'have you got me into?'

Costain was physically no match for Flynn, even now, and he knew he was beaten in this contest. Even so, he sneered at him, showed no fear. 'What the hell d'you mean?'

'I've been kidnapped and beaten up because of you,' Flynn said. 'Look at my face! What is going on?'

'Nothing you need to know about.'

'I'm in it, I'm part of it. I don't want to be, but I am,' Flynn growled, spittle flying from his bust lips, pink with blood. 'I want to know what's down in the water.'

'Fuck you,' Costain said – and spat into Flynn's face.

'Well then, let's do this the hard way . . . been wanting to do this since I laid eyes on you . . .'

From behind, flashlights suddenly lit up the scene; shouts and the sound of a big dog barking.

Two cops had arrived. One had his gun drawn in one hand, a

strong torch in the other. The second cop was doing his best to hold back his German Shepherd dog, desperate to sink its fangs into human flesh.

Karen gently eased Flynn's blood-stained Keith Richards T-shirt over his head and dropped it into a wash basket. He winced as the neck of the shirt brushed against his swollen lips and bashed eye.

'You wuss,' she chided and took a step back to look at him. She had seen his upper body naked before, but not from such close quarters. Despite the scars of his battering, the raised weals, the scratches and cuts, she caught a little breath in her throat, then raised her eyes to his.

'I know – I'm a real soft arse,' he admitted miserably and sat down creakily on the edge of the bath. 'Been a bad night.'

They were in the bathroom of Karen's rented apartment on the Avenida de Gran Canaria, on the steep valley side, overlooking the commercial centre in Puerto Rico directly below and, to the south, the port. It was in a fine position. It was the first time Flynn had ever visited.

She moved to stand in front of him, put her fingertip underneath his chin and gently raised his face to the light.

'Crikey,' she said.

'You should see the other guys,' he said, then thought through that little quip. Maybe not: one dead, skewered by a chair, one with a very broken nose, another shot and very probably dead. And more, he thought. This was not likely to end well, so he added, 'Perhaps not.'

'Is this all about the Costain guy?'

Flynn nodded and told her of his adventures, sticking to the truth mostly, leaving out the dead men bits which she did not need to know. Then his escape from the luxury villa – leaving out the Lamborghini – and his hunt for Costain which ended in a scuffle in a seedy alley where the participants were separated by the cops – fortunately with no arrests made.

'Good job you turned up when you did,' Flynn said. 'I didn't seem to be able to shake that young lady off.'

Karen grinned. 'As I came into the bar with my friends I saw you escorting Costain out through another door, then I saw her follow you. Thought you might need help . . .' She paused, her eyes playing over him.

'Have you had a good night?' he asked.

She pouted. 'So-so.' She seemed to brace herself to blurt something. 'I wish you'd turned up, though.'

'Didn't want to spoil the party.'

'You'd have made it,' she said deeply. Her hands slid on to his broad shoulders. 'I don't really want to go back to England, you know?'

'Thought you had big plans?'

'I'd rather be here.'

'Not much opportunity for advancement in anything here,' he said.

'Oh, I don't know . . .' She leaned forward and kissed him softly, making him wince again. 'Did that hurt?'

He nodded and swallowed. 'Agony.'

'How come you never made a move on me, Steve Flynn?' she whispered.

'Because that's all it would have been – a move, a conquest.' He arched a sore eyebrow. 'I'm not into the long haul.'

'Things change . . . people change . . . you never know . . .'

'I don't want to hurt you.'

'Or is it that you don't want to hurt yourself?'

Flynn grimaced at the words and the perspective – and truth – she described.

'Whatever, Steve,' she said softly, 'you need to move on . . . and so do I, and I'll tell you one thing, big guy . . .'

'What's that?'

'I'm not leaving this island until we've made love.'

Flynn rose slowly from the side of the bath. Karen took his hand and led him through to her bedroom. He followed meekly. Then she turned to him and slowly pulled her T-shirt over her head, dropped it, then slid her hand behind his back and crushed herself against him. He could not deny that her touch, her skin, her nipples hardening against him, felt so very good.

Then, all the pain in the world, all the villains, all the conspiracies, all the doubts, had to be put to one side as she tilted her head to him and they kissed hard and passionately.

NINE

Henry Christie was up with Alison at six. She had guests in who wanted an early start and breakfast had to be got under way, so Henry took full advantage of the food being prepared. He wasn't normally a fry-up breakfast kind of guy, usually opting for equally fattening croissants, but he knew he needed to fuel up for what was going to be a long day and that the rest of his meals would probably be taken on the hoof. So he snaffled bacon, sausages, fried eggs and toast and two cups of the best filter coffee he had ever tasted. As he ate he planned the day, knowing that, whilst planning might be divine, where an SIO is concerned it usually goes to rat shit.

He had decided to use the new purpose-built Major Incident Room facility at Blackpool where he would be by seven to have a heads together with DCI Woodcock. Work out how to get the incident staffed – always a problem – then there would be the first briefing and tasking at nine a.m., post mortems at ten a.m.; somewhere in there he needed to have a detailed conversation with Lisa about Percy's frantic phone call. The post mortems would probably take in excess of four hours, he guessed, and although this would slow him up he decided he had to be there to know every detail of the double murder. Yesterday he had delegated this task to the DCI, thinking they might have been carried out last night – but that was when he'd been feeling dead to the world; now, feeling almost chipper, he wanted to go personally, then get back to the incident room to be briefed on progress, which he assumed would be slow.

But he would not allow it to go slowly. He knew the first seventy-two hours were crucial and if it went beyond that, the investigation could hit the rocks. There was literally no time to lose and, as dramatic as that might sound, it was the truth.

The big thing in his favour was that he had come face to face with the killer.

Not that he'd had much time to study the guy's features – Henry had spent most of his time in the man's company fleeing from him – but he *had* seen him, still held something visual in his mind's eye, and it was his intention to get the description down on paper, spend time putting an e-fit together and get it circulated quickly.

Henry had already scheduled a meeting with the e-fit people for eight a.m. so that he would have something to show at the briefing an hour later.

He finished his food and five minutes later he was in his car.

The road out of Kendleton was deserted as Henry pushed the Audi along the tight highways he had come to know so well over the last months, enjoying the speed whilst listening to the latest Rolling Stones CD, recorded live in Hyde Park.

As he listened, though, his mind drifted, his thoughts criss-crossing as he mulled over yesterday, even up to the point where Alison had climbed into bed with him and told him about the American visitor.

Henry narrowed his eyes. The car slowed as he approached the junction with the A683, where he stopped. In his mind he recreated the moment Alison had mentioned the American and the moment he had come head on with Percy's forensic-suit-clad killer.

You shouldn't have seen me . . . I've nothing against cops.

I'll show you mercy if you come out now.

I'm wearing night vision goggles, so I will be able to see you.

Henry remembered the man's voice.

At the time it had been all excitement and fear and although he had understood the words, what he hadn't taken in, in his blind panic to stay alive, was one vital thing: the accent.

Not northern, or southern. Not Geordie or Scouse or Cockney. Not from anywhere in the UK.

The guy had been speaking with an American accent, for Christ's sake.

'Shit!'

Henry punched the centre of the steering wheel, jammed the accelerator down and pulled out on to the main road, heading for the motorway at junction 34. At the same time, he dialled a number he knew well on his new mobile phone, which was slotted into a holder on the dashboard and linked to Bluetooth.

As ever he felt like a pretentious twerp when he curled the earpiece and mic around his left ear. He thought he should have got used to it by now.

A sleepy, croaky voice answered. 'Who the fuck is this?' it demanded.

'Who the fuck is that?' Henry retorted playfully.

The man cleared his throat. 'Whaddyawant?' Henry heard him yawn loudly.

'Information.'

'Right,' he drawled. Henry could imagine him rubbing and distorting his tired face. 'What sorta information?'

'Information on a killer.'

Flynn stirred, lay there, trying to get a measure of his body and how he was feeling.

Some parts good, others not so good. No doubt about it, he ached and was very sore from head to toe. The pounding his skull had endured in the moments after being thrown into the Mercedes was pretty much how a football must feel after ninety minutes of being booted around, but he was certain that no damage had been caused internally. The remainder of him also felt intact, but battered, everything repairable.

He opened his eyes.

He was on his back, his left arm trapped under Karen's shoulders, and she lay on his bicep as if it were a pillow, her face turned towards him, still asleep, breathing deeply and regularly.

Although Flynn had opened his eyes, only one of them – the right one – actually came open. The other was still swollen and closed. He touched it carefully with his free hand, confirming the size of the swelling – big, soft to the touch like rotten fruit, and tender.

'Yuk,' he said. There was the possibility that a doctor might have to have a look at it.

To more pleasant things: Flynn focused on Karen's face and recalled the night they'd had.

A silent 'phew' passed his busted lips. To say it had been incredible was a bit of an understatement. Flynn's lips curved into what probably looked like an evil leer but was meant to be a half-smile at the memory and what it might mean to them both.

Karen's eyes flickered and she caught him looking.

'Hi, babe,' she said dreamily, 'is that the one-eyed ogle?'

'Yes . . . and hi to you, gorgeous,' he said, feeling slightly self-conscious at his use of the lovey-dovey term. Flynn wasn't really in touch with his romantic side. He was a man of action, a doer, and part of that psychological profile, the 'doing' bit, meant he loved 'em and left 'em. It didn't make him feel proud but he knew he had been avoiding any form of intimacy beyond the actual bedroom, so he was a little afraid that this woman was already changing that.

'Your face is a mess,' she informed him, 'but I still think you're handsome.'

'That's both a reality check and reassuring.' He paused unsurely, urging himself on. 'And I think you're beautiful . . . actually have done for months now.' He almost choked on the words, but he did mean them.

She raised herself on to one elbow, allowing the blood to flow back down Flynn's arm. His fingers tingled. She leaned forward and kissed him lightly. 'Last night was great,' she said.

'It was . . . I need to get going,' he said.

'Yeah, I know . . . but don't even begin to think you're running out on me. That's not going to happen, you do know that?'

Flynn swallowed. 'I know and I'm not.'

'Not least because I want you inside me again.' She held his gaze as she reached down under the single sheet and grasped him. He responded instantly.

Henry headed for Blackpool nick first and the poky office he had there as part of the FMIT presence on the Fylde coast. He kept his brewing tackle in a locked cupboard behind his desk, so he dug out his small kettle, his mug and some coffee and got things under way. Then he sat at his desk and corralled his thoughts whilst gazing out of the window overlooking the rear of the Sea Life centre, over which a huge shark was affixed that he had nicknamed 'Dave' after an old boss of his.

He raised his mug to that bastard's memory, spun back to his desk, opened his A4 size notepad and started writing.

With the help of aspirin and paracetamols, the pain had subsided slightly throughout Flynn's body as he made his way on foot from Karen's apartment. He was wearing a T-shirt she had found in her wardrobe that he suspected might have belonged to an old boyfriend. Anyway, it fitted him. She promised to boil wash the blood-stained Keith Richards T-shirt even though Flynn did think it added a little something to it. Blood and Keith seemed to meld well together.

The sun, even so early, was rising nicely in the sky, promising another day of swelter. It felt good on him.

What also felt good was the feel of Karen's hand in his as she walked alongside him. The last time he had walked holding the hand of a woman was over four years ago, so it felt good, but also strange – and he liked it.

He knew that something had withered and died in him when he had lost Gill Hartland, but as he strolled along with Karen that 'something' deep inside was starting to stir again. When he thought back to Gill he remembered it had taken both of them too long to be brave enough to admit their feelings for each other, and then it had been snuffed out in an instant; the time they'd spent together had only been fleeting.

Flynn knew he could not make that mistake again. He squeezed Karen's hand and peeked at her. She knew he was looking but kept her profile to him, a proud smile on her face.

They walked down the steep steps from the apartment into the commercial centre, their plan being to stroll down to the marina and grab a lovely breakfast at one of the quayside cafés in the small shopping centre nearby.

First, though, Flynn wanted to call in to his villa, which they would pass on the way. They trotted across the road near the police station. Karen touched his arm, pointed and said, 'Look. What sort of car is that?'

The yellow and black Lamborghini was being chain-hauled on to the back of a breakdown truck, its front end mangled massively.

'It looks like a Ferrari,' Flynn said innocently. This had been an area that he hadn't shared with Karen when he'd told her about his abduction: he'd just fudged how he'd got from the villa back to Puerto Rico.

'What a shame.'

Flynn swallowed. It was a shame. The damage was extensive and seriously expensive. Two cops watched the car's slow journey on to the back of the truck as they listened patiently to another man. Even from this distance, Flynn could tell he was upset and having a right rant and rave, gesticulating as he spoke to the cops. The owner, Flynn supposed. His pride and joy, stolen and wrecked. Serve him right for leaving it unlocked and with the key in, Flynn thought.

They crossed the road and reached the exact point at which Flynn had been bundled into the Mercedes. He carried on walking with Karen through the public gardens.

His villa was set on the right, its small terrace behind a high rattan fence, giving it some privacy. He went through the gate and stopped dead. The sliding door was open and he knew he had left the place locked up. Karen bumped into him, not expecting the abrupt halt.

'What—?'

Flynn held her back and gestured for her to stay put as he approached the door, then stood on the threshold looking into the open plan living and kitchen area of what, essentially, was nothing more than an upgraded holiday apartment.

The settee and two chairs had been tipped over, their cushions slashed open. The flat screen TV had been ripped from its wall mountings and smashed to pieces on the tiled floor. In the kitchen area he saw that all the crockery had been broken, the cutlery thrown everywhere. He stepped carefully inside, once more feeling the rise of rage at this invasion of his life. What instantly made it worse was the fact that this place did not belong to him. He was the custodian and had promised to care for it on behalf of the German owner, one of his clients.

The walls had been spray-painted with loops and whirls of black and red metallic car paint, almost impossible to remove. It had also been sprayed all over the furniture.

'Hell!' Karen said behind him. 'Kids?'

Flynn didn't reply but walked carefully through the up-ended furniture into the bedroom beyond, which had had the same treatment, as had the bathroom.

Flynn inhaled, exhaled, trying to hold himself together, but struggling as the implications of this invasion also struck home.

'I've been half-arsed about this, Karen, tripping through the streets like a lovelorn teenager. This is a dangerous game I'm in and there are people out there who mean me real harm for whatever reason. I'm not sure it'll be a sensible thing for you to be associated with me for a while, until I get this sorted . . .'

'What d'you mean?'

Before he could answer, Karen's mobile phone rang out. She almost cancelled the call, but saw that it was Adam Castle, her brother, phoning.

'What . . . ? Right . . . yes . . . we'll be there . . .' Her eyes became frightened. 'Five minutes,' she said and hung up. 'That was Adam . . . we need to get to the marina . . . someone's wrecked *Faye*.'

'Put Rik on . . . I said, put Rik on,' Henry insisted. 'Jeez.'

Rik Dean came on the line. 'Henry – what's going on, what've you just told her? She's really upset.'

Henry explained he had just phoned Lisa to ask exactly what Percy Astley-Barnes had said when he'd called the evening before last. Henry had somehow wanted to avoid breaking the news of Percy's horrific death to her, but had been left with no options and had told her more bluntly than he had intended. This had set Lisa off 'on one'.

'He's dead?' Rik said.

'Professional hit,' Henry confirmed. 'And I might have been killed too, had it not been for my excellent nautical skills.'

'Ey?'

'Never mind. Look, I know he phoned Lisa and it may be that she was the last person to speak to him . . . I'm gonna start my timeline with that phone call and work backwards and forwards from there, so I need to know exactly what was said and the exact time he made the call.'

'Right, let me talk to her,' he said dully. Henry picked up on something not right in his tone.

'You OK, pal?'

'Nah . . . he phones her and not the cops . . . just makes me wonder.'

'Wonder what? If she doesn't love you, or if she's still playing the field?' Henry asked straightforwardly.

'Well . . .' Rik drew out the word.

'It's bollocks, I'd say. Percy was clearly into something he couldn't handle and desperate for some guidance . . . I'm pretty sure it was just a panic phone call and he knew she would get me to call him.'

'But she's so upset!'

'Rik, he's been murdered . . . let her have a sob and some hysterics, it's a big deal. I'd be upset if you were murdered.'

'Mmm . . . OK, I'll get back to you.'

Henry hung up, then stood up, grabbed his jacket and left the office. He was on his way over to the MIR.

Time to get hunting.

* * *

Two hundred and fifty miles to the south, another man employed in the business of law enforcement, but on a much broader scale than Henry, was entering his own office in the American Embassy in London after a short but tedious commute into the city from a small town to the west of the capital. He stood at the threshold, shook himself out of his jacket and tried to throw the garment across the room, hoping to get it on to the coat stand next to his desk.

Unlike James Bond, he missed. The jacket flopped to the floor and the man shook his head miserably. 'Story of my life,' he thought. He picked up the jacket, hung it up, then slumped down on to his chair.

Karl Donaldson was essentially a man of action but, like his hero James Bond (he liked the books, not the films), when he hadn't had too much action recently his spirit went into decline. His life, he thought miserably, had become humdrum, homebound, office-bound. Fucking boring.

He had once been an FBI field agent but for the past fifteen years he had been a legal attaché working from the FBI office at the US embassy. At the moment he was still working from the Grosvenor Square building, but a move to new, swanky premises was looming – and that thought filled him with dread. All glass partitions, water coolers and open plan office life . . . sent a shiver down his spine.

His basic job was to act as a collector, collator, analyser and conduit of criminal intelligence through various police forces worldwide but mainly in Europe, where he had close links with Europol and Interpol, as well as state police forces, including those in the UK.

Since 2001 his job had been mainly to chase, sift and sort for intelligence relating to international terrorism. Although he loved the job and had been responsible for bringing many evil men to justice – and some to the end of their lives – he had become bored and listless.

True, there had been occasions in the past few years when he had found himself back in the field, physically chasing bad guys, coming head to head with some and almost losing his life in the process once. But for too long now he had been operating from behind a desk, getting increasingly involved in the tittle-tattle of petty office politics. Worst of all, he had started dreading the daily commute in from Hartley Wintney, sometimes having to stand all the way on a packed train, eyeing all the other zombie-faced commuters and wishing one of them would pull a gun and start shooting so he could disarm the bastard.

His worst fear was that he might be the one to pull the gun.

He had access to firearms. He was getting psychologically damaged by his humdrum existence and was only one step away from mowing down a carriage-full of innocent people. Or were they really innocent?

Another thing that did bother him – killing fellow commuters was just a heavenly fantasy – was that although he was completely committed to hunting down terrorists, he was actually 'brassed off' with it all. (Donaldson, though a Yank through and through, did have a penchant for collecting and using British colloquialisms, and 'brassed off' was his current favourite.) He was particularly bored by seeing nothing but Islamic names passing over his desk.

He was, in fact, missing everyday crime and criminals.

Robbers, rapists, drug runners, murderers, gangsters, extortionists. Good old-fashioned hit men who didn't have bombs strapped to their bodies, even.

Where was the Mafia these days? Don Corleone – where the hell was he?

The answer to that, he thought cynically, was that they were operating with impunity. The FBI, Homeland Security, the CIA and a plethora of agencies with three or four initials, hastily cobbled together with little thought of strategy, were now strongly focused on preventing and disrupting terrorism, sending in unmanned drones to launch missile attacks on mud huts in Afghanistan whilst they watched on monitors half the earth away, dancing around, giving high fives as a house was obliterated, and never getting their hands soiled.

Donaldson knew this was all a necessity, did not question that, and he knew that others *were* still investigating organized crime, and he would do his utmost to find, seek, disrupt and destroy enemies of the USA. That was what was required of him.

But hell! He missed criminals. Pined for them.

Which was why the phone call that had woken him from a bad night's sleep earlier that morning had triggered a glimmer of excitement in him. It also served to remind him that, important as his own job was, life did still go on in 'normal' land and innocent people took bullets and professional hit men still got contracts – and cops still hunted bad guys down.

It had been a while since he'd heard from his old friend Henry Christie, whom he'd met too many years before for comfort, when he, Donaldson, had been investigating American mob activity in the north west of England. They had been firm friends since and even worked together occasionally.

So, though Donaldson had been Mr Grumpy with Henry, what his friend had asked him to do had been of great interest.

Donaldson sat back in his office chair after logging on to the FBI intranet. He interlocked his fingers, stretched out his arms, cracking his knuckles.

The computer screen came lazily to life.

He rocked forward, entered his complex password, then wriggled his fingers like a maestro pianist about to launch into a concerto.

In his case, though, the only tune he would be playing was 'Hunt the Hit Man', a little known ditty which he had performed hundreds of times to great acclaim.

Flynn had never felt such intense fury. It seemed to build into a crescendo as he stepped slowly, deliberately across *Faye*'s deck, into the cockpit, then beyond into the galley, stateroom and sleeping quarters beyond.

'Bastards,' he hissed.

It looked as if the boat had been damaged by a herd of rampaging bulls armed with sledgehammers and spray paint, smashing and defacing everything in their path.

The control panel that housed the sonar, GPS, radar, radio and other electronic devices – all massively expensive – had been hammered to pieces, just wanton destruction. The locked cupboards had been prised open, their contents dragged out and crushed to pieces.

In the galley, all the kitchen fittings and fixtures and equipment had been smashed, too; then beyond, the luxurious furniture in the stateroom had been shredded with a knife and the walls and windows sprayed with the same metallic paint he had seen on the walls of his villa: same people.

Flynn surveyed it all with his good eye, then walked slowly back through the mess to the deck to see Jose leaning over the rail, pulling something on to the deck.

Flynn growled as he saw what it was. One of his treasured fishing rods, twisted, bent and mangled.

Jose looked at him wretchedly, holding the broken piece of equipment in both hands. 'They broke into the equipment locker,' he spat. 'All the rods are missing . . . I think they're in the water . . . this one snagged on the side.'

Flynn did a quick mental calculation. Ten of the best rods and reels. Looking at twenty thousand euros just there.

He looked at Karen on the quayside, anxiously biting her thumb nail.

Flynn sidestepped the open engine hatch, then knelt to peer into the compartment to see the oil filler caps missing from both engine blocks, empty sugar bags thrown on to the floor below. Sugar in the engines. The damage from that little act almost irreparable, other than by taking out the engines, completely stripping them down and cleaning them off. A mammoth undertaking. The cost of that repair was almost incalculable.

The boat was ruined and Flynn felt like crying – just for a moment.

'Did we get Costain's address?' he asked Karen.

She nodded. 'You think this was him?'

'He's my starting point – and I'm now going to finish a conversation I started last night that was rudely interrupted by the arrival of two cops and a nasty looking police dog.'

It wasn't a bad start: twenty-five detectives from around the county, a support unit team, two dog men, and three admin staff to kick start the computer system; plus an office manager, an allocator, an exhibits officer . . . great. Henry was fairly buoyed up about things as he gathered up his briefing notes and other paperwork, then walked in front of the murder squad and began the briefing to get a major investigation under way.

Henry and Woodcock had spent most of the last hour working on the strategy for the investigation and starting the murder book properly, in which all decisions, actions and reasoning would be recorded as it all progressed.

Within the hour everyone was deployed and Henry retreated to the SIO's office just off the main briefing room. As he went he beckoned DC Jerry Tope in with him. Tope was from the force intelligence unit and had worked for Henry on several recent cases. Although he was regarded as a bit of a 'surly bleeder' and was insubordinate on too many occasions for comfort, Henry liked the guy and knew he was a particularly valuable asset, not least for his impressive computer skills.

Tope was going to run the intelligence cell on this investigation.

He trudged glumly behind Henry into the office. DCI Woodcock came with them.

'Mornin' Jerry.'

'Henry.' He nodded. 'How are you?'

'Good – sit.' The pleasantries were over. Tope sat, Woodcock sat. Henry poured them both a coffee from the filter machine that came with the office (coffee not included), then sat behind the desk and considered Tope. 'Quite a few things for you to be doing here.'

Tope nodded.

'Just off the top of my head,' Henry said, looking skywards and counting off with his fingers. 'Phone records . . . Percy's mobile wasn't found at the scene but we have his number.' Tope nodded: easy enough. 'Percy and Charlotte went away recently . . . Canaries and Florida . . . could these trips be connected to their deaths? Let's find out where they went, when they went, et cetera.' Tope nodded: easy. 'Finance and business records need unearthing and analysing. Was the business OK or going tits up? That could be a big factor, and maybe what he said when he phoned Lisa.' Henry shrugged. 'Know what I'm saying?'

'Who else, family-wise, is connected to the business?' Tope asked.

'Father was, but isn't now. As far as I know Percy was the sole owner, but I'm not one hundred per cent on that. Find out, eh?'

'Will do,' Tope said confidently as his mobile phone rang. He balanced it on his folder and peered at the screen with a frown.

'You need to get that?' Henry asked.

Tope picked up the phone and peered closely at the screen. Henry saw his eyes widen with shock and then Tope quickly stabbed the 'end call' button to sever the connection. 'Nope,' he said brusquely, but gave Henry a sheepish look, placing his hand guiltily over the phone.

Henry returned a puzzled expression but said, 'Right, let's get on . . . I'm going to have a few more minutes with the e-fit people, then head off to the post mortems.' He looked at Woodcock and screwed up his face. 'Will you just kick ass around here for the time being, then go out and see Percy's father again? I think we're going to have to keep plugging away at him and hope for some lucid moments because I think he knows more than he's capable of telling us . . . that OK?'

Woodcock looked slightly discomfited by the request, but said, 'Yeah, no probs.'

'OK – meeting over.'

Tope and Woodcock left the office. Henry sighed and began checking through his action plan for the day before setting off to see the e-fit people again at Blackpool nick. From there he would be going to the hospital for the PMs.

Outside the office, Jerry Tope stalked angrily across the incident room, out into the corridor beyond, where he tapped the keypad on his phone and returned the call he had refused to take a couple of minutes earlier. He put the phone to his ear, waited for the connection, then whispered dramatically, 'What the hell do you want? Thought I told you never, ever, friggin' call me again . . . bastard.'

TEN

'That's no way to speak to an old mate, is it?'

When Scott Costain and Trish did not show up at the allotted time for their charter, Flynn declared to Adam Castle, who was waiting with him, 'They're not going to return to the scene of their crime, are they?' Flynn got their address from Karen's booking records, memorized it and, with a snarl firmly fixed to his face, set off back to his villa on foot. Here he intended to jump into his Nissan Patrol, parked up under an awning around the back, and drive to Costain in order to confront him.

On the way he made the call.

'You,' the man at the other end said nastily, 'are no friggin' mate of mine . . . and, would you believe it, I was in a meeting with your nemesis when you rang.'

Flynn stopped dead. He had reached the digital time/day/date/ temperature display board on the promenade at the back of the beach, not far from his villa. The temperature had already reached twenty-eight degrees.

'Henry Christie, you mean?'

'The very same.'

Flynn sneered at the name – a conditioned reflex. 'Why were you in a meeting with him?'

'Got a double murder on our hands . . . argh, bah! Why am I telling you this? What the hell do you want? It better not actually be anything because I think you've taken all this using me too far, all this phoning me when you want something. I've given you too much already. Almost lost my job over you.'

Flynn listened slightly guiltily to the tirade, surmounted his guilt and said, 'Are you still happily married to the lovely Marina?' There was silence at the other end of the line.

Flynn knew how cruel and unfair he was being.

He and Jerry Tope went back a long way and somewhere in that dim, distant past, the two had once been good friends. So much so that Flynn had once taken the blame for an indiscretion on Tope's part when his wife, Marina, suspected Jerry of an infidelity. Flynn had stepped up to the mark and saved the marriage. Of course, Tope now owed Flynn a big debt and rather cheekily Flynn had used the threat of revealing the truth about one sordid night in Preston to make Jerry, occasionally, tell him things that he shouldn't. Like stuff that can only be discovered on police computers.

'Yes, I am still happily married,' Tope said frostily.

'And would you like to keep it that way?' Flynn teased.

'Yes.'

'In that case you need to look into your crystal ball – i.e. your computer – and tell me everything there is to know about Scott Costain.'

'Why, what's Costain got to do with you?'

'Nothing you need to know about. In fact, the less you know, the better.'

'I don't know . . . I could get in the crap . . .'

'Yeah,' Flynn said heartlessly, 'either way, personally or professionally. At least you can justify an Intel search on Costain, whereas there is no way of you justifying a grab-a-granny night twenty years ago in Squires, Preston, is there? You know what to do. Get back to me.' Flynn ended the call. He realized that he needed to stop holding the infidelity card over Tope's head when it suited . . . but it was so useful to have tucked up his sleeve in times of desperation.

Flynn continued to his villa wondering what the best approach was with Costain. Part of him warned, *back off*. Flynn had unwittingly become involved with some seriously nasty people and common sense told him he should go to the cops and throw himself on their mercy. Problem with that was that it would probably lead to more complication and, maybe, the rest of his life rotting in a Spanish jail cell. He did not have much faith in the Policía and to go looking for them and say, 'I've just killed two men' might be a step too far. He did not want to find himself in the horrible grind of the Spanish justice system.

Another option was to do nothing and see what happened.

If the people who kidnapped him were real players then it was always possible they were into something so deep they might have disposed of the two bodies in the villa or simply left them, done a runner, and possibly nothing would ever come of it with regard to Flynn's involvement.

Except that Flynn would always be waiting for that tap on the shoulder and he might turn round and see cops or he might turn and see villains.

To Flynn, therefore, doing nothing was too iffy. He knew he had to make the running because it was in his nature. He had to go and rattle cages, because that was how he'd always operated. He liked kicking shins . . . and the appearance of Jack Hoyle on the scene was an added factor in that equation. Just what and who had the double dealing, wife stealing, thieving bastard got himself involved with? Flynn wanted another confrontation with him, but one where he could take his time over beating the living crap out of his ex-partner. There was a lot of pent-up anger in Flynn where Jack Hoyle was concerned and it had just been reignited.

As Flynn unlocked the Nissan Patrol, he had pretty much decided what he was going to do.

First – crack Costain's skull open and finish off what he'd started yesterday. Second – trace the boat he'd encountered, the one where the people on board had not welcomed him with open arms. Third – and maybe at the same time as number two – track down Jack Hoyle; fourth – get some answers.

Flynn didn't immediately get into the Nissan. Instead he slid back the driver's seat and unlocked the hidden panel under the carpet in the floor of the car. It opened into a long, thin, specially engineered space running underneath the front seats. A good place to hide things – such as a Bushmaster rifle, cushioned in bubble-wrap.

All Flynn did was touch the weapon to reassure himself it was still there if needed. It was and he knew it was loaded. Not the most practical weapon in the world, especially for close-quarter work, but reassuring nonetheless.

He clipped the panel shut, pulled back the carpet and then climbed into the car and started the diesel engine. It was about a twenty minute drive to Costain's address; time, Flynn thought, to mull things over properly.

The night it all went sour was branded into Flynn's brain. The drug raid that went wrong when a cop got shot and a million pounds' worth of takings went missing – into Jack Hoyle's pocket. Then, subsequent to all that, the revelation that Hoyle, Flynn's trusted partner in the cops, had also been screwing his wife behind his back. Then the year of shame and denial until Flynn decided it was best to leave the job because the pressure on him – driven by a certain Henry Christie who had been tasked with investigating the allegation of the missing money (and could not prove that Flynn had had any part in its disappearance) – was so intense.

Which was why Flynn fled, virtually penniless, to Gran Canaria and cadged a job on a fishing boat owned by Adam Castle. Flynn was due some police pension but it was a long time before he could draw it – age fifty-five – and money had been tight. But he had worked hard and eventually cleared the air and his name with the ever suspicious Henry Christie, whom he'd encountered a few times since in the intervening years.

At one point, Flynn had actually tracked down Jack Hoyle. Having faked his own death, Hoyle had made his way to the United States, forged a new identity and was working on a sportfishing boat out of Key West.

And how fucking ironic was that, Flynn thought bitterly.

He and Jack Hoyle had shared two passions in their lives.

They had been mad-keen fishermen.

And both had been sleeping with Flynn's wife, Faye.

At the memory, Flynn punched the steering wheel as he drove the Nissan east along the coast towards Maspalomas along GC1.

'Bastards, the both of them,' he said.

Although Flynn had managed to track Hoyle down, he had fled before Flynn could properly confront him and had not been seen since.

Until now. Until he had abducted Flynn off the streets and tried to talk to him like he was an old mate. The feel of his forehead crashing into Hoyle's nose was amazing.

Henry was quite pleased with the likeness generated by the e-fit and circulated it straight away so that within minutes all the operational cops in Lancashire had the image on their mobile devices. He also sent one, via his phone, to Karl Donaldson.

Next for Henry were the post mortems.

He drove across the resort to Blackpool Victoria Hospital and parked close to the public mortuary alongside a very spiffing restored E-Type Jaguar that belonged to Baines, the Home Office pathologist, who was already kitted up and pulling a pair of latex gloves on to his bony hands. Percy's naked body was laid out on the stainless steel slab.

Henry nodded at Baines, put on a smock and a face mask just as one of the forensic team members came in, her job to collect items for analysis. Also present was a CSI to record the whole of the PM on video and she was already setting the scene with a few shots of Percy's body and close-ups of the head wounds.

Baines, with his own recording microphone fitted to his ear, began talking into it so that everything said over the course of the PM would be recorded. He began by describing Percy's body in a cold, clinical manner . . . name, sex, age, weight, height, general appearance, skin colour, race and any identifying marks or scars . . . then looked closely at the bullet wounds and said what he thought of them.

Henry watched and listened, asking and recording questions as they occurred to him, making his own notes and feeling quite sad, as ever, at being present at the post mortem of someone who had been taken before their time.

The villa was on a small estate in Maspalomas, almost on the immense and justly famous sandy beach near the lighthouse at El Oasis. Flynn knew this urban district, a small enclave of nice villas, mostly holiday rentals, in an area surrounded by similar estates, all quite pleasant. He'd had charter parties staying around here and it had been part of his service to pick them up and take them down to the boat, then do a return journey at the end of the day's fishing.

Flynn climbed stiffly out of the car, feeling his battered body tightening up. He took a moment to rub the caked-up pus out of his left eye, picking it off delicately, like grit. He could just about see through the swollen lid now, but the vision was slightly blurred.

He rolled his shoulders, realizing that, strong and healthy as he was, recovering from a beating took longer the older he got. He took a breath of the warm, sweet air. Ahead were the famous Maspalomas sand dunes and, to his left, the busy resort of Playa del Inglés, a place he tried to avoid.

He hesitated – another age-related thing. Last chance to make his decision: fight or flight, in essence.

If he went and knocked on Costain's door he would have to accept and deal with what came through it head on.

Now was the last moment to back off and see how it all played out without his further involvement.

It was simply not within him to do so.

He pushed open the gate that led to the villa complex and found Villa Elisabet, which stood in its own grounds, separated by a high hedge from the others around it. Very private and pleasant, much too good for someone like Scott Costain, Flynn thought.

There was a terrace with dining table and chairs on it to his left, the pool beyond just on the other side of the villa. The main door to the villa was straight ahead.

Flynn noticed the curtains behind the patio windows were still drawn.

He walked to the front door and rang the bell, stepped back and waited. He rang the bell again, hearing it echo hollowly somewhere inside, but no one answered.

He tried again – still no response – then knocked loudly. The door itself was a thick, heavy chunk of PVC and although it appeared closed at first glance Flynn saw the tiny gap around the edges showing it was actually very slightly ajar.

He pouted, then put his knuckle to the centre of the door and pushed it slowly open, revealing a short, tiled hallway leading to an open plan lounge and kitchen area.

'Hello,' Flynn called. No response.

Something unpleasant crept down the back of his neck. The dormant cop sense kicking in, reliving the moments in history when he had done something similar as a cop. Knocking on a door, opening it up . . . that creepy feeling . . . knowing when something wasn't quite right, that a dead body might just be lying in wait.

Or it could simply be that Costain was not in, had inadvertently left the door open. Maybe he and Trish had done a midnight flit.

Flynn sniffed. His nose had been bashed about last night but he still had his sense of smell and something hung in the air.

'Hello,' he called again. 'It's me, Steve Flynn, from the boat.'

The words echoed across the tiles and back from the painted walls. He stepped in and walked into the lounge, checking the kitchen area to his left. Everything seemed to be in order. Except for the smell.

To his right was a hallway with three bedroom doors off it, and a bathroom.

He called out again; still nothing came back.

He walked slowly down the hallway. The bathroom was on his right, behind a sliding door, half open. All OK in there. Next on his left was a bedroom door. He looked in and saw twin beds still made up, not slept in. After that there was another bedroom with twin beds again, both made up and tidy.

One room left, directly facing him, behind a closed door.

Flynn guessed this would be the double with an en suite. He knew the layout of villas like these was much of a muchness.

Flynn tapped on this door.

That smell.

'Hello,' again. His voice echoed. No reply.

His hand turned the door knob, pushed open the door. He was correct – this was the master bedroom. Double bed, sparsely furnished, nice but basic holiday accommodation.

Flynn said, 'Shit.'

Costain's girlfriend, Trish, lay spread-eagled and naked on the bed, but with her limbs also twisted and unnatural. She was face up, her dead eyes staring at the white ceiling, and was lying in a bed saturated in her blood, blood splattered up the wall behind the bed, pools of it on the tiled floor next to the bed.

She had been shot dead.

To Flynn it looked as if someone had placed the muzzle of a gun against her left temple and pulled the trigger, the exit wound then having taken off the whole left side of her face.

And there were three bullet wounds in her front, two in the chest, one in the lower gut. Possibly these had been the first ones fired and had flung her on to the bed and probably killed her, rendering the head shot superfluous and simply brutal, just to make sure she was dead, even though it was probably plainly obvious.

And the smell.

Not that of a dead body – she was far too fresh to smell just yet. The aroma was cordite from the discharge of the weapon.

Flynn swore under his breath as his mouth dried up. He did not move, just remained where he was, looking through his one good eye at the scene of death. He was reluctant to step into the room to see if Scott Costain's body was somewhere just out of sight because he didn't want to spoil any evidence but, more importantly, did not want to taint himself with anything either.

Already, he wanted no connection with this killing.

Even so, he squatted on his haunches to look under the bed and then rose on tiptoes to peer into the en suite, the door of which was slightly open. From where he stood, he could not see Costain. He might not be there anyway, but Flynn thought he'd better check.

Reluctantly he edged around the room, ensuring his trainers did not touch any of the blood splashes.

There was no sign of Costain.

Flynn backtracked out of the room by the same route, gave one last look at the girl's body, his face now angry.

He walked into the hallway and back out of the villa, not touching anything, not closing the door. He was pretty sure he hadn't left his mark on anything.

Outside, he exhaled, not realizing he'd been holding his breath.

His instinct was to run for it, or at least walk very quickly away in a non-suspicious manner.

But the fact that Scott Costain wasn't there troubled him.

Even though Flynn had tagged Scott as a fairly mindless bruiser, he hadn't come across as someone with the wherewithal to murder his girlfriend in cold blood. So where was he?

Not inside the villa, for sure. It was only a single storey building with no upper floor or roof terrace and Flynn had checked the rooms.

Flynn walked to the patio/eating area, beyond which was the small swimming pool – which was where he found the answer to the nagging questions.

Scott Costain was floating face down in the pool, dead. The back of his skull was simply a gaping, ragged crater, reminding Flynn of an opened tin of baked beans with the lid twisted back to reveal the contents. It was a huge exit wound, maybe two bullets having passed through, and the very still pool water was clouded pink. A beautiful blue dragonfly hovered over Costain's busted head, seeming to look down and inspect it. Then, as if repelled by what it saw, it zipped away.

Flynn walked to the edge of the pool and went down on to his haunches again, noticing Costain's gun on the pool floor, the one he'd threatened Flynn with on the boat. He rose, feeling slightly dithery. He was a tough, hard man, but even he was affected by these two brutal deaths and the swirl of thoughts and possibilities mashing through his own head.

It didn't take a genius to work out he could easily be the next one on the list. He had been lucky last night, managed to escape . . . but two of his abductors were dead and Flynn knew their colleagues would not be likely to let him survive.

He turned, breathed out slowly, having held his breath again. And at that exact moment eight armed cops emerged like ghosts from the bushes around the villa and surrounded him. All dressed in black overalls, ballistic helmets, soft boots; each was carrying an H&K machine pistol and all eight were aimed at Flynn.

One of the cops then screamed instructions at him in Spanish, which he only half heard and understood, but the message was very clear indeed.

Some of the words he knew.

Manos – hands. *Arriba* – up.

When the instruction was given to the accompaniment of the unmistakable jerk of a weapon's barrel, Flynn got it: *Hands up.*

Then, *En el suelo* – on the ground ground; and *bajar* – down.

Flynn guessed there would be the Spanish equivalent of 'fucking' somewhere in amongst that – 'Get down on the (fucking) ground.'

Lento – slow.

Flynn did not need telling twice, even in Spanish. He raised his hands very slowly, then began to bend his knees and take himself to the ground.

Tumba – lie down.

He went to his knees, keeping his expression fairly deadpan, then dropped forward on to the palms of his hands.

From that moment it was plain sailing.

Four of the cops then leapt on him, driving him down on to the terrace, pulling his arms behind his back and fastening his wrists with plastic cuffs – and when they had him, they backed off.

Flynn's cheek was on the tiles and he could look up through his good eye.

He recognized the man in plain clothes who threaded his way through the uniforms. Last time Flynn had seen this guy was when he had delivered a message to Flynn, telling him of Gill Hartland's sudden death.

He was a young detective with old eyes, but Flynn could not recall his name.

'Señor Flynn,' he said.

'I don't know what the fuck you're . . .'

The detective placed a finger over his lips. 'Shhh . . . you are under arrest for murder, señor . . . double murder.'

He was transported to the police station in Puerto Rico, sitting snugly between two burly uniformed cops in the back seat of a big saloon car, his hands now cuffed on his lap. The car was driven by an equally burly uniformed cop and the detective, who was called Romero, sat in the front passenger seat. They had Flynn hemmed in and he sat there silent and sullen, trying to work out his plan of action.

First problem was that Romero had not been specific about which double murder Flynn had been arrested for. Two guys up in a villa in the mountains, or Scott Costain and Trish?

Flynn would wait for Romero to iron out that point.

Second problem was that he was in the custody of the Spanish police, and despite the fact that Spain was a fully paid up member of the European Union and its constitution and all the things that went with that – such as human rights – horror stories still came screaming from the cells and sometimes people who had been arrested languished for a very long time without charge or reason, and got forgotten about.

As the car dropped into Puerto Rico Flynn glanced across to the marina, shook his head despondently and wondered when he would next set foot aboard *Faye*, or see Karen Glass again.

The car wound down the hill. Flynn blinked with surprise when he saw that the low-loader with the damaged Lamborghini was still parked up near the police station, and he wondered if they were going to try and stick that one on him, too. The police car turned into the secure rear yard of the station and the gates closed automatically behind.

Flynn was now definitely where he did not want to be – ensconced in the Spanish justice system.

ELEVEN

I t was a tough four hours, by the end of which Henry was drained. He had sat through many post mortems in his long career and had never had any great problem dealing with them. He had found that the secret was to be interested in what was happening and learn something, not to be afraid of the gruesome – which they always were – or the fact that it was a fellow human being lying there on the slab.

If there was anything that bothered him, it was the lingering smell that clung to clothing for days after. That problem was pretty much a thing of the past these days, though. In the more health and safety conscious environment, everyone attending a PM had to be properly kitted out – masks, gloves, smocks – and the smell of death did not get through to the clothing as much.

At the end of this session, however – two dead bodies, two hours each, two intricate examinations – he felt like he'd had enough.

Finally, it had got to him.

He realized it could be a combination of factors such as tiredness, age, that pension hovering there if he wished to take it, the fact that he had only just survived the gunman who had murdered these two people, and his subsequent drenching and boat trip. Lots of things . . . and a little bird telling him that maybe these should be the last two post mortems he should ever attend.

Professor Baines refitted the rib cage he had earlier removed from Lottie's chest to give him access to her heart, lungs, liver and kidneys. (Although the cause of death was obvious – massive trauma to the brain caused by gunshots – he still had to do a full PM that included an examination of all vital organs and stomach contents.) He folded her skin back over her ribs and the mortuary attendant began to sew her up.

Henry lounged at the back of the mortuary, making up his own notes and observations, wanting to get out of here.

'Are you OK, Henry?' Baines asked. He pulled down his mask as he walked over to Henry.

Henry pulled his face and drawled, 'Yeah,' doubtfully.

Baines peeled off his latex gloves. 'Had enough?'

Henry looked at him levelly and repeated the word. 'Yeah.'

'Time to go?'

'Yeah.'

'Just a quick observation – if you don't mind?'

'Fire away,' Henry said.

'The world needs people like you and me, Henry. People who make a difference, people who clear up the dross, and sometimes it gets hard to deal with . . . I know you can retire, but the world will be a worse place for that. Dead people need people like us, and so do the living.

'I know there comes a time to go, and it's only right you should, you've earned it . . . fuck, I don't really know what I'm trying to say,' Baines conceded, 'except – are you still shagging that barmaid?'

'Well, at least the philosophical moment has gone.' Henry grinned at Baines, who had always been fascinated by Henry's see-sawing love life and was always a bit disappointed when not much was happening in it. 'The answer is, yes.'

'You're going to spend your dotage pulling pints, aren't you? And sleeping with a landlady?'

Henry sighed contentedly. 'Yeah,' he beamed. It was a different kind of 'Yeah' from the earlier ones. A dreamy, rose-tinted one.

'Go for it then, you lucky fucker,' Baines said, 'and leave all the dead bodies to some other poor sucker. I'll email you the formal results in about an hour.'

Whilst Henry had been at the PMs, DCI Woodcock had been in charge of proceedings. He had taken control of the office, got various people into various roles, overseen the allocation of tasks to detectives and other staff and, when he was sure these cogs were turning without too much effort, jumped into his car and headed out to see Percy's father, the dementia-racked Archie Astley-Barnes, at his farmhouse in Out Rawcliffe.

He drew up on the lane and climbed cautiously out of the car and approached the front door.

It opened a crack before he could knock.

The gap was dark and Woodcock could only just make out the grey, grizzled features in the shadow. What he could clearly see were the double, side-by-side barrels of the twelve bore shotgun shoved through and angled upwards at him.

'Hold on there, old man,' Woodcock said.

'Who the hell're you and what the hell d'you want?'

'I'm a police officer – a detective . . .'

'Yeah – heard that shit before.'

'I am – really. Let me show you my warrant card, my ID. I need to get it from my jacket pocket.'

'Slow . . . do it real slow,' Archie instructed like a Wild West gunslinger.

Woodcock took the card out and held it up to the opening in the door. 'I'm working with the detective who came to see you yesterday, remember? Detective Superintendent Christie?'

'Not necessarily.'

'We're investigating your son's death.'

'My son?'

'Yes – Percy.'

'Percy?'

'Fuck me,' Woodcock thought unkindly, 'this is going to be hard work.' But he smiled and was secretly pleased it would be tough.

The double muzzles dropped. Woodcock heard the security chain get drawn back and the door came open.

'You'd better come in, lad,' Archie said, gesturing with the shotgun. Warily, Woodcock entered and followed Archie into the lounge area.

'What's all this about?' he demanded.

'How about you get me a cup of tea first, eh, old man?' Woodcock said. He looked Archie straight in the eyes, and said, 'Do you know who I am?'

Archie frowned and peered hard at him. 'You that detective who came yesterday?'

'Yeah – that's me,' Woodcock answered with a cruel smile. 'Now how about that brew, eh?' he said with a wink.

But as Percy walked out, he turned to Woodcock and said, 'You know, I'm sure I do know you.'

Woodcock was waiting for Henry when he landed back from the post mortems, and followed him into his office off the MIR.

'How did they go, boss?'

Henry slid his jacket off and hung it over the back of his office chair. 'They went . . . nothing we didn't already really know . . . what was left of the bullet fragments have been bagged and tagged and are on the way to be analysed,' Henry said. 'I want them fast-tracked, don't care how much it costs.' He arched his eyebrows and Woodcock nodded. 'The longer we leave stuff on this, the less chance of anything, I'd say.' He slumped into his chair. 'The killer's probably long gone anyway.' He shook his head. 'How did you get on with Archie?'

Woodcock snorted. 'Nothing . . . memory like a sieve . . . doesn't even remember you calling yesterday.'

'I think we need to look into getting him some care sorted . . . what's the rest of his family doing?'

'Spread far and wide. I'm pretty sure Percy is the only one directly connected to the family business up here and they don't seem to have much contact with dear old daft Dad. Ron Timpson's trying to make contact but I don't think they'll be of much help, to be honest.'

'What about business partners, shop managers and the like?'

'Actually very few staff, pared right down to the bone from what we can see. One manager oversees all the shops and just a few experienced sales people on the shop floors. Apparently Percy made a few redundant recently and there's talk, according to Ron –' Ron Timpson being one of the DCs on the murder inquiry – 'that one or more of the shops might be closing.'

Henry digested this information, linking it back to Percy's phone call to Lisa: *I've done something really, really stupid.* Henry speculated, 'Business failing? Does that equate to a bullet in the head? Desperate situation, desperate measures?'

'Both staff and the books need a close look, I'd say.'

'Yeah,' Henry agreed, 'but yet Percy still had time to take Lottie to Florida and the Canaries.'

'I wonder who will benefit from Percy's death?'

'Don't yet know. Not found a will or anything that could be construed as a will.'

'I'll task someone to talk to his solicitor,' Woodcock said.

The discussion continued, the sort of roundabout chat that as an SIO Henry had had on numerous occasions, just generally tossing ideas around. From these discussions, lines of inquiry often emerged that became hypotheses that were investigated, analysed and followed up or discarded – but never forgotten. Even the most unlikely scenarios had to be kept bubbling on the back burner because there was one thing Henry had learned well over the last thirty years of a bumpy career: fact was stranger than fiction, and sometimes even the most outlandish idea could turn out to be the right one.

Henry stood up, suddenly needing to pee – and then grab another coffee. In that order. Woodcock stood up, but Henry stopped at the door and turned to the DCI. 'You remember that kidnap?'

Woodcock's face changed to an expression Henry thought must have been puzzlement, although for a moment he looked worried.

'Uh – which one do you mean, boss?'

It was Henry's turn to frown. 'The tiger kidnap we managed to disrupt; we locked up some serious players.'

'Yeah, yeah, course,' Woodcock said, relief in his voice.

'Need to task a couple of good, hard jacks to visit those guys in jail, see what they have to say about Percy's death.'

'Retribution, you mean?'

Henry nodded. 'I've known people murdered for less. The fact we managed to prevent it happening might still rankle with some folk.'

'I'll get Bob Wade and Trevor Taylor to find out which prison these guys are in and follow it up.'

'Yeah – they sound just the right sort . . . and on that note . . .' Henry said, his bladder urging him to move quickly. But he stopped again and said, 'I really need to have an in-depth with my sister, too. She went out with Percy for a while and she might be able to tell us some things about his lifestyle. Problem is she's in Lanzarote until the middle of next week.'

'Nice jolly for the boss?' Woodcock suggested.

'Mm . . . however, need a pee.'

Woodcock sourced some excellent coffee and by the time Henry returned from the loo a hot mug of medium roast was waiting for him. He thanked Woodcock profusely and sipped the coffee as he meandered around the MIR. Two HOLMES 2 terminals were up and running, staffed by specially trained personnel who had been brought in from their usual places of work to input the data that was starting to arrive as the investigation got rolling. Henry chatted to them – two ladies who worked in admin at Blackpool nick. Then he moved on to the office manager, an experienced DS, tasked with the smooth running of the room; then he went on to the allocator and exhibits officer. The jobs were still allocated by hand, recorded on triplicate forms, one of which went on file, one to the officer(s) doing whatever the job was and one to the HOLMES 2 operators for inputting into the system.

There was already a binder half full of tasks and Henry had a quick sift through them just to get a feel for what was happening. He was reasonably happy with the way it was going so far, but things could never really move quickly enough for him. He hated being one pace behind a killer.

Next he moved on to check the timeline that had been posted on the wall, basically four sheets of flipchart paper, A3 size, turned to 'landscape' and stuck on the wall. A black line – literally the timeline – was drawn with a thick felt tip right from one end to the other, across the middle of the paper. At its central point was a cross and a time and a date – the moment Percy had phoned Lisa.

The next point along the line marked where Lisa had called Henry and the next one indicated where Henry himself had visited Percy's house, disturbed the killer and then gone sailing.

Henry moved on and looked at his e-fit of the murderer. He looked at it for a long time, wondering if he'd done a good enough job of it.

He had.

There was also an e-fit of a full length portrait of the killer wearing his forensic suit, although Henry doubted it was much use unless he used it as everyday attire.

On the wall opposite were photographs of the crime scene and Henry spent some time looking at these dreadful images, sad at two unnecessary and brutal deaths.

He had reached the bottom of his coffee. He wandered back to his office and sat for a while doing what superintendents do best: thinking, hoping he was doing enough to cover his arse.

He hoped he had the most important things covered and racked his brain to see if he could tease something out he had missed. He rocked forward and stood up, pulling his jacket off the back of the chair and on to his own back.

As much as he would have liked to be out and about, knocking on doors – or preferably kicking them down – he knew he had to go back and revisit the relatives of the two murder victims and let them know the results of the post mortems, another of those tasks the SIO had to take on, although Henry knew a few who happily delegated this to others.

Stepping into the MIR he called across to Woodcock, who was writing at one of the desks.

'Pete – I'm off to visit the parents again, bring 'em up to speed with where it's at . . . I'll do Lottie's first.'

'Oh, OK . . . I could do Archie if you wanted?'

Henry shook his head, already on his way out. 'No, my job, I'll sort it,' he called over his shoulder, 'after which I'm back to the crime scene.'

Lottie's family was in deep mourning.

The atmosphere in the house was very grave and Henry felt like an intruder, even though a family liaison officer (FLO) was present, a young police woman who was acting as a conduit between the family and police, but also as an evidence gatherer. Henry chatted to her first and, although she had been well trained to take on the role, she was still inexperienced and just a little tearful. The family's grief had rubbed off on her.

Henry then spoke to Lottie's father, this time in the kitchen. He looked to have aged significantly overnight. His eyes were expectant and fearful; the thought of what his daughter's body had just undergone was terrifying his imagination. Butchered on a slab.

'It was as we expected,' Henry said, knowing that the best way through all this was for him to be honest and direct. A 'cruel to be kind' scenario. 'Lottie had been shot through the head, twice. She must have died instantly, as the trauma to the brain from either round would have killed her outright.'

The father said, 'You were present . . . at the post mortem?'

'Yes I was.'

He looked at Henry, nonplussed, trying to form words. 'Was she . . . I mean . . . ?'

'She was treated with dignity and compassion,' Henry assured him.

'OK, OK,' he murmured, this seeming to answer his unspoken question.

'She would not have suffered,' Henry said, referring to her death.

'Except in the time leading up to her death,' the father said. 'Then she would have been terrified beyond belief.'

'Yes,' Henry said, 'she would have. I can't deny that.'

The man nodded.

'I'm so sorry, but I will get him. Now, Mr Bowers, if it's all right with you, while I'm here I'd like to take the opportunity to have a look through Lottie's things, if I may? Up in her room. Just a glance for the moment, but I'd like you to give me permission to take away anything I feel might assist the investigation. I will send someone around a little later to do a more thorough job, though.'

'You have my permission. There's nothing to hide, so take what you need.'

There wasn't much, as far as Henry could see. Her bedroom was fairly typical of a single young woman's, he guessed, still living at home.

Some traces of childhood and teenage years – a doll, a poster of a pop star – but mostly just a modern feminine looking room. Three-quarter size bed, nice self-assembled furniture, a desk, dressing table, TV and laptop. He would let someone else seize the laptop.

'This is it,' her father announced, looking into the room over Henry's shoulder, then backing away quickly, overcome with emotion. 'I'll leave it to you,' he said in a voice that sounded tearful.

'Thank you.'

Henry stepped in and closed the door, entering the world of Charlotte – Lottie – Bowers, feeling a bit like a burglar.

As if he was at a crime scene, he jammed his hands into his pockets and simply stood there, taking it all in, letting his eyes do the walking, trying to imagine her there. Back home after a failed marriage, would she still have the same habits as always? Would she keep a diary? Looking at her laptop on the desk, Henry guessed she would be social media savvy, would have Facebook and Twitter accounts, probably. Would have e-mail and could well have other accounts, such as Instagram, maybe. They would all need checking.

Nightmare, Henry thought. Social media sux.

He sat on the tiny office chair at the desk and looked at it. Perfume bottles, nail polishes, nail polish remover . . . a photo of her and some of her friends in a 'Forever Friends' photo frame. A photo of her and Percy stuck on the wall with Blu-tack, looking all loved up.

Henry didn't touch it, but looked closely at it.

Percy was quite a bit older than her – into his forties – and he'd been quite a bit younger than Lisa, maybe ten years either way. He'd been a toy boy in one relationship and a cradle snatcher in another, even though Lottie was in her thirties.

But they looked like a good couple, a good fit, nothing out of place about them.

Henry's eyes scanned the desk and behind one of the photo frames he saw a small digital camera. He dragged it towards him, then switched it on.

He wasn't great with new technology, but even he could manage to find his way around a digital camera and soon started to flick through the photographs stored on it, starting with the most recent first, then going backwards in time.

The first of the photos were of her and Percy, a vast array of those 'couple' photos taken when they hug each other and one or the other of them, arm extended, takes the picture. Lots of smiles and laughing. Having a great time photos.

Then Henry came across a few photographs of a fishing boat . . . he thought the type of boat he was looking at was called a sport-fisher, but couldn't be certain. He had no great knowledge of anything maritime, as his excursion into Morecambe Bay had adequately demonstrated. And he liked to be fishing with his feet firmly on the ground.

Quite a few of the shots were of a marina which looked very nice, crowded with row upon row of very sleek, expensive looking power boats and sportfishers. The whole place looked extremely plush and wealthy.

He went through the photographs slowly.

A few were of Percy and Lottie, arms around each other, on the deck of a fishing boat – Henry now knew it was a fishing boat, because he could see fishing rods stacked up . . . sometimes he amazed himself that he could put such clues together. And quite a few of these photos were obviously taken by a third person.

There were more photos of the boat itself, one of which was taken from the quayside where the boat was moored. It showed the back end of the boat and its name emblazoned across it and its port of origin.

The boat was called *Silverfin* and the port was Key West.

So the trip to Florida the couple had taken, Henry put together brilliantly, was to do some sea fishing. Did they catch marlin and huge tuna fish from Key West, Henry half-recalled? He had studied Hemingway at school and seemed to think that the writer had lived in Key West at some stage in his life and had owned a fishing boat there.

Percy did not strike Henry as being an angler.

Maybe it had been one of those secret ambitions but, if the business was floundering, wasn't it a bit of an extravagance to zip over to Florida to treat his girlfriend to some deep sea fishing? Henry sighed and continued to flick through the photos, then stopped at one and peered at it.

He knew enough about digital cameras to be able to focus in on sections of the screen and enlarge them.

The photograph that had piqued his interest was the only one so far in which there was someone else other than the couple. It was a shot of Lottie standing on the deck of *Silverfin* and behind her was the cockpit of the boat with the wheel and the instrument panel behind it.

Bending over and giving a shadowy profile to the camera was a man dressed in a T-shirt and shorts, a baseball cap on his head.

He looked familiar.

Henry angled his head at the camera and peered closely at him. The photo wasn't all that clear, he was just a guy in the background behind Lottie, in the darkness of the cockpit, not focused on, just the usual collateral damage in an innocent photograph. Probably a crew member.

Yet . . . he looked familiar to Henry, although he knew this could not be the case. Henry simply did not know anyone in Florida. Full stop. Yet . . . he tried to enlarge it again, but it didn't seem to help.

Frustrated, Henry flicked the button so the screen returned to normal, and in the corner of the same photograph he saw the edge of what looked very much like a bicycle wheel, which also seemed slightly odd. He didn't get time to ponder as his mobile phone rang and he answered it immediately, not checking the caller ID, still looking at the photograph of Lottie's happy face.

'Henry Christie,' he said.

'Henry – where the hell are you?' It was DCI Pete Woodcock, his voice sounding urgent, and Henry could hear footfalls and heavy breathing.

'Lottie's parents.'

'Good . . . look, I'm on foot, Blackpool town centre . . . ditched my car . . . certain I've just spotted a guy who's a dead ringer for your e-fit of the murderer we're after . . . got patrols closing in . . . it's all over the PR.'

'On my way,' Henry snapped.

He took totally inappropriate leave of Lottie's parents' house, saying he was sorry but he had to rush, that he'd borrowed her camera and would return with a receipt if that was OK. He hadn't waited for an answer, just tore rudely out through the front door and leapt into his car, which then screeched down the avenue.

Lottie's family lived in the village of Singleton, not too far away from Blackpool, and within a minute Henry was on the A586, Garstang Road, heading west towards the resort.

As he drove, he reached into the glove compartment, fished out his personal radio and switched it on, hoping the battery was charged up. It was, and the radio was already tuned into Blackpool's frequency; the first voice he heard was that of Woodcock, directing operations. Henry visualized his location: somewhere near to the railway station, Blackpool North.

'Exchange Street,' Woodcock was transmitting. 'Last sighting, Exchange Street, walking in the direction of the town centre.' He sounded out of breath.

'Alpha Six, got that,' a mobile patrol shouted up. 'Dickinson Road, heading to the town centre.'

One of the town centre foot patrols shouted up that he was on Springfield Road, which Henry knew wasn't far away from Exchange Street. There was a good chance that if the suspect was going in that direction he could well end up in that particular cop's arms.

Henry called up, driving one-handed, his Audi touching seventy. 'Detective Superintendent Christie, presently Garstang Road, direction of the town centre. What's the description of this man?' he demanded. 'And patrols to be aware that if this is our suspect, he is extremely dangerous and will not hesitate to injure a police officer.'

Woodcock piped up, 'Six foot, medium build, short brown hair, wearing a brown zip-up leather jacket, blue jeans, trainers.'

'Roger that,' the comms operator acknowledged.

A series of mobile patrols also acknowledged receipt of this information.

'No sign Exchange Street,' Woodcock gasped.

'Nor Springfield Road,' the officer on foot said.

'A patrol needs to make for the railway station,' Henry butted in. He had weaved through the traffic, zapped cheekily around the busy roundabout at Little Carleton and was speeding down Westcliffe Drive, only minutes from the railway station himself.

Woodcock shouted up, his footfalls pounding as he ran, 'I'm at the station now . . . I'll check it out.'

'Be careful,' Henry said.

'Roger.'

'Alpha Six, I'll continue towards town, check out the bus station.'

The foot patrol said, 'I'll do High Street, Talbot Road area.'

Henry powered on and then he was at the top of Talbot Road, driving towards the centre, having slowed right down and adopted cop cruise mode. His eyes searched hard, looked at every single person.

Woodcock chirped up over the radio, 'In the railway station.' Then, 'No sign.'

Henry felt deflated. He called up comms. 'How many more patrols do we have free and within a couple of minutes of the town?'

He knew that people being chased could disappear very quickly and time was critical. The longer it took to get cops to the area, the less chance of a result.

'Just two town centre foot patrols and one more mobile.'

'Roger . . . keep them deployed in the area for at least another fifteen minutes if possible . . . DCI Woodcock, location?'

'Railway station.'

'One minute.'

Henry caught up with him on the concourse outside the station. He was doubled over, hands on his knees, gasping, red-faced.

'I mean . . . I couldn't be exactly certain . . . I was on Dickinson Road, saw the guy out of the corner of my eye . . . looked just like the e-fit. Time I turned round, he'd scarpered. I combed the streets, then spotted him on Exchange Street, then got blocked by a bin wagon. Ditched the car, ran . . . fucking lost him . . . sorry, boss.'

'You win some,' Henry said. 'I wonder why he was walking around the town centre.'

'Dunno, I'm just sorry I couldn't grab him . . .'

'He's likely to be elusive . . . he won't be easy to nail or catch.' But why was he strolling around town? Henry wondered again. Was it possible he had digs around here? It wasn't unknown for felons to get their heads down in some grotty bedsit in Blackpool.

'That's if it was him,' Woodcock said. 'Bloody looked like him.'

Henry gazed around. 'Any CCTV in this part of town?'

'No,' Woodcock said sharply. Then more softly, 'No . . . don't think so.'

'Pity . . . just check to see if there is. You never know . . . could strike lucky.' Henry patted the DCI on the shoulders. 'Never mind, mate.'

Having got his breath back, Woodcock stood upright and asked, 'How did you go on at Lottie's?'

'Er . . . not sure really . . . got some recent photos on a digital camera which I'll get printed and enlarged . . . might be nothing.'

'And old man Archie?'

'Didn't get round to see him. Might be tomorrow now . . . I'll give you a lift back to your car.'

TWELVE

Steve Flynn was naked.

He stood in the centre of the cell.

The door opened and he glared at the gaoler, who noted the expression and hesitated slightly.

'Señor,' the gaoler said, tossing a bundle on to the floor. 'Put these on.'

Flynn glanced down at what looked like a roll of rags, then devilishly back at the gaoler, who retreated quick-time and slammed the cell door shut, leaving Flynn alone in the semi-darkness, the only light cast by a dim, flickering bulb behind toughened frosted glass over the door.

He picked up the pile. It was a very old pair of prison dungarees and they looked as if they hadn't seen washing powder for years. They were grey to start with, a slash of hi-viz neon yellow across the chest and back, and the lack of cleaning did nothing to help that colour.

Flynn peered into the crutch. It was soiled, marked with dried shit.

Much of Flynn's self-respect had already evaporated with the invasive strip search he'd had to endure and to some extent he was past caring, but there was no way he was going to dress in shit-soiled clothing. His own had been seized for scientific examination and he would probably never see it again, he assumed.

He dropped the dungarees, stepped over to the wall and jammed the heel of his hand on the 'call' button set into the cell wall, and didn't release it. He could hear it ringing somewhere in the cell complex.

'At least it's annoying someone,' he muttered, his rage starting to rise again.

Footsteps approached along the cell corridor, then the inspection flap in the cell door clattered open and the round, moustachioed face of the gaoler appeared. 'Si?'

Flynn pointed at the dungarees and said, 'Not. Wearing. Them. Shit. On. Them.' Then he added, 'Sucio,' meaning 'dirty'.

The gaoler pouted. 'Y?'

'Limpio – por favor,' Flynn said. *Clean, please.*

The gaoler harrumphed with annoyance. 'Por qué?'

'Porque sucio.'

The hatch slid up and slammed shut. Then the gaoler's footsteps began to recede and Flynn slammed his hand back on the call button again – but this time nothing happened. The gaoler had obviously deactivated the button from the outside of the cell.

'Bastard,' he hissed and started to smash the side of his fist on the cell door, but eventually gave up, twisted his back to the cell wall and slithered down so his naked buttocks were on the cold, hard concrete floor. He rested his forehead on his drawn-up knees and wrapped his arms around his shins.

Having arrived at the police station in Puerto Rico he had been almost instantly transferred to the main police station for the island in Las Palmas where he had been roughly manhandled throughout the whole process, but acquiesced silently with the farce that was his arrest and detention. Then his clothing had been taken from him, he'd been full body searched – which included having to part his arse cheeks and display his anus to the searching officers – then been tossed into a stinking cell, the toilet in which was blocked with evil smelling faeces and toilet paper.

It was a grim place, but Flynn knew he could put up with it.

He had been given no rights, no phone calls, no offer of a lawyer and nothing to eat or drink, but he was pretty sure that was par for the course. He knew that Spanish cops still operated with impunity and dealing with a suspected double murderer clearly meant it was OK to deny rights, humiliate and rough handle him.

Flynn didn't care. He knew he could hack it.

He raised his head as footsteps came along the corridor. Two people approaching. Flynn could already recognize the ones belonging to the gaoler; the other set he did not know, but guessed they belonged to the detective, Romero. The key went into the lock, the cell door creaked open.

Flynn was right. Romero stepped into the cell. Flynn stayed where he was, just looked sceptically at his captor.

'Señor Flynn – you have a complaint about the clothing we have provided?'

'Literally, it's shit up.'

Romero tutted. He walked into the centre of the cell where the dungarees had been dumped and pretended to look at them, as if he hadn't known what state they were in. Flynn guessed this might be an olive branch moment, the showing of some compassion.

Romero's face turned angrily from the soiled clothing to the diminutive gaoler. There then followed a heated exchange in Spanish that Flynn struggled to understand, although he got the gist. At the end of a short rant from Romero, the gaoler looked crestfallen. Romero turned back to Flynn and reverted to English.

'You have my most apologies about this, it is not right. These clothes are disgusting and I will ensure they are replaced immediately.'

Flynn continued to regard him unimpressed, not taken in by the sudden kindness.

'Your welfare is paramount, Señor Flynn,' Romero cooed.

Flynn grunted and stifled what would have been a very loud guffaw.

Romero threw the dirty dungarees at the gaoler, who caught them delicately and scurried away.

'We need you to be comfortable, for interrogation,' Romero said.

One of Flynn's eyebrows arched high. 'Interrogation – or interview?'

'Are they not the same beast?'

'Hardly. Interrogation smacks of fingernails being pulled out – you know, like they did when Spain was ruled by fascists. Third World torture. Interviews search for the truth.'

Romero considered Flynn and his words, then said, 'Whichever is suitable.' He gave Flynn a dangerous grin.

*   *   *

'Never mind,' Henry commiserated again. 'You win some . . .'

They were back in the MIR, in Henry's office.

'I'm just gutted,' Woodcock said, still shaking from the exertion, but took a swig of tea from the mug Henry had made for him. 'I'm certain it was him.'

'Wonder what the hell he was doing strolling through Blackpool?' Henry pondered out loud – again.

'Christ knows.'

'I'll get someone to check CCTV footage,' Henry said. Woodcock looked at him sharply. 'Yeah,' Henry conceded, 'I know there isn't much coverage where you spotted him, but there's a rake of cameras all the way from the railway station into town. Maybe one of them picked him up.'

Woodcock looked doubtful. 'I'll get that checked, if you want? After all, it was my mess.'

'OK, that'd be good.'

'So you didn't get to see Archie, then?' Woodcock said, changing the subject.

'No; like I said, I'll catch up with him tomorrow. One cop a day's probably enough for him anyway.'

The DCI nodded his agreement to this course of action.

'Oh – everything wasn't a total loss, though.' He pulled out the camera he had taken from Lottie's bedroom. 'I rushed out with this, need to give them a receipt, mustn't forget . . . it was on her desk in her bedroom.' Henry switched it on and Woodcock came to stand by his shoulder. 'Photos of her and Percy on a trip to Florida.' Henry flicked through them. 'Mostly just of each other, but there is one . . .' Henry continued to flick through the images, also seeing some of high, remote looking cliffs that didn't seem to look like Florida at all. When Jerry Tope walked in the two higher ranking officers glanced up, then returned to their task, paying him no real heed. 'Here, this looks interesting.' He held the camera so Woodcock could see the screen properly.

'Lottie on a fishing boat?' Woodcock said.

'Yeah – but the guy behind her in the shadow, in the cockpit or whatever they call the bit where the steering wheel is . . .'

Woodcock peered at the image, pouted. 'Nah . . . what about him?'

Henry looked again. 'I thought . . . dunno . . .'

'Want me to look?' Jerry Tope ventured.

Henry held out the phone for him and he took his turn. Henry saw the subtle change in expression on the DC's face. His eyes widened, then he looked at Henry. 'I know who that is!'

Henry waited for the revelation.

'Do *you*?' Tope said.

'Just tell me,' Henry said crossly.

'Well . . .'

'Don't screw me about.'

'If I was a betting man – which I'm not, but if I was – I'd lay good money down on that being Jack Hoyle.'

The next pair of dungarees was straight out of the packet. As clean as they'd been made and straight from the factory, probably some grubby sweat shop in a Madrid back street. The only problem was that they were about three sizes too small for the tall, wide, muscular Steve Flynn. Years hauling in big fish such as marlin, with his feet jammed against the foot rail of the fighting chair in the stern of *Faye*, had built up his thighs to be wide and muscular in a natural way and he knew as soon as he started pulling the garment on that it was going to be a very tight squeeze. The material and seams almost screamed their displeasure. It did not help either that they were about six inches too short.

Flynn knew this was just another move in Romero's psychological chess game with him, another attempt to weaken his defences. First the transfer from Puerto Rico, manacled up in the back of a van, then the undignified strip search, then the seizing of his clothing, then the unhygienic cell in which he'd been left naked, then the clothing fiasco. Romero would have an answer for it all, if it came to it, but Flynn had pegged him as a slippery sod who would get away with maltreatment easily.

Flynn knew the game: keep belittling, make 'em feel worthless, treat 'em like shit. But he didn't care. He could ride it.

Now he was having his fingerprints and photograph taken, having just had a swab of saliva taken from the inside of his mouth for a DNA profile.

He smiled ingratiatingly at the digital camera as a uniformed cop snapped his photograph.

Romero appeared at the door of the tiny fingerprint room. A quick-fire exchange took place between him and the cop, then the detective looked at Flynn.

'I now wish to interrogate you,' he said.

'Interview, you mean,' Flynn corrected him.

Romero's bulbous, sleepy Spanish eyes blinked slowly like a toad. 'Semantics,' he said. 'I ask, you answer, and we see where it goes.'

Flynn gave a 'whatever' shrug, then followed the detective.

'OK, what have we got?'

Henry posed the question to Jerry Tope. They were in his office with DCI Woodcock and a DI called Matterson.

'Only had the chance to skim through things so far,' Tope began unapologetically. 'I've accessed Percy's personal bank accounts – but please don't ask me how, or even tell anyone, because we haven't yet served the order for access.'

Henry rolled his eyes. Tope was very adept at hacking into computer systems without their owners realizing it. It was a useful, though sometimes dodgy, skill. He was so good that the FBI wanted to poach him and already the newly formed National Crime Agency was sniffing around him. Henry was reluctant to let him go, even if he was a grouchy bastard and usually insubordinate. One day, though, a 'can't refuse' offer would come Tope's way.

'These are only his day to day accounts – a current account, a savings account and a business account relating to the shops. He may yet have more, be surprised if he doesn't.'

'First impressions?'

Tope shrugged. 'I'm not an accountant or businessman . . . I'll hand this stuff over to the financial guys . . . but his current account looks healthy enough, a fair wodge in the savings account, but the business seems to be operating on a massive overdraft.'

'How massive?' Woodcock asked.

'Quarter of a million, thereabouts.'

Henry rocked his head from side to side. He was no businessman and hated being even fifty pounds overdrawn, so a quarter of a million seemed a lot to him, though maybe it wasn't. 'Speak to his accountant,' he told Tope, who nodded, 'armed with this information, but don't let on you know . . . try to get a big picture of the business. Anything else?'

'Tracked down the travel bookings for the flights to Florida and the Canary Islands and I've got into one of Percy's email accounts . . . but all I've got from that are the flight reservations so far, nothing else of great interest at first glance.'

'OK. Phone records?' Henry asked.

'The telephone unit's on that now.'

Henry glanced at the other two detectives. 'Any thoughts?'

Neither had anything to add.

'OK, Jerry, that's brilliant. Keep plugging away,' Henry said, then leaned back and posed the question, 'What d'you think to this Jack Hoyle thing? Do you think it's something we need to follow up?'

'Don't know,' Tope said. 'He did disappear with a million quid, supposedly, and we still need to speak to him about that.'

'Mm . . . he was Steve Flynn's big mate and partner, wasn't he?' It was a rhetorical question, because both he and Tope knew the answer to it. Then Henry added naughtily, 'Yeah, Steve Flynn, your mate.'

Tope coloured up like beetroot.

'You heard from him recently?'

'No, no, boss.' Tope coughed as though something thick was stuck in his craw.

Henry didn't pursue Tope's obvious discomfort, but made a mental note not to forget and went back to the issue of Jack Hoyle.

'So, Jack Hoyle – accident or coincidence?' He dropped forward again. 'I like coincidences,' he declared. 'I like them very much because coincidence is what usually trips up the bad guys, and Hoyle is definitely a bad guy. I have no doubt he stole that money way back and now he's on a boat with two people who later end up dead. Coincidence my buttocks.'

The interview/interrogation room was as grotty and unpleasant as all the other rooms in the police station.

Flynn sat on a plastic chair screwed to the floor at a similarly affixed table, opposite Romero. He could feel the stitching in the dungarees stretching taut against his muscles, reminding him briefly of the Incredible Hulk. If he got angry enough, Flynn thought, he was sure he could burst out of the garment and probably turn green.

Underneath the thick, slug-like moustache, Romero's mouth twisted into a supercilious grin.

Flynn eyed him blandly.

'These are the rules,' Romero said. 'This is my police station and I say how things go. You will answer my questions, you will tell me the truth and admit to these murders and things will remain . . . pleasant.'

'I think you need to explain to me exactly what you're getting at.'

-'The English couple in the villa. You murdered them.'

'Which couple?'

'There are others?' Romero said, rolling his eyes as though Flynn was being stupid. 'The couple at the villa where you were arrested.'

'I don't think so.' Flynn shook his head.

Romero paused, then said, 'How did you come about your bodily injuries?'

'Which ones?'

'All of them. The face, the eye, the chest, the stomach . . . you are extensively injured.'

'I'm clumsy. I fell.'

Romero gave a short shake of his head. His eyes never left Flynn's. 'I can see you are going to be awkward, Señor Flynn.'

'You asked for the truth, you got it.'

Now Romero sighed. 'You are Stephen Alexander Flynn?' Flynn nodded. 'You live in a villa on Doreste y Molina – correct?'

Flynn: 'Correct.'

'You work on a charter fishing boat and you are a former police officer from Lancashire in England, si?'

'Si.'

'And you came to Gran Canaria, say, eight, nine years ago after leaving the police on suspicion of stealing a large amount of money, si?'

Flynn didn't particularly like that. It riled him enough to make him say, 'A suspicion never proven.'

Romero gave a slight, 'don't care' shrug. 'Last night you had an altercation in Puerto Rico's commercial centre with Scott Costain and his girlfriend.'

'Is that a question?'

'It is.'

'Then yes, I did.'

'What was that about?'

Flynn knew he had to tell the truth but only the bits he wanted the Spaniard to know – otherwise things would get very complicated indeed.

'I was annoyed by the way in which he had elbowed a client of mine out of the way by intimidating him, then taking his place on the boat. I learned how that happened from the original client last night.'

'And it became a fight?'

'He started it,' Flynn said petulantly.

'According to eye witnesses in the Irish bar, you were seen to drag Mr Costain bodily out into a side alley.'

'Did they see him punch me first in the bar?' Flynn fibbed. 'I dragged him out so there wouldn't be a problem inside.'

'So you fought outside?'

'Yes, we did.'

'Hence your injuries?'

'Some of them. Like I said, I fell. But as regards Mr Costain, I bit off more than I could chew.'

'Por qué?'

'He was a better fighter than me.'

'But he is much smaller than you.'

'Better at it.'

'So the police come, the fight is broken up and you are sent your separate ways?

'Correct.'

'But you still haven't finished with him, have you, Señor Flynn?'

'I'd had my say.'

'And this morning you visited him and killed both him and his girlfriend.'

'No.'

'You brutally murdered them. Shot them to death.'

'I think you'll find I didn't.'

'I think you did. If not, why were you there?'

Flynn swallowed. It was a good question, yet to tell Romero the whole truth could end up very badly for Flynn and he certainly didn't want to go down the road of telling him everything that had happened. To claim he had been kidnapped and had then killed two of his captors, then escaped by stealing a Lamborghini that he trashed. When those two deaths were discovered, Flynn hoped there would be no route to him, but to give the cops a lead would be suicide. He hadn't killed Costain and Trish and he was sure the police had no real evidence to prove otherwise, but to give them two other deaths instead would just be silly.

'OK – I went there because I was still mad,' Flynn admitted. 'They were dead when I got there and I'm sure your scientific people will be able to pinpoint their time of death. I have an alibi for every moment since last night's fight. I don't have a gun. You won't find any gunshot residue on my hands from firing a weapon.' He held up his fingers and hoped he'd washed his hands thoroughly enough since handling the gun last night in the villa. He also hoped that the cops, having seized his Nissan Patrol, hadn't searched it properly and found his hidden Bushmaster. It wasn't the type of gun that had killed the couple, but it would show that Flynn did have access to a weapon and would muddy the waters for him. He knew he had to keep his story tight. 'I simply didn't kill them. I found them dead, that's all.'

Romero listened patiently, unimpressed. 'How well did you know Mr Costain?'

'Before yesterday I had never met him in my life.'

'You are a liar. Convincing, I admit, but a liar.'

'You have the truth before you,' Flynn said.

'Will I have to beat the truth out of you?' Romero threatened in a low voice.

'Now that would be interesting,' Flynn said and looked deep into the Spaniard's eyes. 'Do the Spanish police really still beat confessions out of prisoners?'

'Only if they have to.'

Henry spent some time completing the murder policy book, although he couldn't keep his mind from wandering back to the photograph with Jack Hoyle in the background.

The Jack Hoyle/Steve Flynn incident had been nothing more than a mere blip in Henry's career. One of those fairly unpleasant but mundane things a senior detective might be asked to investigate to assist the Professional Standards Department, which was the modern guise of the Discipline and Complaints Department. Or the 'Rubber Heel Squad' – the cops who investigated cops. It had been a fairly messy affair, with lots of counter-allegations being made, and in the end nothing was proved, not even that the million in missing money even existed.

Because of it, though, Flynn and Hoyle left the job under a cloud.

Flynn had come to hate Henry, but the two of them had crossed paths a few times since and a tolerable truce ensued between them, although under the veneer Henry still actually had little time for Flynn. He believed the police service was much better for Flynn not being in it.

Hoyle had left under similar circumstances, then faked his own death, and consequently Henry had had no encounters with him since. Flynn had claimed that he had tracked his ex-partner to the United States where he was working on a fishing charter boat, but Hoyle had managed to do a runner, or so Flynn alleged. Henry had only Flynn's word on that.

But going by this picture, maybe there had been some truth in what Flynn had claimed. Henry snorted derisively at that thought. He and Flynn rarely saw eye to eye and, as Henry had once said to Flynn, 'Call me a cynic, but I don't fucking believe you.' It hadn't helped matters that Flynn was looked upon with some fondness by Alison, which made Henry think, *grrr* . . .

And yet, that aside, here was an up-to-date photo of Hoyle. Henry's eyes hadn't deceived him. Jerry Tope confirmed it.

Henry lay down his pen and stared vacantly into space, then scooped up his desk phone and dialled an internal number to the one and only Jerry Tope – who was actually only sitting in an office just on the other side of the MIR. If Henry had stood up and gone to his office door, he could have seen Jerry's door.

'Intel Cell, Jerry Tope.'

'It's me.'

A hesitancy, then, 'Hello, boss.'

'So when did you last speak to Steve Flynn?' Henry asked cheekily.

If Tope had had a mouthful of anything, he would have spluttered it out. 'I . . . I haven't, boss.'

Henry chuckled. 'Whatever. Look, Jack Hoyle . . . do some digging, get everything you can about him, please. Same applies for Steve Flynn. Dig out their old personal files and everything you can about that missing money.'

'Why Flynn?'

'Because I say so. I'm a detective superintendent, or didn't you know that?' Henry blasted him, but only jokingly. It was rare for Henry ever to pull rank, but occasionally he had some fun with it. Otherwise what was the point?

But Tope did not see the joke. 'You know Flynn's not involved.'

'I don't know anything of the sort. The guy is a thoroughly bad egg.'

'OK, I'll see what I can do. Incidentally . . .'

'Yes?'

'Can you send the cleaner round to stick a broom up my arse? Might as well do her job, too.'

'I can think of something much more painful to stick up there.' Henry smiled. From the office window he could just see the top of Blackpool Tower. He hung up.

'You know you can't prove anything,' Flynn said with a confidence he didn't really feel.

'It isn't what I can prove,' Romero said, 'it is what I can convince a criminal court to believe.'

'Fuck you,' Flynn snarled.

The two men were now standing on the threshold of Flynn's cell. It still stank and the toilet had not been unblocked.

'What exactly do you want?' Flynn said.

'To clear up a brutal murder, a double murder in fact. This is a peaceful law abiding island and you seem to attract violence to it. You should be in prison, Señor Flynn.'

'You know I didn't do it.'

'Then tell me who did.'

'If I knew, I would. Maybe you need to do some digging into Mr Costain's background. There might be some answers there.'

'I will, but until then . . .'

'I'm under arrest?'

'Very much so.' Romero gestured into the cell.

Flynn walked in, then stopped suddenly and spun around. 'Time for my phone call, please. And if you are seriously going to do a background check on Costain, you might want to speak to a detective I know in England, in Lancashire.'

'Who might that be?'

'Christie, Henry Christie . . . he's a detective superintendent. He'll know about Costain, and then maybe you'll be able to apply some fundamental investigative thinking to all this instead of just grabbing the first fall guy you see – me!'

'What do you mean?'

'Find out how a man lived and you'll find out why he's died.'

'That sounds like something your grandmother might say,' Romero said scathingly and slammed the cell door shut.

Flynn's nose was only inches from it. He stood there for a moment, then turned and walked over to the bed muttering, 'At least I wouldn't have to teach her how to suck eggs.'

THIRTEEN

The debrief for the murder team that evening was upbeat and Henry gave and felt a sense of positivity. One of the main things was that a Porsche 911 had been found abandoned in Poulton-le-Fylde, up someone's driveway, and a Nissan Note had been stolen from nearby, but both reports had come in late. First, the Porsche in the driveway of a big, detached house was only discovered when the house owner and his wife returned from a short break to find it impossible to get their Mercedes up the drive. Second, the Nissan had only been reported stolen by the owner, a nurse on a night shift at Blackpool Victoria Hospital, when she actually stepped out of her house to go to work that evening.

Fortunately, with regard to the Porsche, the comms operator receiving the report had been well briefed about the double murder and linked the Porsche to it so that, as well as the murder team being informed, a local bobby and a CSI were dispatched to the scene. Then, when the Nissan was reported stolen from a street nearby, the same operator did the sums – one car abandoned, another stolen – and sent the same bobby to report it and bear the possibility of a link in mind.

Good work, for which Henry had gone into comms at Blackpool and thanked the operator.

The details of the Nissan were duly circulated and a note attached saying that if it turned up anywhere, burned out or otherwise, a CSI had to be sent to it immediately.

The Porsche – as Henry had recalled seeing when he had gone to Percy's house – was on hire from a well-known car hire company in Manchester and a detective was going to visit their office next day.

A lot of work had been done at the crime scene, and details of Percy's business dealings and money transfers were now being scrutinized officially; the e-fit image of the killer was widely circulated and Henry reported to the squad he expected to hear something back from the FBI soon regarding the American accent angle – hopefully. The full results of the post mortems were revealed and a video of the actual examinations was made available.

So Henry was feeling reasonably sanguine about it. The juggernaut was moving in the right direction and everyone was hanging on to its sides.

He dismissed the team after taking questions and they all dispersed, ready to have a pint or get off home, whichever floated their boats.

As Henry watched them go, his mind actually returned to boats.

He went back into his office and reached for the desk phone, which rang just before he picked it up.

'Hi, Henry.' It was Donaldson.

'Hey, Yank, I was just about to call you.'

'Got in first . . . been doing some rootin' for y'all,' Donaldson said, exaggerating his twang for Henry's benefit. 'And you ain't gonna like it.'

'Try me, I'm a big boy.'

'From what you told me and from the e-fit, this guy fits the description and MO of a hood operating for a low level mobster in Miami. To put it plain, he's an executioner.'

Despite being a big boy, Henry suddenly went cold and fearful. 'Name?' he asked.

'Hawke, with an "e". Jason Hawke. Hawke by name, hawk by nature. He looks like your e-fit and our intelligence has it that he "suits up" for his jobs and uses a revolver as opposed to a semi-automatic pistol. Thirty-eight calibre. Soft points.'

'Suits up?' Henry said.

'Paper suit, forensically aware, been arrested several times and he's very savvy so he has always walked.'

'Sounds like him,' Henry said dully.

'Boston born, mob background in the Big Apple, evolved from a gofer into an enforcer and then a hired killer. Served time as a teenager for putting two rounds into a guy's head, but pleaded and was out in two years. Guy he shot was a scumbag, anyway.'

'So that makes it OK?'

'Absolutely,' Donaldson laughed. 'In fact Hawke's name has popped up in connection with lots of gang-related hits. Was arraigned for one, but a witness got queasy, then dead. Seems the only way to make anything stick with this guy is to catch him in the act – which is what you did. But what the hell is he doing whacking some two-bit, legitimate jeweller in the north of England?' Donaldson finished.

'That is the question I would have asked myself.' There was a pause while both men mulled over this conundrum, then Henry said, 'How far away from Miami is Key West?'

'One hundred and sixty miles, give or take,' Donaldson said knowledgeably. His last posting as an FBI field agent had been in Miami, so he knew his way around Florida.

'It's down at the far end of the Florida Keys, isn't it?'

'Next stop, Cuban cigars,' Donaldson said. 'Why?'

'I've got a photo of our dead couple on a fishing boat in Key West. They were there a couple of weeks ago . . . thing is there's a guy in the background of one of the shots that I recognize.'

'That *you* recognize?'

'Yeah, ex-cop, disappeared with a big wodge of drug dealer's money . . . Jack Hoyle . . . I think you know the story.'

'Jack Hoyle, Steve Flynn – that story?' Donaldson did know of it, had even met Flynn a few times.

'That's the one. Hoyle's in the background of one of the shots . . . fortnight later, they're dead . . . maybe at the hands of a mob killer from Miami.' Henry's ring piece nipped sharply together as he said these words, his physical concession to his excitement – a twitching arsehole.

'You got the name of the boat?' Donaldson said.

'Uh . . . it's on another photo . . . just hang fire.' Lottie's camera was still on his desk (and Henry mentally castigated himself for not booking it in with the exhibits officer). He switched it on and found the photo of *Silverfin*, from the port of Key West. He told Donaldson.

'Hold on while I search for it,' Donaldson said.

'How do you mean?'

'An Intel search on the FBI system . . . we have a database of boats on it . . . bit like a mini-Google.'

Henry could hear computer keys being tapped whilst Donaldson hummed.

'Whoa!' Donaldson uttered.

Henry's bottom did another tightener.

'Just to backtrack, I said that Hawke is a mob hit man . . . well, what I didn't tell you was that the mobster he works for in Miami is called Giancarlo Fioretti: small operator, big ideas. I came across him a few times when I worked there.' Donaldson exhaled quite loudly into his phone. 'And he owns a sportfishing boat in Key West called—'

'*Silverfin*,' Henry ventured.

'Which means your vics were recently on a boat belonging to a crime boss in Florida.'

Henry's arse then slammed so tightly shut he felt it would need to be prised apart with a jemmy.

Henry's breathing was unsteady, his heart hammering, his throat dry, as he impatiently watched the monitor of his desktop PC, which was logged into his work email account. Then, with a magic Henry the Luddite still did not understand, an untitled email appeared from Donaldson, with various attachments.

Henry moved his forefinger, about to press and select and open it, when his mobile phone rang. With an irritated shake of the head he answered it.

He hurtled through the corridors out into the secure car park, where he leapt into the Audi and set off, annoyed by the slowness of the rising security barrier.

'C'mon, you . . .'

It rose and he accelerated through. Minutes later he was abandoning the car in the ambulance only parking area outside the entrance to the A&E department at Blackpool Victoria Hospital, a place where, he thought, he'd spent far too much of his police service.

He trotted quickly into the emergency treatment area just beyond reception and literally grabbed a passing nurse, one he half-recognized. He pulled out his warrant card and said, 'Archie Astley-Barnes – just been admitted from his home address in Out Rawcliffe . . . seriously assaulted.'

Henry drove the Audi cautiously over the rutted track leading up to Archie Astley-Barnes's farmhouse in Out Rawcliffe. He stopped on the edge of the yard at the front of the building. Drawn up and abandoned at various untidy angles were three police cars (one a CSI van, one a local patrol and the other DCI Peter Woodcock's Vauxhall Insignia).

Henry paused in the driver's seat, looking at the farmhouse, all lights blazing, the front door wide open, security lights on.

The expression on his face was one of grim anger as he wondered what sort of person could have beaten a frail old man within a hair's breadth of his life . . . and maybe, if Archie didn't regain consciousness and the life support machine that was keeping him going was switched off, to death.

The only good point about it was that Archie, despite his frailty and mental state, might well have given his attacker more than he had bargained for.

Henry climbed out and shivered, his mind still full of the image of the old man in the A&E unit, a crash team working furiously to keep him alive and then stabilize him.

Woodcock emerged from the front door, already dressed in his forensic suit. He came over to Henry, his expression very much matching Henry's.

'Boss,' he greeted Henry.

'Pete . . . what have we got?'

'The guy who lives in the next farm along the track was driving past about an hour and a half ago, saw Archie's lights on, front door open, which was odd, apparently. Usually all the doors are closed up, shutters down, just the hint of a light. So he stops and checks. Finds Archie in the living room, badly beaten up but still breathing, with his shotgun in his hands . . . blood everywhere, but not all Archie's. Neighbour called the ambulance and police and the paramedics ferried him to BVH.'

'Neighbour saw nothing?'

'Not a thing.'

Henry winced, his shoulder suddenly hurting. 'What do you think?'

Woodcock shrugged. 'Burglary gone wrong, maybe. Archie surprised someone who attacked him but managed to get to his shotgun, and looks like he blasted the intruder . . . the shotgun's been fired and there's blood flecks around the door and frame. He could be just winged, could be an arse shot . . . there's a blood trail across here.' Woodcock indicated an area of the front yard that had been marked out by tape. 'Could be minor or major . . . whatever, I reckon this could be linked to Percy's death, that's my guess.'

'Why?'

'Just a feeling.'

'Anything stolen that we know of?'

'Hard to say . . . there's a tray full of diamonds in the bureau that seems untouched.'

Woodcock's view that it was linked to Percy's death didn't quite seem to fit with this scenario to Henry, but he could have been wrong. It had been known.

'How are the rats?'

'Looking hungry and nasty.'

Henry sighed, rotated his jaw, then said, 'So we have a wounded burglar on the loose?'

'Looking that way. I've got two dog men en route, going to start searching the fields nearby. Already alerted A&E at BVH and Lancaster Royal, although he could have had a car to get away in. The way the trail of blood ends suddenly suggests that.'

'How many offenders?'

Woodcock shrugged.

Henry considered all this, sifting and filing it, putting it into logical order and thinking the very worst – that this could become another murder and he could well be standing on the edge of another murder scene, which might – or might not – be connected to what he was already investigating. His gut feeling was that this was a completely different sort of thing and, as Woodcock had suggested, could be a burglary that had gone wrong. 'I want the circus out for this, Pete. There's every chance that Archie could die and I don't want to get caught showing my arse, so let's do this right from here.'

It was an old mantra, but one drilled into Henry's brain: *You don't get a second chance at a crime scene.*

He raised his eyebrows at Woodcock. 'You're the man on this, OK?'

Other than getting an overview of the potential murder scene by being walked through it by Woodcock and a CSI, the only thing Henry actually did was to oversee the seizure of Archie's tray of diamonds for safe keeping. He had them photographed as a whole, then individually – not that Henry could tell one rock from another – and had them bagged and sealed, then conveyed by two uniformed cops to the safe in the major incident suite, where they would then become the responsibility of the exhibits officer. Although he didn't really want them in police possession he knew it would be foolhardy to leave them vulnerable at the scene where, with the greatest respect to all concerned, light fingers could be attracted to shiny things.

With Woodcock, Henry counted a hundred and sixty-two diamonds, all cut and finished. Henry could not even begin to imagine their retail value. A thousand pounds each, maybe . . . he didn't have a clue, but knew that when they were fitted into a ring or necklace, they could easily sell for five grand each.

Either way, the sums were astronomical.

'What are you going to do with them?' Woodcock asked.

'Keep them safe and see how Archie fares. Let's just hope he recovers and, if he doesn't, that he's made a will. We need to find his solicitor and hand them over as soon as possible . . . if we can't do that, I'll get them put into a safe deposit box . . . I'll work on it. Whatever, I don't like the thought of them being with us for longer than necessary.'

On a cage perched on the bureau top, one of Archie's rats surveyed them, its eyes as black as anthracite.

Henry gave it a wink. 'RSPCA for you, mate.'

The scene was secured at midnight. The police dogs had not found anything of interest in the surrounding fields, which tended to firm up the belief that the offender had escaped in a car. Henry left a fully briefed uniform cop outside the farmhouse in a vehicle and made the decision to resume in the morning.

He then phoned BVH and after much arguing – because he wasn't an actual relative of Archie's and therefore no information concerning his condition could be released – was eventually put through to the consultant who was treating Archie. She had no problems in talking to Henry and informed him that Archie was very, very poorly, not expected to survive the night.

Henry assured her the police were doing their best to chase down relatives. They chatted on about the incident itself and Henry was a little surprised that she hadn't been told to keep an eye out for anyone turning up at A&E with possible shotgun injuries. She put Henry on hold just to double check with reception, came back a few moments later to say that the department had been informed but had been given a mobile phone number to contact, rather than the police station.

'OK,' Henry said tiredly. He was fading fast and his brain wasn't operating as well as it should have been. He gave the consultant his mobile number to call if there was any significant change in Archie's condition.

He drove away from Archie's, down the narrow lanes that brought him out on the A586, where he had a decision to make. If he turned

right he would head back to Blackpool, left would take him towards
Lancaster where he could soon be on the A6, then on to the M6,
on his way to Kendleton.

In one place – the house he owned in Blackpool – he would be
cold and alone, but be in bed in less than twenty minutes; in the
other, which was probably forty minutes away, he would be able to
spoon up to his wife-to-be, all warm and fuzzy after a nightcap.
He'd actually told Alison he would be home by nine, but events
had conspired against him and he had phoned to apologize and she
had been lovely about it. Disappointed, but lovely.

In one place he would wake up with no food in the house; in the
other he could have another great breakfast waiting for him.

'No contest,' he shouted to no one in particular. He turned left
and floored the Audi, slamming on for the speed cameras when
necessary.

He also figured that the drive would give him a chance to mull
things over and plan ahead.

He had reached the point where the A586 met the A6, and the
nose of the Audi was just pulling out to go north, when his phone
rang. As he hadn't connected to the hands-free system, he drew on
to the forecourt of a service station and answered it.

'Mr Christie?'

'Yes.' Henry recognized the voice of the nice lady consultant –
and a feeling of dread coursed through his system.

'This is Kelly Longton . . . we spoke a few minutes ago regarding
Archie Astley-Barnes?'

'Yeah?' he said dubiously.

'I'm afraid I have some terrible news . . . I'm sorry, but he has
just died. The brain trauma from the assault was too severe, we
think he had a blood clot there, too, but he's just suffered a major
heart attack and we couldn't save him.' Her voice was choked.

Henry stared ahead into the distance, completely devoid of
emotion.

His house felt chilly and inhospitable. The heating had been left on
a programme which only activated the system if the outside temperature dropped below a certain level. No one had been in the place for
over a week and it was beginning to feel slightly neglected. Even his
youngest daughter Leanne, who had a tendency to use the place as
a hotel when things weren't going too well in her love life, hadn't

been near for a while. She was 'shacked up' (as Henry derisively called it, much to her annoyance) with her latest badly chosen boyfriend, but so far they hadn't fallen out. Henry wondered what she would do when the house was sold and she had nowhere to run and hide when the relationship went south, which it surely would.

Henry closed the front door behind him and stood in the hallway, then walked into the living room and sat down heavily on the sofa. Quite a lot of the furniture had now been disposed of, mainly to charities, but the basics would remain until the house was sold. That included a bottle of Jack Daniel's in the kitchen cupboard, which Henry suddenly remembered was there.

He poured himself a large measure into a cheap glass and wandered through to the extremely cold conservatory overlooking the back garden and farmland beyond.

From here, late at night, Henry had often seen foxes, stoats, deer and badgers. It had been a good place to chill and he and Kate had often cuddled up close in the darkness.

The JD tasted good, setting his throat warmly alight.

He filed away the memories before he became maudlin, necked the JD and went to pour himself another, realizing how far his life had moved ahead, even in the relatively short time since Kate's death. Maybe the biggest change was that Alison lived and worked miles away in the country and his work was usually in Blackpool or Preston or Blackburn, the big towns of Lancashire, where the biggest crimes were usually committed. Although it was nothing more than a commute, the hours he put in were still often horrendous, especially when a big job kicked off, and it was bound to have a negative impact on the new relationship.

Putting the job first was the one mistake he did not want to make with Alison. Kate had often suffered in silence and that would never happen again.

Nor did he like sleeping alone.

Standing there in his marital home he determined to solve the murders he was working on, tie up loose ends, then call it quits, no matter what carrot might be dangled in front of him to get him to stay. He wanted to be with Alison full time.

That was his future, not attending A&E units at midnight to see the sad spectacle of an old man who had been beaten to death, probably just for the sake of some chunks of compressed coal.

It had been a pathetic sight.

After the phone call from the consultant Henry had rushed back to A&E so he could follow Archie's body down to the mortuary and start a chain of evidence. Once there he had helped the uninterested, pasty-faced mortuary attendant strip the old man, bag and tag his clothing for evidence and heave him, covered by a muslin shroud, on to a tray which was then inserted into the body chiller, then slam the door shut.

Another one for the coroner.

Henry was at least glad he had made the decision to treat the crime scene as a murder scene and keep it secure.

By the time he had finished at the hospital it was just after two a.m. For Henry it was too late to drive all the way back to Kendleton. What he realized, though, standing in his kitchen with a bottle of booze in his hand, was that if he didn't have this house as a crash pad, then he would have no choice but to drive all the way to Kendleton.

'So why am I here?' he asked out loud.

He was just about to tip the JD into the glass, but stopped short. He did not want to be alone, chilly, melancholy.

It would take a fair chunk of time to get to the Tawny Owl and he would hardly get any sleep before he had to get up again, but that was where he belonged and going back was the right thing to do, both for himself and Alison. And it was what he wanted to do.

He screwed the top back on the JD, decided to take the bottle with him and left the house. Two minutes later, he hit the motorway.

The roads were virtually deserted and he made good time and drove into the car park at the front of the Tawny Owl forty minutes later. Five minutes after that he crawled into bed with Alison, who acknowledged his arrival with an irritated murmur.

FOURTEEN

'How exactly do I work this thing?'

Henry had been avoiding the moment, but it had arrived. He held up the iPad and showed it to Ginny, Alison's stepdaughter. Most of the senior officers in the constabulary had been issued with one but Henry had studiously avoided using his although he was sure that the benefits were, well, beneficial.

Ginny laughed patronizingly, took it from him and switched it on. 'That always tends to help,' she winked.

Henry gave her his best pissed off look.

'You use a laptop, don't you?'

'It's in the office.'

'This is much the same, really.'

'Mm. Even though I have a phone that has a touch screen or a swipe screen or whatever the heck it is, I have a bit of an aversion to it. I think my fingertips are far too thick.' Ginny gave him a look and he said, 'Don't you dare say a word. I just have a heavy touch.'

She sat down next to him and said, 'Look . . .'

It was six forty-five a.m. the following morning. Henry, Alison and Ginny were in the dining room of the Tawny Owl, the two ladies about to kick start the day in the hostelry, which included being ready to serve six breakfasts for walkers who had landed last night without warning.

Henry munched his way through a bacon bap, having decided to forgo the full English. Two days running might have slammed his ventricles shut, but the smell and quality of the cooking made him slaver like Pavlov's dog. As he ate he watched Ginny with the iPad. She had reached the point where he had to input his password to get on to the constabulary system.

From there he sort of understood things.

Ginny stood up, left him to it, but was replaced by Alison, who came up behind him and draped herself over his shoulders, kissing his ear.

'I'm glad you made it home last night,' she said.

'Yeah, me too. Good decision. Not a lot of sleep involved, though.'

She stuck her tongue in his ear, then walked away chuckling dirtily.

With a grin, he continued with the iPad and logged on to the email system. Since his last check, he had received eighty-one messages. He groaned, especially annoyed at those senders who had the audacity to mark their particular one as urgent.

He went to the one from Karl Donaldson he had been about to open at his desk in the MIR just as the call came in about Archie's assault. He opened it and saw there was a photograph attached to it. Before clicking on it Henry read the email, which told him nothing more than he already knew about Jason Hawke.

As he touched the screen to open the photograph the internet connection went down, as it often did in this remote area where gas pipes were quite a new thing, let alone broadband.

The hotel phone rang somewhere in the kitchen. He heard Alison answer it.

He folded the last piece of the bacon bap into his mouth, then picked up his coffee, refilled it from the filter jug and turned to head outside for an early morning intake of fresh air.

It was a nice, cold, dark morning. His eyes widened as he spotted a huge male red deer strolling arrogantly across the village green. He watched in awe as it stood there for a moment, threw back its head, then with one bound leapt across the tiny stream to the other side of the green; then it was gone like a ghost into the mist of the morning.

Henry exhaled appreciatively.

'For you, David Attenborough,' came a voice from behind him. Alison handed him the phone.

'A deer,' he mouthed, with the excitement of a kid.

'I know,' she said, unimpressed. 'There are hundreds of the buggers around here.'

'I know, but . . .'

Alison spun away shaking her head, whilst Henry thought to himself, *Never ever allow yourself to become numb to the wonders of nature.* Into the phone he said, 'Superintendent Christie.'

'Red deer or fallow?'

'Eh? Oh – red,' Henry stuttered.

'Beautiful . . . anyway, sorry, boss . . . Chief Inspector Carney, FIM,' the man at the other end introduced himself. FIM stood for Force Incident Manager, the officer in charge of the main control room for the constabulary at the comms room at headquarters at Hutton, near Preston. The FIM controlled major incidents, deployed appropriate personnel and was responsible for turning out specialist officers according to the on call duty rotas. 'Sorry to call so early, but I know you're interested in the Costain family and I thought, possibly, you might want to deal with this, or at least decide how it is dealt with.'

'Go on,' Henry said.

'We've just received an email, which I've verified, from the police in Gran Canaria. A detective called Romero says he's investigating the murder of a man called Scott Costain and his girlfriend Trish Mason. Apparently they've been shot to death in their villa in Maspalomas and this detective would like us to do background checks on the two victims and, of course, inform the families.'

'Scott Costain?' Henry mused. He knew the Costains very well – was in the process of doing all he could before he retired to dismantle and disrupt their criminal enterprise. But Scott's name wasn't familiar. 'I don't know him.'

'I've just checked him out on PNC, too.'

'OK. Is there anything more, is this something I can look at when I get in to work?'

'There are a few things, actually, boss. This detective, Romero, actually mentions you by name.'

'Oh, right,' Henry said cautiously. 'Should I be flattered?'

Carney chuckled, 'Maybe, but there is a killer to this, if you'll pardon the expression.'

Henry waited.

'They have someone in custody for the murders.'

'That's good, isn't it?'

The chief inspector chuckled again. 'You're going to like this.'

'Go on.'

'Ex-cop of this parish, Steve Flynn.'

'The Steve Flynn?'

'The one and only.'

'Well, I'll go to the foot of our stairs,' Henry said, almost laughing with glee.

'There is something else that you might, or might not, need to know too.'

'What's that?'

Carney told him and, just as he had finished, there was a terrible scream and a crash from inside the pub.

'I'll call you back,' Henry said, whizzed his coffee dregs and ran inside to see what accident had happened in the kitchen.

Alison was holding Henry's iPad gripped tight between her hands as though she was attempting to snap the device like a huge bar of chocolate. The expression of horror on her face stunned Henry. 'What is it, love?'

She was shaking terribly. Behind her stood Ginny, also speechless and terrified. Henry crossed to her and took her arm. 'Babe, what is it?'

'This . . . this man,' she said shakily. She tilted the iPad towards Henry. In the time he had been out for his morning coffee it had reconnected to the internet and continued to download the photograph Donaldson had sent, the one of Jason Hawke.

'What about him?'

Henry glanced at the mug shot, instantly recognizing Hawke as definitely the man he had seen at Percy's house.

Alison could hardly get her words out and Henry could see she was having what he assumed was a panic attack. He prised the iPad out of her grip, laid it on the table, then gently manoeuvred her into a chair and went down on his haunches in front of her, holding her hands between his. Tears streamed down her face.

'Henry, you really have to leave the job . . . I don't know if I can stand this happening again.'

'Stand what, sweetheart?'

'This . . . that man . . . you remember I told you about an American having breakfast here a couple of days ago?'

'Yeah.' Henry felt a sudden thump in his lower belly.

'It was him,' she said. 'The photograph . . . it was him . . . he was here. In my pub . . . sitting over there.' She looked up at Henry with pleading eyes. 'Henry, not again, please not again.'

FIFTEEN

Flynn stared at his breakfast, a churro – a fried stick of batter liberally sprinkled with sugar. Churros are usually served with thick, hot chocolate, into which they are dipped, but the cuisine in the police station did not stretch that far. Flynn's was served with a steaming plastic mug of hot coffee, sweet and milky.

He devoured the churro – the first food he'd had since his arrest almost twenty-four hours before – and he was ravenous. Then, with the rough blanket a gaoler had provided for him after much complaining wrapped around his shoulders, he sat back on the bench alongside the curled-up figure of his new drunken cellmate and savoured the brew. It tasted wonderful.

Eventually, sadly, he finished it.

The man next to him farted wetly. It stank. Flynn wafted away the aroma but could not be bothered to move away. He felt stiff and very sore, the injuries from his assault and abduction seeming to ratchet him up tightly. He needed a shower and a proper sleep, but before those luxuries, he needed a lawyer.

With that in mind he forced himself to stand up, crossed to the wall and stuck his thumb on the call button.

Alison had previously been the target of a man Henry had been investigating, resulting in her suffering a serious assault. The image of her smashed-in face being held up against a car window to taunt Henry was always imprinted on his mind.

She had been chosen and targeted because of her connection to him, and had suffered dreadfully. In fact Henry had almost expected to find her dead and now, maybe, it was happening again.

Someone he was investigating had turned up on her doorstep and, unwittingly, she had chatted openly to him about her fiancé and their future.

'And now you tell me this man is a friggin' hit man?' Alison's voice rose towards hysteria again. 'A hit man? Sitting, eating my full English, talking to me? A fucking hit man!'

One thing Henry had noticed about her was that when she got upset or stressed, her use of language sank right down to gutter level. He tried to tell himself he loved it, that it was just another interesting quirk to her character.

'He won't be back,' he started to reassure her.

She cut in, blazing. 'Call me a cynic, but that's utter cock and bollocks. You cannot be certain of that.'

'I can. I promise you he won't be back.'

Noticing that his language, too, had sunk to drainage level, Henry bellowed down the phone, 'I'm fucking authorising it, that's who,' at the belligerent traffic sergeant in the Operations Department at headquarters. 'No, actually, the chief constable is authorising it, so if you want to pop along to his office and ask him, then be my fucking guest.'

'But sir—'

'No *but*s, mate. It's happening . . . now give him the keys.'

'Yes sir. When do you expect we'll have it back, then?'

'When we catch a killer, that's when.' Henry slammed down the phone and, unfairly, said, 'Moron.'

He could feel himself shaking like a volcano about to erupt, from his toes to his cranium, furious at himself, furious with everyone, furious with the world.

'Here, darling.'

He turned. Alison stood there with a fresh mug of coffee in her hand, offering it to him. Unlike him, she had pretty much recovered from her earlier shock and upset, although she looked drained.

Henry took a steadying breath, reached out with a dithering hand and took the mug. 'Thank you. I'm really, really sorry about—'

'Hey, not your fault.' She moved in close and put the tip of her forefinger over his lips. 'OK? He's a bad man and you're probably right, he wouldn't dare come back.'

He nodded, but knew different. What Alison had not seen was the detailed background on Jason Hawke that Donaldson had sent through as a file attachment. His obsessive, violent behaviour, his ruthless hunting down of people who had wronged him, his cold-blooded ability to kill people and leave no witnesses or evidence behind. Henry now knew he was on Hawke's list, and probably Alison and Ginny were too. Henry knew that Hawke was suspected of obliterating a family in witness protection he had hunted down for a crime boss. He had killed each one, father, mother and two young children.

At this moment in time, therefore, Henry and his new family were easy meat for this guy.

And at this moment, Henry was struggling to get anyone to help him and until he did, he wasn't going anywhere.

Protecting people was difficult at the best of times. It was complicated and, if done properly, very expensive in terms of staff hours.

So far all he had been able to achieve was snaffling a traffic car from Ops and getting someone to sit in it outside the pub, a uniformed presence. That had been the subject of the phone call he had just made to the uncooperative sergeant.

Henry had hit on the idea of assigning the underused PC Bill Robbins to this task. Bill had been a firearms officer until he'd had a nervous breakdown after some particularly nasty incidents and no one really wanted him on their staff, so he found himself mooching around various headquarters departments, basically killing time. Henry's idea was to put Bill in a traffic car and get him to drive to

Kendleton, park in front of the Owl and act as a deterrent of sorts. Even that had taken threats and pulling rank.

Henry slid an arm around Alison's waist and they hugged, Henry trying not to spill his coffee. They were at the bar in the pub, close to the fire Alison had just lit with logs from the woods.

'I've managed to get a traffic car to park up outside, but he's the best part of an hour away. I've also got an Armed Response Vehicle coming from Lancaster to drive past and a mobile to keep cruising as and when possible. It's just a stop-gap for the moment; then I'll get something more permanent – until we catch him.'

Alison stepped backwards. 'You need to get in to work to do that, don't you?'

'I do, but I'm not going anywhere until you and Ginny are protected. It would help if there was a local bobby, but we know there isn't.' He looked pointedly at her and she nodded. The last one in Kendleton had never been replaced; now the police house in the village was deserted and the people of the village did their own policing, up to a point. The nearest cops were in Lancaster, a good fifteen minutes away.

'I'm sure I'll be fine,' Alison said. 'You go in, get hunting.'

'Not until that traffic car is parked up outside and I've seen an ARV drive by at least once, and a section mobile . . . only then and maybe not even then.'

Henry glanced past Alison's shoulder as the revolving doors swished and four men entered the pub, each one carrying a double-barrelled, twelve bore shotgun.

'Oh my good—'

Alison smiled and said, 'This is why I'll be all right.'

The relief that coursed through Henry was so intense he almost cried – but he kept it together.

'Well?' the first man through the door demanded, brandishing his firearm. 'Where is the bastard and where do you want us?' This was a local farmer called Singleton, also a regular in the pub, as were the three others. One was the local doctor, Lott; another a gamekeeper from the nearby estate owned by the Duke of Westminster; and the final one a young lad who worked in an abattoir. Henry knew each and every one of them well and, whilst they were not friends as such, they weren't a million miles away. He had served them all drinks from one side of the bar and drunk with them on the other. Each was a respected member of the local community. They supported their local hostelry with ferocity but, although their hearts were in the right place, Henry could not allow this, as much as he would have liked to.

'Guys,' he said, 'lower the weapons for a start.'

Singleton – flat cap, large ruddy face, a stereotypical farmer – took a menacing step towards Henry.

'I knows what you're going to say, Henry, so don't even start. This lass –' fortunately he chose to point at Alison with an arthritic finger rather than with the barrels of the shotgun – 'this lass is one of us now and we love her. This place belongs to the village and we protect each other out here, which you should know by now. We're all licensed to own and carry these guns, we know what we're doing with them and we're here to protect Alison and Ginny. Not that bothered about you, yet. Only if you arrest us will we back off. Otherwise –' he glanced at the three others, who came to a sloppy sort of attention – 'we're here for as long as necessary, understand? And we've decided to call ourselves the Wild Geese.'

Henry blinked back his tear, then said, 'You wonderful people.'

Two hours later, after a flurry of activity, Henry sat down at his desk in the MIR and checked through his 'to do/have done' list. His finger worked its way down it until he reached the bottom two items: 'Archie Astley-Barnes' and 'Steve Flynn – murderer!'

He heaved himself out of his chair, went to the office door, leaned out, caught Pete Woodcock's eye and beckoned him in.

'Close the door.'

Woodcock sat down across from Henry.

'Archie,' Henry stated.

'Boss?'

'First impressions – I don't believe it's connected to Percy's murder, but I am willing to be proved wrong.'

'I'll bet it is, somewhere down the line,' Woodcock said.

'Absolutely . . . maybe, maybe not . . . however, I want you to run with it, Pete.'

The DCI's face lit up. 'Really, boss?'

'Yeah. I'll keep going with Percy and Lottie and we'll run Archie's death alongside them from here, just in case there is a link, and so we can keep an eye on everything. You pull a small team together in addition to those we've already got and we can share resources. I know it'll be a tight squeeze, but the HOLMES system is already up and running, so it'd be daft not to. But you run it, yeah? Chase down the blood samples from the house – those that don't belong to Archie – and the PM is down to you and that's later today.'

'OK, thanks, boss.'

'Scoot.' Henry flicked his fingers at Woodcock, who left quickly, closing the office door behind him.

Henry then glanced at the last item on the list. Steve Flynn. Arrested for murder in Spain. The one bright thing in Henry's horrific day and he couldn't help but grin at the prospect of Flynn being incarcerated in a Spanish hell hole.

Finally, he thought.

But before he did anything he made another call to the Tawny Owl.

'Hi, babe, it's me.'

'OK, Henry, enough is enough,' Alison said. 'This is the third call since you left. I'm OK, OK? I'm surrounded by people who would lay down their lives for me. There's a cop car parked outside now, and I've seen two others drive past, flagged them down and fed them. I'll be OK, you just concentrate on catching the guy.'

'OK, OK,' Henry said.

'And I do love you.'

'Me too, love you, that is . . . er, watch out for me on TV later . . . big press briefing in an hour, all channels I think.'

'I will, so don't forget your lines.'

'I won't . . . hey, don't give any of those gun-toting yokels any beer. They're likely as not to shoot each other, rather than a bad guy.'

Alison giggled. The phone call ended when Alison cut Henry off after about a dozen back and forth *Byes*, like they were teenagers. Henry stood up and went into the MIR, which was buzzing with renewed activity. He passed from desk to desk, chatting to each person, asking how they were getting on.

It was obvious they all liked working for Henry. He was a good boss who took time with his staff, mostly. When he'd been a local DI on CID, there had always been a mad scramble to get on his team.

As he moved around, he was pleased by the progress.

Then he went into the office marked 'Intel Cell' where he found Jerry Tope with his head down at the computer.

'You got a mo?' Henry asked when Tope finally looked up.

'Uh – yeah, sure.'

'In my office, two minutes? Bring two brews.'

Tope nodded, Henry retreated.

A few minutes later Tope backed in through Henry's office door bearing two mugs of instant coffee. He sat and shoved one across the desk. Henry took it with thanks, cleared his throat, had a sip.

'Thanks,' he said, surveying Tope across the rim of the mug.

Tope returned a cautious look, unsure why he had been summoned, albeit in such a pleasant way.

'You know how much I like coincidences, don't you?'

'Er, yeah, sorta . . . why?'

'Got a phone call this morning from the FIM, who in turn had just got a message from the police in Gran Canaria, of all places.' Henry let the words permeate into Tope's massive brain.

'OK,' the DC said.

'Mm,' Henry said, starting to draw out what he hoped would be a time of mental torture for Tope. The man's Adam's apple rose and fell in his scrawny throat. 'They have contacted us to say they are investigating a double murder.'

'Some connection to us?' Tope ventured.

Henry gave a shrug. 'To us, maybe, not necessarily to this investigation. The police there have asked me to contact the families of the deceased and also give them any background we can about the victims, a man and a woman.'

'A man and a woman,' Tope echoed.

Henry took a deliberately loud slurp of his coffee, which he thought actually tasted shit. 'And, like I said, I'm a man who likes coincidences.'

Tope furrowed his brow. 'So how can I help? I presume I can?'

'I'm certain you can.'

Tope shifted nervously.

'I take it you are aware that when a senior officer does an Intel check on any person, the system automatically flags up to the senior officer the names of the last three members of staff who also carried out a check on that person.'

'I'm aware of that.'

'OK – so, earlier this morning the FIM received the request from the police in Gran Canaria about a double murder, naming both victims, as you would expect,' Henry said. Tope nodded along. 'So what I want to know, Jerry, is this: bearing in mind my penchant for coincidences, how is it that you had the foresight to check out the name of one of the victims before that person was even dead?'

'I check out a lot of people. It's part of my job. Anyway, who are you talking about?'

Henry noted that Tope now looked decidedly unwell.

'Scott Costain,' Henry revealed like a trump card, although he was pretty sure Tope knew what was coming. 'You checked out the name of someone who was going to become a murder victim. Now that, to me, is one hell of a coincidence. What are the odds of that?'

'We have an ongoing investigation into the Costains. You are almost single-handedly smashing their organization, so checking one of them is . . . is . . .'

'Is what, Jerry?' Henry's voice was cold and clinical.

'A . . .' Tope hesitated, dreading to say it, '. . . coincidence.'

'OK,' Henry then said evenly, 'let me lay one more on you before I actually ask you why you checked Scott Costain. The police in Gran Canaria have a suspect in custody for the double murder.'

Tope's skin actually changed colour at this revelation.

'So guess who that might be?'

'I don't know,' Tope said, his lips hardly moving.

'I'll give you a clue. He's a mate of yours and you've been known to give him sensitive information in the past.'

'Flynn?' Tope whispered.

'Right in one! Now what am I supposed to do with this?' Henry asked. 'Tell me why you checked Scott Costain –' Henry leaned on his desk and pointed at Tope – 'and if you don't come clean, I promise you we'll do this the hard way and the first thing I'll do is seize your mobile phone and check on all numbers dialled and received and see if I can get the Spanish cops interested in you as an accomplice. How does that sound?'

Tope's eyes dropped and he stared into his coffee.

Henry sighed. 'Shit, Jerry.'

'I didn't actually give him any information. He did phone me, yeah, and asked me to give him anything on Costain, but though I looked I never got the chance to call him back with anything, so I haven't done anything wrong this time.'

Henry laughed starkly. 'You imbecile . . . what was it? The same old ruse? "I covered for you when you shagged some bird other than your wife?" That one? Isn't that a bit long in the tooth now?'

'I didn't pass him any information.'

'Deal's done, though, innit? As soon as you type in that name and press "enter". It's all about intent, mate.' Henry shook his head. 'Jerry, Jerry, Jerry, what am I going to do with you? You've teetered on this precipice before, haven't you?'

Tope nodded dumbly.

'Right, I want you to make contact with this detective in Gran Canaria and tell him we're on with his request and that you and me will personally go and tell Costain's relatives of his death, and also the girl's if she's local enough.'

'OK.'

'Scott Costain? He's not on our radar, is he?'

'No he isn't. He was brought up in Northern Ireland, where his convictions are.'

'But it seems his home address is on us?'

'LKA up on Shoreside with the rest of the clan.'

'I'll send you a copy of the email from Gran Canaria. You get some Intel together for them, then let's go and break some bad news. If nothing else it'll be an excuse for me to have a look into the wasps' nest . . . after the press briefing, that is. Oh, and Jerry? Watch your arse, OK? You know what I mean.'

Tope scuttled out of the office red-faced and terrified.

The press briefing took place at Blackpool police station and went well. All sections of the media were present and hungry for this sort of thing, a grisly double murder, one of the victims a well-known local businessman – and a confirmed suspect, a hit man from America no less. The journalists were almost slavering as they recorded Henry's words and were particularly interested in fuelling speculation about Percy's dubious business dealings, although Henry refused to comment on that. It lasted the best part of an hour and Henry fended off questions about Percy's father, stating that at the moment there did not seem to be a link to his son's murder, but he was keeping an open mind on the subject.

After they dispersed, Henry made his way back to the MIR and settled down in his office for five minutes of getting his head together. That was his plan, anyway, but there was a knock on the door and a very sheepish Jerry Tope slithered in, clutching a file of papers, eager to make amends.

Henry regarded him stonily, then gestured for him to take a seat. 'Fire away.'

'Scott Costain and his girlfriend, shot to death in their holiday villa. Steve Flynn was found at the scene and arrested and is still in custody. Seems Costain and the girl chartered Flynn's fishing boat and they had a falling out about something, ending up in fisticuffs in Puerto Rico town centre. They were sent on their way by cops, then the morning after the police attended a report from a neighbour and found Steve at the scene.'

'Steve Flynn shot two people to death?'

'Well, he was at the scene of the murder.'

'He is one nasty piece of work,' Henry said.

'Capable of killing two people in cold blood?'

'Capable of anything, though I wouldn't have thought daft enough to get caught. Still, not our problem, is it?'

'Don't you think he deserves some help?' Tope said in disbelief.

'Nah, not really. We'll just do what's been asked of us and deliver some death messages, shall we?'

'We?'

'Yes, you're coming with me, pal.'

'What about me?'

A large figure had appeared at the office door and, despite the man's size, neither of the two had noticed his approach. Henry looked up quickly; Tope's head swivelled.

'What the hell are you doing here?' Henry demanded, rising from his chair and smiling.

'Sounds like you're gonna need a bodyguard. I'm your man,' Karl Donaldson announced.

Donaldson had never intended to travel north, or 'oop newerth' as he liked to call it now, mimicking a Lancashire accent. He'd thought that getting some information for his friend Henry Christie was just a diversion and as far into the criminal world as he could go, then it would be back to the grindstone of terrorism.

That morning he had risen at six to get ready for work – commuting by train from his local station, into London at seven-ish. He had actually boarded the train and was trying not to imagine gunning down his fellow travellers.

To get his mind off it, he fished out his mobile phone and called Henry Christie's number. Since sending Henry the email the night before concerning Hawke, he'd heard nothing from his northern pal.

The call went straight to voicemail and Donaldson left a short message.

Then he checked the time and wondered if Henry had even set off for work yet, so he called the landline number of the Tawny Owl, knowing his friend was virtually part of the furniture there now.

This time it rang out for a long time. This was fairly unusual because Donaldson knew Alison was a stickler for answering the phone quickly as part of her business. 'You don't get a second chance to make a first impression,' she had quoted continually, 'especially in the hospitality trade.' She was particularly keen on an almost corporate approach to answering professionally, so he let it ring, knowing it would get answered, which it was.

A gruff, deep, northern, yokel voice said, 'Th'Owl.'

Donaldson said, 'Excuse me?'

'I sid, th'Owl.'

'Do you mean "The Tawny Owl"?'

'What I sid, int it?'

'Who am I talking to, please?'

'Ahm Jack Singleton . . . who're yew?'

Donaldson grinned, able to visualize who he was talking to. Since Henry had become resident up there, Donaldson and his wife had also stayed a few times as guests of Henry and Alison. On those visits he had got to know some of the locals quite well, Jack Singleton being one of them. In fact Donaldson and Singleton had been on rough shoots on Singleton's land a few times.

'Jack, it's me, Karl Donaldson.'

'Ooo?'

'Karl Donaldson, the Yank, the FBI man – you remember?'

'Oh aye, big, good lookin' guy . . . fit wife.'

'The perfect description.' Donaldson smiled. He staggered slightly as the train jerked. 'Is Henry there?'

'No, gone t'work.'

'How come you're answering the phone?'

''Cos we're all 'ere, protectin' Mizz Marsh.' Singleton's voice dropped to a confidential hush. 'Mafia hit man's been here and could be comin' back, but he won't get through the Wild Geese.'

Donaldson leapt off the train at the next stop, legged it over the bridge at the station and managed to catch a train going in the opposite direction. Twenty minutes later he was reversing his Jeep out of his tiny garage and speeding to the M4.

He had made the unilateral decision to put terrorism on the back burner for a day or two.

'The cops down there scanned Costain's travel documents and emailed them to me,' Tope said, opening the file on his knee and extracting a thin sheaf of papers, handing them over to Henry, who sifted through them. There were two e-tickets and printed-off boarding cards for flights from Manchester to Gran Canaria, copies of Scott Costain's and Patricia Mason's passports and a booking confirmation for a villa. 'None of the documents actually has an address on, but oddly enough he's put an emergency contact name and address in the passport, something I know I've never done.' Tope gave this scanned document to Henry.

'Nor me.'

He and Tope were in the back of Donaldson's Jeep; at the American's insistence, he was going to be driving Henry about for the foreseeable future. Henry had given him the address and directions.

Henry had a good look at Scott's photo on the passport but was fairly sure he hadn't come across him before, despite his dealings with the family. One thing Henry had learned was that the Costain family tree was like a monkey puzzle and relatives were always popping up unexpectedly. There were many of them and although they had been firmly rooted in Blackpool for almost thirty years now, they did have connections across the Irish Sea and, more tenuously, to Romanian gypsies.

Henry took it all with a pinch of salt.

To him they were simply a big bad family, the male members of which didn't know how to fit condoms, and who were deeply involved in criminal activity that over time had become more organized. One of the things that Henry wanted to achieve prior to retirement was to bring the criminal side of the Costain family to its knees because they had been such a nuisance over the years and no one had ever grasped the nettle and throttled them. This was why he was taking just a teeny chunk of time out from his murder inquiry. Not because he thought, or even imagined, there was any link here to Percy's murder, but because an excuse to step over the Costain threshold should always be grabbed.

Donaldson drove on to the Shoreside estate. This was the largest council estate in the resort and also one of the poorest and most crime-ridden in the whole of the UK. Its unemployment rate was ninety-seven per cent, it was a wild and dangerous place for the unwary and the Costains had ruled it by intimidation, theft, burglary and drug dealing for too many years.

Henry eyed what looked like a bombsite, in actual fact the rubble that remained of a row of shops systematically demolished by the youth of the estate and never rebuilt. That meant to buy anything, get a haircut or a newspaper, people had to leave the estate. Henry knew a lot of residents had started buying online from supermarkets and having orders delivered to their doors. That too had become a problem, because Henry also knew that in the past month, four supermarket delivery vans had been ambushed on the estate and emptied of their contents.

'Next right, we're there . . . it's on the left,' Henry directed Donaldson.

He stopped outside the Costain homestead, two semi-detached council houses knocked together to form one very large house to accommodate the sprawling generations of the family. A black Mercedes Viano was parked outside.

Henry re-read the message from Gran Canaria, then slid out of the car with Donaldson, leaving Tope in the back seat.

Henry eyed his friend.

'I'm gonna be your shadow,' Donaldson said.

'Right,' Henry said. He walked to the front door and rapped on it with his knuckles. A cop-knock.

Footsteps, then the door opened and Henry was greeted with the sight of one of the most stunning women he had ever seen. Cherry Taylor had been the long-time girlfriend of Runcie Costain, briefly head of the clan before his short reign came to a tragic end in a hail of bullets from a rival gang. Cherry, it seemed, was still part of the furniture.

She was in her late thirties, but a raven-haired beauty who had been a stripper, lap dancer and hooker in the past. She was wearing tight cut-off jeans and a baggy, low cut top, and her hair and make-up were all mussed up as though she had just got out of bed.

Scowling, she flattened her hair and spoke to Henry, whom she recognized instantly.

'Didn't I show you my fanny last time we met?'

'You certainly did, Cherry, and a marvellous sight it was,' he said, recalling the moment when, just as a tease, she had presented her finely shaved pubic area to Henry, with the promise of a freebie. He had been impressed, but declined the offer – not least because he had been in hot pursuit of Runcie at that very moment.

'Wanna see it again?' She grinned lewdly.

'I'll pass,' Henry said.

'So whaddya want, copper man?'

Henry squinted up at her. She was quite tall to start with and was standing on the threshold, one step above him. 'May we come in, Cherry? I have something . . . delicate . . . to discuss.'

She eyed him suspiciously. 'You're not gonna bust me?'

'No – promise.'

'OK, then, why not?' She spun like a lap dancer and led the way in.

Just before Henry followed, Donaldson leaned over his shoulder and whispered, 'You never cease to amaze me.'

Henry gave him a knowing wink.

Flynn had sat in his cell all day in the tight dungarees. His drunken cellmate had sobered up, was sick, then was yanked out of the cell never to be seen again, leaving Flynn alone. The blocked-up toilet was never attended to but Flynn was given the concession of being allowed to use one along the cell corridor next to the shower block, where he had to sit and perform under the scrutiny of a gaoler. Then he was banged up again with the overflowing sewage and a slowly flooding cell floor.

He closed his eyes and dozed, leaning back against the cold wall, drawing his knees up to his chin.

The cell door creaked open and Romero stood there, his nose twitching with disgust. He gave Flynn a thumbs-up gesture.

'You're free to leave, amigo.'

The lounge had a more modern look to it than Henry remembered, even had a bar in the corner. He recalled horse brasses adorning the walls, lots of nods and winks to the alleged gypsy heritage. Leather chairs, thick carpets. They had all gone. The carpet had been replaced by laminate flooring and the furniture was much more functional and up to date, something like IKEA might do. It seemed a practical upgrade to Henry as he stepped into the living room, which was divided from the dining room beyond with new sliding doors that met in the middle.

Cheryl took up a position in the centre of the room and turned to face Henry and Donaldson. She had fierce green eyes (though they had a hint of mischief about them) and Henry got the feeling she could be very intimidating and forceful, especially when she was fully awake.

'So what have we done this time, officer?'

'Nothing, I don't think, unless you want to admit to something now and save time.' Under the circumstances Henry knew he should not have been so facetious, but the Costains did have a bad effect on him and he instinctively rose to them.

Cheryl shook her head. 'Can't resist, can you?'

'No,' he admitted. 'Look, Cheryl, I need to speak to an actual member of the Costains, a grown-up fully functioning member I can have a serious conversation with . . . no disrespect, but is that possible?'

She pouted demurely.

Henry heard some movement in the dining room, behind the sliding doors, a kind of whirring noise. Then it stopped and another whirring noise began, rather like an electric motor, then the doors opened slowly, rather like a stage curtain, revealing the dining room beyond.

They also revealed the very old man sitting in a state of the art wheelchair, who said with a slight Irish lilt, 'I may not be fully functioning, but I'm grown up and a member of the Costain family – so do I meet your criteria, detective?'

SIXTEEN

F lynn emerged into the warmth at the end of a Gran Canarian day, having had most of his property returned but no offer to take him home, nor any real explanation as to why he was released, just a fudging, 'We're still investigating and no doubt I will be speaking to you again shortly,' from Romero. 'I shall keep your passport, and we have not finished with your car yet and will keep your mobile phone too and, of course, your clothing.'

The detective waved Flynn's passport under his nose.

'Where did you get that from?'

'A search of your home address—'

'Which revealed?' Flynn asked.

'Who knows?' Romero said mysteriously. Flynn knew: nothing.

'Am I on bail, then?'

'No, but you cannot leave the country.'

'So I'm not a free man?'

'Semantics, as ever, Mr Flynn. You are free to go about your business, but not free to leave Gran Canaria.'

Flynn had started to protest until Romero held up a finger and said, 'If you wish to be a guest of the Spanish justice system, then that can be arranged. I'm investigating a double murder and you still are the prime suspect, but until my scientific results come back . . .' He shrugged.

Flynn scurried out of the police station, feeling an argument over the matter would not go his way.

Stepping into freedom he reflected that he had been unaware up to that point just how good it felt – even if it looked as though he would be thumbing a lift home because, as he flicked through his wallet, he saw that the twenty euros that had been in it were gone. He wondered how easy it would be to cadge a lift dressed in tight-fitting dungarees, no shirt, no underwear, no shoes. Knowing some people who lived in Puerto Rico, Flynn thought there could easily be a queue forming of very nice men who were willing to pick him up.

He stood still and raised his face to the low sun, now desperate for a drink and some food. Problem was a lack of funds, and not really knowing anyone in Las Palmas.

He was about to step off the kerb when a car pulled in. It was Karen's beat-up Fiat Panda with the roll-top roof and rickety windows that wouldn't quite close.

'Flynn,' she called, leaning across and opening the passenger door. He leaned in and she took in his chest bulging against the too tight top of the dungarees. 'Get in or you'll have the whole gay population of the island baying for your body. Let me take you home.'

As much as he was a tough guy, a wave of relief flooded through him and he dropped into the passenger seat with a sigh. 'God, it's good to see you . . . how did you know . . . ?'

'Adam's been on to them all day and they finally let him know you'd be released at this time.'

'Good man,' he said.

Karen sniffed up. 'You've got a bit of a whiff about you,' she said, wafting her hand in front of her face.

'You should smell the other guy.'

'What say a shower and food and drink, then a bit of storytelling?' she suggested, pulling the Panda into traffic, doing a hairy U-turn and heading back towards Puerto Rico.

'Sounds good.'

She drove on to the GC1 and floored the little car. Then she said, 'Did you?'

'Did I what?'

'You know, Steve. Don't play games with me. Adam's been to-ing and fro-ing all day, trying to get you out, pleading your innocence with that nasty detective, who is convinced you killed them, even if he can't prove it.'

Flynn shook his head. 'They were dead when I got there. If I had killed them I wouldn't have hung around long enough to get locked up, trust me.'

'So you didn't?' Karen looked at him fearfully.

'No I didn't, darling.'

She held his gaze for a moment, tears filling her eyes – until a movement caught Flynn's peripheral vision. He grabbed the steering wheel and yanked it down. With a howl of its horn the other car swerved but at least there was no collision, and they also avoided ploughing into the back of the truck ahead of them.

'Eyes front,' Flynn ordered.

Henry looked at the old man, amazed at how shrivelled and prune-like his skin was. His hands, controlling and manoeuvring the wheelchair, were arthritic and gnarled and looked extremely creepy. But he was dressed immaculately in a tweed jacket and bow tie with brown brogues on his unmoving feet. He edged the wheelchair through into the lounge and Henry now understood why the carpets had been replaced by laminate – to allow this machine and its occupant to drive from room to room without snagging on pesky shag pile.

He drew the machine up in front of Henry and slowly held out one of the shrivelled hands.

'My name is Liam Costain.'

Henry took the twig-like hand and shook it, believing he could have crushed it without any great show of strength.

'Don't believe we've ever had the pleasure,' Costain said.

'Detective Superintendent Christie.'

'Ah yes, I have heard of you, in a very negative context where my family is concerned.' The old man's grey eyes twinkled.

'Really?' Henry said, taking an instant dislike to the weird guy, who had a neck like a tortoise and reminded him of a Disney cartoon character whose name evaded his mind at that moment. It would come to him. 'And what context might that be?'

'Death,' the old man said. 'So why are you here, officer?'

Henry fleetingly wondered if he would still be able to draw his pension if he decided to tip him out of his wheelchair.

'Because I need to speak to an adult relative of Scott Costain.'

'I am his grandfather. His father was Runcie, whom I believe you knew,' Costain said. 'Why do you need to speak to someone?'

'Do you know Scott's present whereabouts?'

'He's on holiday in the Canary Islands with his girlfriend. Has he been arrested or something silly like that?' Cherry asked.

Henry glanced at Cherry and said, 'You might want to sit down.'

'I'll stand.'

'I've been contacted by the police in Gran Canaria and they have asked me to visit you . . . I'm very sorry,' Henry said solemnly, 'but Scott and his girlfriend are dead. There is no easy way to say this, but they have been murdered. I'm sorry.'

And he really was, because as much as he despised the Costains he didn't wish any of them dead, although they seemed quite capable of bringing that on themselves.

'My God,' said the old man, shaken. 'I don't believe it.'

'I'm afraid that's all the information I have. I don't have much detail, but it seems they were murdered at their villa.'

'Is this a joke, a cop wind-up?' Costain demanded. 'If so, it's in very poor taste, something that a cop like you, who has his knife very firmly in the ribs of a decent hard working family like ours, would say. Just for fun.'

Henry almost rose to the insinuation. 'I don't play games, Mr Costain. I'm delivering a genuine message. Scott and his girlfriend have been murdered and I do not like delivering such news to anyone, even your family. What was he doing out there?'

'Taking a holiday, like I said,' Cherry cut in, sensing the growing tension.

'Yes, as she already said,' Costain snarled, revealing a very badly fitting set of false teeth that dropped slightly from the gums. 'What are you implying?'

'I'm asking a valid question.'

'It was just a holiday,' Cherry insisted.

'Most people who go on genuine holidays do not get murdered,' Henry said.

'I do not like your chain of thought,' Costain said. He jerked the joystick on his wheelchair and the vehicle shot forward and rammed into Henry's shins. It hurt.

'Ow.' He jumped back, but the old man jerked the stick again and ran into him again. 'Oi, do that again and I'll tip you out of that chair.'

'You'd assault a cripple?'

'Depending on the circumstances.'

'Well, at least I now know what sort of a man I'm dealing with.'

'I'm just doing my job, delivering a message on behalf of another police force, that's all. They asked me to ask you what he was doing out there, simple as that.'

Costain reversed the wheelchair away, still staring angrily at Henry.

'I have a telephone number, a direct line to the detective in charge of the investigation. He speaks good English, I believe, so there won't be a problem with communication. He's called Romero. There is every chance he will want you to travel out there to identify Scott formally.'

'I will be going,' Costain said.

'OK, I need to go and see his girlfriend's parents; they live in South Shore.'

'We can do that,' Costain said quickly.

Henry shook his head. 'I don't think so.' He balanced a slip of paper on the arm of the settee. 'This has Romero's number on it and my work mobile. We'll leave you now.'

He turned, as did Donaldson, who had remained a silent presence during the interaction. Cherry followed them to the door and as Henry stepped out on to the front step she said, 'Sorry about that, he's very upset, I can tell. Sometimes my husband just goes off on one.'

'No prob . . . your husband?'

'Yes, we're married.'

'Well, congratulations then,' Henry said, unable to disguise his surprise – and scepticism.

'Two months,' she said, and added quietly, 'and I'm not in it for the sex.'

'Not my business,' Henry said, 'but, back to why I came here, if you do need any sort of help with this, give me a call.'

'What, so you can pry even further into our business?'

'Unfortunately, Cherry, your business is criminal.'

'True,' she conceded, then her eyes narrowed, 'but that doesn't mean to say that you and me shouldn't fuck, does it?' As she spoke she leaned forward and whispered into Henry's ear. 'No one would know . . . it's still shaved, you know?'

'I'm sure it is,' he said, backing off and thinking, *Once a hooker . . .*

He and Donaldson walked back to the car – and then it came to him. 'Jiminy Cricket.'

'Yes, I see that,' Donaldson agreed.

Cherry closed the door and re-entered the living room.

Costain, in his wheelchair, was still in the centre of the room.

Now, behind him, stood Jason Hawke, a gun in his right hand, hanging by his thigh.

'I could have killed him where he stood,' he said with frustration.

'You're both fucking idiots,' Cherry said in a low voice. Their faces turned to her with surprise. 'That guy out there is your worst enemy and the worst thing you can do is rile him. You know he's got it in for us and yeah, good idea, annoy him so much that he decides to come back mob-handed and then we've had it.' She scowled fiercely at them. 'You do know what we've got upstairs, don't you?'

Costain's old face seemed to curdle. He did not like being told what to do, but saw the logic.

Cherry ploughed on. 'He's already managed to close down two of the clubs and the last thing we want is for him to start digging . . .'

'I still want to kill him,' Hawke said. 'And that smug bitch he lives with.'

'Then do it,' snapped Costain. 'Just kill him . . . get it done. It's a shame you didn't manage to do it when he turned up, because your face is all over the news and if he does get hold of you and starts digging from your direction, this whole thing's going to blow up in our faces.'

'Yeah,' sneered Cherry. 'You'd have thought it was easy enough to put a bullet in someone.'

Hawke glared, then raised his gun. 'You'd think so, wouldn't you?'

'Stop it, you fools,' Costain said. 'We need to think about Scott now.' He regarded Hawke thoughtfully and said, 'Maybe Christie should be put on the back burner for the time being . . . more urgent things require your attention now.'

DCI Peter Woodcock had been relieved to see Henry leave the MIR with Tope and the big American stranger on some totally unrelated fool's errand up on Shoreside. He had been sitting at the far end of the room, pretending to be busy getting things together for the murder investigation he had been put in charge of, that of Archie Astley-Barnes, the victim of what certainly, on the face of it, appeared to be a burglary gone wrong.

He gave Henry five minutes, then left himself, desperately trying to hold down the feeling of nausea that gripped his whole being.

He tried not to rush out of the room and actually gave a smile to one of the female members of staff who had been brought in to spend time sifting through the CCTV footage that was coming in and amassing by the hour from the town centre cameras, searching for footage of the man Woodcock had chased on foot towards the railway station. She smiled back, then her brow creased as she rewound one of the discs and zoomed in on a short scenario taking place on the screen. She fiddled with the computer, enhancing what was a fairly poor picture.

When she glanced around, Woodcock had gone.

She returned to her task, focusing in, sharpening everything, and although the image became clear she wasn't entirely sure what she was looking at.

The bedsit was in a large terraced house in Severn Road, behind the Pleasure Beach complex in South Shore. Woodcock drew up outside and sat in his car for a few minutes, checking his phone, ringing a number that did not get answered. The street was quiet, which was just what he needed. He walked quickly from his car and straight through the unlocked front door of the house into a dank hallway, then, without hesitation, up the uncarpeted stairs to the first floor and into flat four on that landing.

The smell was a bad one, even worse than outside, and it hit him even with the flat door only slightly open. Woodcock realized, with some relief, what it was: death. The gagging aroma of body odour, expelled gas, shit and urine, a real Chanel Number Five.

He twisted quickly through and closed the door. Ahead was the bedsit. There was a tiny bathroom to his left, then beyond that the squalid living accommodation consisting of a camp bed, one ring cooker, portable fridge, an old armchair and, the big necessity of life, a large screen TV. Life at the shit end of the street.

One glance into the dirty bathroom. Blood was smeared all through it, all round the toilet, in the wash basin and shower cubicle. And from the bathroom there was a thick trail of it across the floor of the bedsit to the figure laid out half-naked on the bed. It was a man, mid-forties, lying face up with one leg on the floor, one arm dangling, the other across his chest. He was naked from the waist down and blood dripped from a wound underneath him on to the vinyl floor, coagulating in a wide pool that looked like tar.

Woodcock exhaled with relief.

He was dead, had bled out.

The visit to Trish's parents was less confrontational because there was no one at home. The address given was in South Shore but in the more salubrious area to the east of Lytham Road, where she lived in a pleasant, substantial, red brick semi. Or certainly had done until she started hanging around with Scott Costain.

Henry and Tope knocked on a few neighbours' houses and were told that the parents were away on holiday, no one seemed to know exactly where, and that the daughter, Patricia, hadn't been seen there for over six months anyway. One neighbour confided to Henry that she had gone off the rails. No one had a phone number for them, so the detectives were unable to pass on the tragic news of Trish's death. Henry shoved a note through the door with his name and mobile number on, asking them to contact him as soon as possible.

'You'd think the girl would have a mobile phone with her,' Tope observed.

Henry agreed. It was something to speak to Romero about.

'See what you can find out anyway, will you?' he asked Tope.

They climbed back into the Jeep, Tope in the back seat, and set off back to the MIR, pulling on to Lytham Road and turning towards Blackpool whilst discussing the recent encounter at the Costain stronghold.

Henry dangled his right arm over his seat so he could see Tope as they all spoke. 'I've never come across the old man before . . . just as I haven't come across Scott,' he said.

'New blood in the clan?' Tope suggested.

'Didn't even know Runcie had a son . . . but Runcie himself came over from Ireland to run the family business.' Henry shook his head. 'They're like rabbits.'

'Maybe the old guy is trying to finish what Runcie started – the professionalism of the family?' Donaldson suggested.

'Seems a bit long in the tooth for that,' Henry said. 'Then again, once a crim always a crim . . . and as a criminal enterprise they are deffo on the ropes.' He had a smug grin on his face as he said that. Henry knew he was making good headway in taking them on, and not always by the most direct route – a lesson he had learned from the way in which Al Capone had eventually been busted: through the taxman. In this case, Henry didn't go for the money, although that was on the cards, but he had managed to close down two nightclubs and a pub they were associated with in Blackpool because of their continual infringements of the licensing laws and (this one he particularly liked) flouting of the non-smoking legislation. Sometimes it was catching the tiddlers that did most harm.

But the appearance of two family members he had never come across before troubled him, even if one of them was now shot dead in a swimming pool. Since his success with the closure of the licensed premises there had been quiet on the Costain front, so maybe Donaldson was right and they were regrouping under the tutelage of old man Liam and moving into other, more subtle areas. Scott being murdered in Gran Canaria was a puzzle. Obviously he was out there for a reason and somehow Steve Flynn had got caught up in the shenanigans. And Cherry being married to someone over twice her age? Her specialism was prostitution . . . maybe there was something in that, Henry mused. Perhaps the family weren't as down and out as he thought.

'Find out what you can about the old guy,' Henry said to Tope, and spun to face the front in his seat just as they passed the junction with Severn Road, his mind dismissing the subject of the Costains for the time being because he now had to focus on finding the killer of Percy and Lottie, and there was no connection between the two. Once he had a killer in his cells, then maybe he'd give it some thought and continue on his pre-retirement crusade to destroy them

– and enjoy watching Steve Flynn plummet to his fate at the same time. Double joy.

A car drew up at the junction as they shot past; Henry only glanced at it but did not take any real notice, his mind full of many other things.

Flynn emerged from the shower in Karen's apartment, fresh and clean, no longer reeking of the sewer, a large bath towel wrapped around his middle. He walked on to the balcony where Karen sat looking pensively across the deep valley of Puerto Rico. She smiled, then began to blink rapidly as her eyes started to moisten with tears.

Without warning she rushed into him, burying her head into his chest. His muscular arms encircled her.

'Hey, hey,' he said softly, stroking her hair, 'what's this all about?'

She tilted up her face, resting her chin on his sternum. 'I don't know, Steve, what is this all about?'

'I don't know,' he admitted. 'It's not something I've asked for.'

'I know . . . look,' she stood away from him. 'We've only just found each other after months of looking at each other and secretly knowing we were right for each other. I don't want to lose you, particularly not in some ridiculous way. Promise me . . .' Her lovely chin began to wobble as she fought back against the tears. 'Promise me you won't do anything stupid.'

'I won't, but things might happen I don't have any say over.'

'Like what?'

'The people who dragged me off the streets – the same people, I guess, who killed Costain and his girlfriend – aren't the sort to leave unfinished business, and I think I'm unfinished business. I don't have a damned clue what they're up to, but Scott Costain did and they think I'm running with him, so they might be back. I need to be ready for them, or I take the game to them, make the running.'

'Steve, what are you saying?'

He could feel his heart pounding because he did not want it to be like this. He wanted to have nothing to do with what had happened. All he wanted was a peaceful life on the island, somewhere to live that was his, his fishing and Karen Glass.

Simple, not much to ask for.

'You're going for them, aren't you?' she demanded.

The look in his eyes told her everything she needed to know.

*   *   *

Henry cradled his desk phone, happy to have discovered that all was well in Kendleton and the Dad's Army of defenders, aka the Wild Geese, were still *in situ* and hadn't killed anyone and everything was as normal as it could be in the circumstances. Several patrol cars had been seen passing and Bill Robbins was still parked up at the front of the Tawny Owl, being plied with food and drink. He exhaled a short blast of relief but, even so, all he wanted to do now was get home.

It was six p.m. and the murder team debrief wouldn't be until eight, giving him two hours to get his head down and see where everything was up to – and that included the extra murder of Archie. On that thought, he looked into the MIR to see if he could spot Pete Woodcock, but he was nowhere to be seen.

Then he remembered: Archie's post mortem was scheduled for five thirty p.m. and Woodcock was attending it, so it was unlikely the DCI would be free until well after seven thirty. There was a good chance of not seeing him at all that evening so, though Henry wanted to catch up with him, it might have to wait until the day after. Maybe a phone call would suffice.

Through the open door of his office, Henry saw Tope and Donaldson walk past. Henry made his way over, sidestepping the desk of the lady who was going through the CCTV footage. She glanced at him and opened her mouth to say something, but though Henry gave her a quick smile he was gone then, into the Intel Cell behind Tope and the American.

Tope's desk was stacked high with binders and receipt books. Very high.

'What's this lot?' Henry asked.

'The books,' Tope said.

Henry gave him a blank look. 'The books?'

'From the jewellery business, seized as you requested. Just from the Blackpool shop.'

'Bloody hell, there's loads of them.'

'According to the team that seized the stuff, hardly anything is on computer. The business seems to have been run in a very old-fashioned way.'

'Is that a good thing?'

'For a computer nerd like me . . . paper, ugh!' Tope shivered.

'Happy reading, mate.'

'What exactly am I looking for?'

'Anything that takes your eye. You know what you're looking for without me telling you.'

'Do I?' he said obstinately.

Henry gave him a devil glare, then said to Donaldson, 'Got a suggestion for you, pal.'

'Fire away.'

'I want to stand the protection down around Alison for tonight. It's impractical and I can't just keep using resources and trading on people's goodwill. I was wondering if you'd go to Kendleton now and dismiss "F" Troop, and when I get word you're there I'll stand down Bill Robbins and call off the other patrolling cops and you can keep an eye on Alison and Ginny.

'I'm up for that – but what about you?'

'Jerry can look after me here.' Henry and Tope exchanged a look which let Henry know that if a bullet was coming his way, Tope wouldn't be throwing himself in the path of it. 'I'll be here until about nine, then I'll run to my car and speed home. If anyone can take me out at a ton on the M6, good for them. Tell Alison to give the guys a free drink each, but only after they've been home and locked away their guns.'

The debrief went well, getting a lot of interest when Henry announced, 'The big news is that our two victims were both recently on a sportfishing boat in Florida belonging to an American gangster called Fioretti. Not only that, we have a photograph of the victims on the boat and in the background is a bent ex-cop of this parish.' That sent a murmur around the room, but Henry didn't elaborate just in case Jack Hoyle still had friends in the force. He didn't want him warned.

It lasted about half an hour – Henry hated to drag these things on – and he dismissed the team with thanks and retreated to his office to get his head together for tomorrow just before going home.

A succession of people waved goodnight to him, including Jerry Tope, whose arms were stacked high with the books.

'Taking them home, if that's OK?'

'Yeah, sure . . . tell you what, give me a few and I'll try and have a skim through some tonight if I get the chance.'

Tope didn't need the offer repeated. He slid off a lot of very boring receipt books on to Henry's desk, then skedaddled before Henry changed his mind.

Henry looked at the pile despondently, then glanced up to see the lady who had been reviewing the CCTV footage standing at his door. She was about to say something, then looked over her shoulder and stepped aside to allow Pete Woodcock to sidle in past her. She smiled shyly at Woodcock, looked at Henry, then withdrew as Woodcock took a seat in the office.

Henry thought nothing of it and said, 'Post mortem?' to the DCI.

Woodcock nodded. 'Yeah, pretty grim, sad too.'

Henry waited for him to continue.

'Blunt force trauma, brain damage, bleeding, possibly something like a baseball bat, battered around the head and body . . . Archie died a pretty horrible death,' the DCI said.

'Any clues regarding the blood?'

'No, not yet . . . samples have been taken from the crime scene. Looks like a big struggle and at some stage Archie managed to get to his shotgun and blast away . . . the wall is peppered with shot.'

'Good for him . . . no one hobbled into a casualty unit yet?'

'Not so far, but I'll be alerted if they do. I've actually managed to get some of Archie's relatives to come up from down south tomorrow, a brother, so an uncle to Percy, too, which will be useful.'

'Well done.'

Woodcock closed his eyes and sagged his head.

'Tired?'

'Exhausted, boss.'

'Well, you've done good. I'm sure we'll get a result on this one quick.'

'Yeah – team up and running tomorrow.'

'In that case, see you,' Henry dismissed him, 'and thanks for your hard work, mate.'

Woodcock nodded and left.

Henry was alone in the office. He looked at the receipt books that Tope had so gleefully unloaded, sighed and dragged them towards him, regretting his hasty volunteering. In truth, there was no way he wanted to haul them home. Tonight had to be a show of solidarity with Alison and the sooner he got home, the better.

Even so, he took the top book off the pile. It was a receipt book logging sales from Percy Astley-Barnes's jeweller's shop in Blackpool. Henry visualized the premises: one of those jewellers with a doorman and two security doors, outer and inner, designed to warn off both robbers and non-serious customers. Henry had been in once to buy an engagement ring for Alison and had left with his debit card thoroughly depleted.

So it was never awash with customers but when they bought, they bought big, as Henry saw when he flipped through the receipt book and saw sales recorded of a thousand pounds, two and a half grand, one for eight hundred (*cheapskate*, Henry thought). Big money, and all the names and addresses of the customers recorded, no doubt to be re-contacted in a year's time to bring the jewels back for spring cleaning. It was a very customer-oriented environment – just one at a time, thank you, please – and Henry had thought it quaint and unusual to have such details written and recorded by hand. He couldn't remember the last time he'd given his full name and address in a shop, apart from Percy's, although they always seemed to want to know his post code and house number.

He skimmed though the book, not really concentrating.

It was only after he had gone past one of the receipts that something clicked and he felt his bottom tighten as his fingers scrambled back through the pages.

A quiet cough made him look up. It was the CCTV lady.

Then his phone rang.

SEVENTEEN

Over thirty years as a cop, many of them spent in the environs of Blackpool and the Fylde, had given Henry Christie an excellent knowledge of a large number of thieves, vagabonds and other miscreants of that area.

Because of this accumulated knowledge he instantly recognized the half-naked dead man on the bed.

'Looks like a slam-dunk,' Henry said, squatting down, knees cracking hollowly, and inspecting the man's misshapen-in-death face. He looked back at Pete Woodcock, who nodded agreement. 'Bled to death,' Henry said, his eyes moving down the body, seeing the back of the man's upper right thigh. 'One of the pellets probably hit an artery inside . . . that is a lot of blood,' he said, looking at the pool under the camp bed on which the man lay; and it was still dripping.

Henry eased himself upright. 'Looks like you've got a few more hours at work after all,' he said to Woodcock.

'At the very least.'

'But he'll be our man for Archie's death . . . like we thought, burglary gone wrong, fight, cracks Archie with that –' Henry pointed to a blood-stained baseball bat on the floor – 'but, bless him, he still manages to blow a hole in the arse of this bastard, who limps home like a mortally wounded animal to die.'

Henry, hands on hips, was looking down at the body of Roland Barclay, one of the better-known felons of the parish, a confirmed and convicted thief and fraudster. Henry knew he was an insatiable shoplifter, but also that he had form for what were known as distraction burglaries. These are where the offender poses as an official from, say, the water or gas board, and cons victims, usually elderly, into letting them into their houses, where the offender then steals money. Sometimes violence is used, especially when the victim realizes that they're being conned and challenges the offender. Henry knew that Barclay had several convictions for this type of offence, and one that included violence towards the victim. He had beaten up an old woman quite badly when she'd had the courage to try and throw him out of her house.

'Every chance there'll be a blood match,' Henry added, recalling the splatter in Archie's front room. 'Good result, except an innocent old guy has died, and try as I might, I can't even start to feel any remorse at this guy's passing. He bit off more than he could chew with Archie.'

'Mm.'

Henry thought Woodcock seemed a bit tight-lipped and less than pleased by this turn-up for the books; maybe he was just tired. The cops had been alerted by the landlord of the block, who had been after Barclay's back rent and had entered the flat to find a blood bath with Barclay dead in the middle of it.

Henry slapped him on the shoulder. 'I'm pretty certain I can leave this in your capable hands . . . nothing spoiling now. Get a CSI up here, then get him down to the mortuary and pick it all up in the morning.'

'Will do.'

Henry had one last glance at Barclay, then left.

Karen had dropped Flynn off at his villa on a sour note despite his reassurances, admittedly half-hearted. He watched her drive away without a backward glance, his mouth twisted. He shrugged and went inside the villa, which was still a mess from the invasion of someone who'd wanted to make a point, and from the police search. He had a small stash of euros hidden inside the fridge, which was still there. He changed out of the clothing that Karen had found for him – again probably left by an ex-boyfriend, he supposed – then got into a pair of three-quarters, sliding his feet into his spare flip-flops. Then he hauled some of the furniture back into place and threw some broken pieces on to the terrace, after which he went on the hunt for some information that was eluding him.

He walked over to the marina on the other side of Puerto Rico, the Puerto Base, from which a row of sportfishing boats operated, all in gentlemanly competition with him.

He wasn't going to the boats but to one of the bars in the small complex on the Porto Grande behind the marina, specifically the Bar Inglés, a seedy, smoke-filled establishment with a dark wood, L-shaped bar and a maritime theme celebrating British sailors and ships. Even so, most of the clientele were locals because the booze was cheap and the atmosphere kept tourists at bay.

Flynn stepped in and went to the bar, ordered a Cruzcampo on draught, which tasted amazing. Apart from when he had quenched his raging thirst after his release, this was Flynn's first real drink. He had yet to eat. He drank it quickly, then ordered a second, which he sipped while surveying the bar.

In a deep corner recess he spotted the man he was looking for. That one person could be found in every bar in every port in the world: the grizzled old sailor with an air of mystery about him, who seemed to just sit and watch life pass by; the old guy who had a history he never talked about unless 'rummed' up; the one who knew everyone and everything that was going on, all the tittle-tattle, the gossip, as well as being able to predict what the weather would be like next week. The oracle.

In this case he was called Eduardo – no one seemed to know his last name – a seventy-year-old Spaniard who had spent his life as a merchant seaman, then in various capacities around the islands on the ferries, skippering a sportfisher and taking tourists out on pleasure cruises. He had been immersed in sea water all his life and also, wisely, perpetuated myths about himself as a gun runner from Morocco and a drug runner across the Straits of Gibraltar, neither of which was true. That did not detract from the fact that he had a deep knowledge of anything seafaring around these parts.

Flynn had spent many a night listening to Eduardo spinning tales of the oceans, and women in every port, whilst he plied him with Malibu and Coke, his favourite tipple. He said it reminded him of the Caribbean.

Flynn ordered the drink and walked over to him. He was sitting alone, smoking an evil smelling pipe.

'Buenas tardes, amigo,' Flynn said.

'Tardes, Flynn.' He coughed through the dense smoke, then took the drink Flynn had brought. 'How can I help you this evening, amigo? An amigo who has *un apuro grande*?' A friend in big trouble.

'Information . . . la información.'

Afterwards Flynn strolled across to the other side of the marina, skirting the beach and finding a spot in his favourite restaurant behind it, where he ordered blind paella, then relaxed to wait for it with a San Miguel and a whisky chaser.

He knew the ultimate answer he was seeking probably lay deep in the dangerous water at the foot of the cliffs that were called Punta de GuiGui. All this stemmed from there, and he tried to recall if Jack Hoyle had said anything significant during the short interrogation, before Flynn flattened his nose.

Just the thought of being dragged off the street made his inner rage fire up to a simmer again and his first urge was to go back to the villa where he had been held captive, all guns blazing.

But he didn't have transport or a gun.

He tried to chill, wondering when he would get both items back. His Nissan had been kept by the police and the Bushmaster was hidden in the secret compartment under the seats. Flynn was fairly certain he would get the car back with the gun still intact and undiscovered. The compartment he had fashioned was hard to find and he doubted if the Spanish cops were good searchers.

It was just a matter of when.

He calmed down, relaxed, then was surprised when Karen dropped into a chair opposite and stared at him, lips pursed.

For a few moments they said nothing. Flynn sipped his beer.

She broke the silence. 'Flynn, I think I understand what you've got to do, though it doesn't mean I'm up for it. But I know I'm crazy in love with you and if you get out of this in one piece, I'll be there waiting for you.'

'OK, sounds good.'

'Do you love me?'

'Yes,' he said quietly.

'Then I want to make every moment count and I'd very much like to screw your brains out. What do you think about that?'

'It's a great idea,' he swallowed, 'but I've just ordered paella.'

Karen leaned forward. '*Faye* is a two minute walk from here.'

Flynn's eyes narrowed.

'I'd say that gives us, say, fifteen minutes of red hot sex, and we can be back here in time for the food.'

Almost before she had finished talking, Flynn swooped across and took her hand, and the caveman who lurked very close to his otherwise sophisticated modern man surface almost dragged her to her feet. 'Best get a move on, then.'

By the time Henry arrived back at the Tawny Owl it was eleven p.m. He had called ahead to tell them he was running late so no one was remotely worried by his absence, but when he entered the bar all the customers turned with their drinks in hand, raised them to him and gave him a huge cheer. Donaldson was behind the bar with Alison and Ginny, serving on.

Henry took a regal bow.

Once he had shouldered his way through the throng and placed all the documents he had brought with him from work on the floor just inside the door leading to the private accommodation, he went to the bar where a drink was waiting for him, plus a meal consisting of a plate meat pie, chips, peas and gravy, which he carried over to a vacant table by the bow window. He was famished and the prospect of early hours indigestion did not put him off eating.

Alison came to sit with him.

'How has it gone, honey?' he asked.

'These people are amazing,' she said, looking at the customers. 'Drunk now, but amazing.'

'They are. You're very lucky. Not many communities like this any more.'

'You're part of it now, you know? Especially after the free drinks offer which, to a man, was taken up.'

'Cheaper than hiring Group Four.'

'What the hell d'you guys think you're playing at?' Donaldson scolded them. 'A sniper's dream, sitting next to a window. You'd get taken out in a doggone moment.' He drew the curtains and sat next to them.

'I've given Karl one of the guest rooms,' Alison said.

'Good idea.'

'Once we've locked up for the night, we should be OK.'

'I would have thought so . . . there will still be a few patrols passing occasionally and the place is very secure.'

Alison said, 'Have you found him yet, do you have any leads?'

'To be honest, no, but his face is all over the media and ports and airports, so he'll either get caught trying to leave the country – unless he is in disguise and has a false passport – or he'll keep his head down until it all dies down a bit, then he'll flee. He knows he's frightened us both, so he might well leave it at that.' Henry tried to sound convincing.

Alison saw his expression. 'Nice try, big boy. If he's going to come, he'll find a way, won't he?'

'He can try, but he is on the run now,' Donaldson said.

'I'll be applying for an arrest warrant for him tomorrow and Karl and I will sort out the American angle so if he turns up across the water he can be arrested, then extradited. He's screwed, love, but yeah, we have to be honest, he could well be nuts enough to give it a go.'

Alison nodded as she took this in. Her chest rose and fell.

'OK,' she said and stood up. 'I'll go and see what the guys want.' She went back to the bar.

'Not happy,' Donaldson said.

'Understatement.'

'So – what's happened tonight?'

'Looks like Archie's murder has been solved, and it doesn't have a link to Percy's,' Henry began, and filled Donaldson in with the details whilst shovelling his meal into his mouth, washing it down with the Stella. 'And there's something else . . . just wait here.'

The food and drink were finished, so Henry took the plate to the bar and held out his pint for a refill. Whilst this was being done he went to the pile of documents from the corridor and returned with a receipt book, collected the fresh beer and went back to Donaldson, handing him the book as he took a seat. Henry explained it was used in Percy's jewellery shop in Blackpool as a record of all sales transactions.

Donaldson opened it, pouting. 'Are we going to do this the hard way or the easy way?'

'Look up two dates, twelfth February first, then twenty-second June, both this year.' Henry sipped the beer.

Donaldson flicked backwards and forwards through the pages. Each one was divided into four tear-out receipts with carbon copies under the originals. The copies were what remained in the books, the top copies having been torn out and handed to the customer. The copies were clear and legible.

'Twelfth of Feb . . . ruary,' Donaldson said slowly, finding the page. His eyes widened. 'Get the fuck out!' he exclaimed, looking sharply at Henry, who looked quite smug.

'Now twenty-second June.'

Donaldson's big fingers scrambled through the pages until he found that date.

This time he whispered, 'Get the fuck out,' in awe.

Henry grinned. 'I like coincidences. They make me happy – although I don't know if there is any relevance to them in this case.'

'So the nasty crippled guy, Liam Costain, bought two lots of jewellery from Percy's shop on two separate dates this year, spent over four grand?'

'Looks that way.'

'Also looks as though Mr Wheelchair Man is going to get a revisit from you very soon.'

'Looks that way,' Henry said and took another mouthful of beer.

As it happened, Flynn and Karen had to reorder paella and pay for the previous one, which was cold by the time they returned to the bar, flushed and very happy from their lovemaking in the stateroom of *Faye*. Rather than the estimated fifteen minutes, they took an hour, and sauntered back to the bar arm in arm, clutching each other.

As they ate the beautiful dish and sipped some very chilled white wine, mostly in a contented silence, both enjoying a bit of post-coital bliss and the warm night drawing in, Karen surprised Flynn by asking, 'Do you want to check out the villa they took you to?'

'I wouldn't mind, but I don't have transport because the cops still have the Patrol.'

'Let's drive up in mine. They won't know it, will they? You could at least see if someone is still there.'

'You sure?' He looked quizzically at her.

'Yeah . . . I want to help you with this. I'm part of it in some way, so yeah,' she shrugged. 'Let's do a drive-by tonight . . . now.'

'It's at the end of a cul-de-sac, you can hardly drive past.'

'I'll drive, you keep your head down on my lap . . . oh, you've already done that, haven't you? Well, you know what I mean,' she smiled with mischief.

Eventually all the customers were herded out of the Tawny Owl. They left unwillingly but good-naturedly and Henry locked the front door behind them. It was shortly after midnight as he turned the key in the lock, and he knew he was ready for sleep.

Alison and Ginny were behind the bar, cleaning up. It was one of Alison's insistences that the bar area was left pristine each night, all the glasses washed and dried, all the shelves restocked.

Donaldson was sitting by the fire which was slowly dying in the grate, looking through the books Henry had brought home.

'Let's do a once-over through the premises, if you don't mind,' Henry asked him. 'Then a nightcap by the fire?'

'Sure, pal.'

Fortunately, and unusually, there were no overnight guests, so Henry and Donaldson could check each bedroom and lock the doors. They crossed paths a few times during this process and ended up back in the bar. Luckily Henry got there just before the shutters were pulled down and locked.

'Nightcap?' he enquired hopefully of Alison. She gave him one of her stares; he came back with his best boyish grin, the look designed to melt any female heart, he believed misguidedly. Not impressed, she relented anyway. 'You'll ruin me,' she said.

'Already have . . . JD for me,' Henry said. 'Karl, what's your poison?'

'Same.'

Alison started to pour the drinks when the front doorbell rang.

Henry cursed, looked at the clock and exchanged glances with Donaldson, who moved swiftly to the bow window and peeked through a gap in the curtains without twitching them.

'It's a woman,' he hissed.

Henry sidled in behind him and peered over his shoulder. It was a woman wearing a duffel coat with the hood up, her face hidden in the shadow. Neither man could identify her.

Henry leaned in front of Donaldson, pulled the curtain back and tapped on the window. She turned to the sound and Henry said, 'We're closed,' exaggerating his lip movement to get the message across.

She flipped back the hood and said, 'I know.'

Henry's eyes narrowed. He recognized her, but she was out of context here and for a moment he could not place her. Then it clicked. 'Bloody hell, what's she doing here?'

'Who is she, Henry?' The question was from Alison, who had joined the men at the window.

'Marion . . . Marion Lang . . . she's just been brought into the murder team to go through the CCTV footage.'

'Better let her in, then,' Alison said.

Karen drove, Flynn alongside her in the old Fiat Panda, out of Puerto Rico into the hills and arriving at the entrance to the small estate of executive villas. It should have been gated and secure, but the metal gates were now missing and had been completely removed since some idiot had driven through them in a stolen car a couple of nights before. The twisted remnants of the gates were stacked on a landscaped area by the road.

Karen drove slowly into the cul-de-sac, past each driveway.

Flynn glanced into the one from which he had borrowed the Lamborghini and saw that the sports car had now been returned – but not repaired. Its front end was as mangled as the gates it had crashed through.

He cringed, wondering how much the damage would cost to repair. More than he earned in a year.

Karen slammed on the brakes and said, 'Is that the car you escaped in? The one we saw in town, smashed up?'

'Might've been,' Flynn admitted.

'Wow – way to go,' she said, impressed.

'I'm actually not proud of causing thousands of pounds' worth of damage to an Italian supercar.'

'You'd be less proud having your ashes scattered.'

'Fair point . . . the villa is the last one on the right.'

Karen drove up to it.

It was in complete darkness and a sign in the garden, which Flynn didn't recall seeing there on his previous visit, announced the property was for up sale or rent.

'I think they borrowed the place,' Flynn deduced. 'Unofficially.'

'Let's have a look.' Karen yanked up the handbrake and switched off the engine. She reached over and grabbed a flashlight tucked in behind the passenger seat.

'We need to be careful,' Flynn warned.

'There's nobody here, you can just tell . . . no car in the drive, no lights inside or out, all the blinds drawn . . . it'll be OK.'

Astounded by her sudden reckless bravery, Flynn clambered out and followed her up the driveway, but suddenly the darkness lifted as security lighting came on at ground level, illuminating the whole of the villa and the grounds.

'Shit,' Flynn said.

'Be OK – bet no one challenges us.'

Flynn looked around the garden and pool area, remembering it well. He went to the door through which he'd escaped, found it locked. The two of them walked around the outside of the house, checking that the other doors at this level were also locked. They were.

Karen stopped at some patio doors overlooking the pool, blinds drawn up behind them. 'The locks on these are usually rubbish,' she said. She handed the flashlight to Flynn, then tugged at one of the sliding doors; it moved slightly in its grooves. She gave it a shake and it rattled loosely in its frame.

'Are you a burglar?' Flynn asked.

'Let's just hope the place isn't alarmed. Bet it isn't.' She stepped right up to the door, put her shoulder to it, took hold of the handle, braced herself, then pushed, lifted and pulled at the same time. There was a click, the door slid open and no audible alarm went off.

'Clearly you should have been,' Flynn said, lighting her face by angling the torch beam up under her chin. She smiled eerily.

She slid the door further open, pushed back the blinds and, taking the torch from Flynn, flashed it into the bare, unfurnished room beyond, then entered with Flynn at her shoulder. There was nothing in the room and they crossed to the inner door, which opened into the hallway that Flynn had run through on his way out. To his left was the door that led to the pool area, to his right was the door to the room where he'd been held captive. Diagonally opposite were the stairs.

Flynn turned right to the room at the end of the corridor and opened it. Karen flashed the torch and Flynn said, 'This is where I woke up strapped to a chair and looked into Jack Hoyle's face.'

The plastic sheet was no longer there. Flynn took the torch from Karen and shone it around the room; he saw no indication of what had happened in here. It had been cleaned up.

He went out, Karen at his heels, and walked to the foot of the stairs where he found a light switch and flicked it on, looked up the steps to that first small landing.

Karen gasped behind him.

'Is that blood?' Karen asked, seeing the smeared red on the wall at the first landing where the man Flynn had shot through the chest had slammed backwards and slithered down on to his backside. The man was gone but the evidence of his probable death was still there.

'Yeah,' he said, 'it's blood.'

Marion Lang, thirty-eight years old, single, admin worker, was a very frightened woman. She was on a stool by the dwindling fire in the bar, Henry opposite her. Donaldson and Alison were at the bar, chatting in low tones.

Frightened, Henry thought, was an understatement.

Terrified was closer to the truth.

She had removed her duffel coat and now sat primly with her hands clasped on her thighs, a coffee on the table in front of her.

She had a pretty but sad sort of face, hair pulled back tightly in a bun. Henry knew she had been with the constabulary for twenty years, mainly doing admin work, and had applied for HOLMES training to liven up her dreary job a little by being drafted on to major incidents and murders. From that she had also developed a skill at reviewing CCTV footage, which required a certain mind-set that most detectives didn't possess. Henry had used her before, which is why she was brought in on this murder following the chase through the streets as Woodcock pursued Hawke. She was a quiet, conscientious person, very suited to spending hours sifting through footage, and Henry liked people like her on investigations.

'I hope I haven't made a mistake here,' she said, mouse-like.

'In what way, Marion?'

'I always go the extra mile, you know?'

'Yes, I know . . . that's why you're on this investigation.'

'People said I could trust you, Mr Christie. I hope I can.'

'Of course you can.'

'Only I was going to tell you something earlier, then DCI

Woodcock went into your office and you seemed very friendly towards each other.'

'We're colleagues and we get on,' Henry said, wondering where this was going.

'Can I trust you?' She raised her face defiantly.

'Yes you can.'

She pursed her lips, then seemed to come to an inner decision. 'As you know, I've been looking at the CCTV footage following the supposed chase on foot – you know, when DCI Woodcock was supposed to be chasing that man who killed the couple?'

Henry nodded but winced inwardly at the word 'supposed' being used twice. It did not bode well. He said, 'There are no cameras in Exchange Street, though.'

'No there aren't,' she agreed. 'But that didn't stop me looking through all the footage from all the other cameras in the area, just to see if I could spot the man, or someone like him, either before or after this foot chase. I go the extra mile, like that.'

'You're a valuable asset to the team,' Henry said genuinely.

She primped proudly at the praise, but then her forehead creased and concern crossed her features.

'What's up, Marion?'

'I hope I'm not going to regret this,' she said.

'It's obviously something vital,' Henry said encouragingly. 'Coming all this way out here at this time of night.'

'I think it's vital, but if you and he are proper friends, then I've had it.'

'Me and the DCI?' Henry asked. She nodded. 'We're not mates, but we are colleagues. I'm his boss, just like I'm your boss. So what's going on?'

She had a manila folder with her which she had placed down by her stool. She picked it up and held it between her hands. 'These are some stills I've enhanced and downloaded from a council CCTV camera on Dickinson Road – timed just a few minutes before the DCI started chasing that man who, oddly enough, never gets found. Also there's a DVD in there that I've downloaded too.'

'OK.' Henry was now feeling concern.

She opened the folder and took out a photograph and gave it to Henry. The time and date stamp confirmed what Marion had just said and the image was perfectly clear.

'I've worked in the Field Intelligence Office for the last two years and I recognized this man.'

Henry stared at the photograph and ground his teeth. It showed DCI Woodcock standing on the kerb by an open car door. It was a Vauxhall Insignia, and Henry knew this belonged to Woodcock. He was talking to another man whose face was turned away from the camera, which was obviously at the top of a lamp-post somewhere nearby. Henry looked at Marion. 'I can see the DCI, but I can't ID this other man.'

Her hand dipped into the folder and withdrew another photo. On this one the DCI was looking away from the camera, showing the back of his head, whilst the man he was talking to was looking the opposite way, now facing the lens.

'Who is he?' Henry asked, even though he knew the answer.

Marion's mouth clamped shut, then she said carefully, 'This is the trust bit. People tell me you're incorruptible but that doesn't mean to say you won't protect your colleagues and, in so doing, screw me – or worse.'

'You can trust me,' Henry reiterated. 'What is this man's name?'

She handed him another photograph. This time both Woodcock and the other man were facing the camera. 'Roland Barclay.'

'Yes,' Henry confirmed. 'You're right, it is.'

'But I do not know if there's any significance in this. A DCI meeting a villain on the streets – it happens.'

'And two minutes later the DCI is chasing another bad guy on foot.'

'Mm,' she said doubtfully. 'I've scoured all the footage regarding that and I'm certain if what DCI Woodcock had said was true, somewhere I would have spotted the man, because I'm good at what I do and, based on what he said, the man should have appeared somewhere on foot – but he didn't. That said, I don't know if the DCI talking to this man is of any interest or if I'm just being silly.'

'Do you have film of the whole of this meeting?' Henry asked. She nodded. 'So what happened?'

'There was a lot of finger pointing from the DCI, who grabbed the other man's jacket at one point and shook him; then the DCI got into his car and drove away. A minute later he was chasing the suspect – allegedly. Barclay crossed the road, probably into Walker Street, and then he was gone. If I had time I could probably track him further.'

'Thanks for bringing this to my attention,' Henry said formally.

'Ahh.' Marion tilted back her head and regarded him cynically. 'End of story, eh?'

'Well, to be fair, there might not be anything to this,' Henry said.

'So I've wasted my time?'

'No you haven't,' Henry said. 'What exactly do you know about Barclay?'

'Thief, con man, burglar, has a violent streak. I know he's assaulted some of the old people he's burgled.'

'Do you know anything else about him?'

'Should I? I just brought this to your attention because I felt uncomfortable with it . . . Just didn't feel right.' She shivered. 'They just seem so chummy at one point, then at another the DCI's angry and shakes Barclay.' Her shoulders fell. 'But maybe it is nothing. Maybe he's just an informant or something.'

Henry held up a hand – the number one stop sign. 'Actually this is important, Marion, and you've done the right thing, but you probably don't know why. Roland Barclay was found dead in his flat in South Shore this evening; you probably haven't heard.'

She rocked forward, shocked, her hand covering her mouth.

'It looks like he died from a shotgun wound.'

'Did he kill himself?'

'No – I think Archie Astley-Barnes killed him in a burglary that went wrong. Barclay managed to get home, but died from his wounds . . . and, Christ! There's something else I've remembered, too.' He shut up, then said, 'You've done a brill job here and you can trust me to get to the bottom of it.'

She beamed delightedly.

And Henry sifted back through his brain. Earlier that day, after visiting the home of Scott Costain's girlfriend Trish in the posher part of South Shore, he'd been returning to the MIR in Donaldson's Jeep along Lytham Road. He saw himself talking to Jerry Tope in the back seat, then swivelling around to face the front and seeing a car pull up at the junction with Severn Road.

Woodcock's car.

EIGHTEEN

Henry was back in the MIR at seven the following morning, jumpy as hell, a horrible sensation running through him. No one else was in and he drifted around the room looking at the timelines and charts he and Woodcock had helped to put together in relation to the double murder. He spent a good long time looking at the mug shot of Hawke that Donaldson had sent him, comparing it to his own e-fit of the guy, which was very close to the real thing. Henry looked into Hawke's eyes, the eyes of a true killer. A professional hit man – but not in the sense of the Jackal; his was a sordid world of back street killing. He swallowed at the memory of just about evading Hawke's bullets and then stepped even closer to the mug shot to look even more deeply into those soulless eyes, wanting to know what drove a man like that on.

'Murdering bastard,' he thought. He was a guy who did it simply because he enjoyed it and was well paid for it.

So why was he here in the UK, killing Percy and Lottie? Just what had Percy got himself involved with? Henry's gut feeling told him he wasn't far from the answer, even though it was still eluding him. Once it all started to unravel it would be quick, he thought.

'Not long now,' he said to Hawke's photograph, and tapped his own nose.

'Talking to yourself, first sign of madness,' a voice came from behind him.

Henry didn't turn. 'Yeah, I'm pretty mad,' he said, and only then did he turn and look at DCI Woodcock. 'Mad at myself, mainly.'

'Why's that, boss?'

'Tell you soon.' He and the DCI were standing across the office from each other and Henry tried – in vain – to look into his eyes, but he was too far way.

'What did you want me to come in early for?' Woodcock sounded edgy.

'Just wanted to run through the Roland Barclay thing with you. I know it's probably going to be straightforward, but I just want to get it all right in my mind so I can concentrate on Percy and Lottie and I don't have to think about it while I hunt this sack o' shit down.' He flicked his thumb at Hawke's picture. 'Come into the office.'

The two men went into Henry's office. Henry sat at his desk, poured two coffees from the jug and pushed one over to Woodcock, who reached for it gratefully and sat down.

'I'm sure it will be straightforward,' Woodcock said. 'I'm sure the bloods will all match and there'll be other stuff to put Barclay at Archie's house . . . bastard.'

'Yeah, I agree,' Henry said, feeling his voice shake.

'You OK, boss?'

'Fine . . . another late night, just basically knackered, I guess.'

'Yuh, know what you mean.'

'I didn't really get a chance to ask you yesterday, but have you ever had any dealings with Barclay?'

Woodcock's face screwed up as he considered this. 'Nah, can't say I have.'

'Ever locked him up?'

Woodcock thought about that one, too. 'No . . . course I knew of him . . . petty con man, basically.'

'When did you last see or speak to him?'

Woodcock fidgeted and took a hurried sip of coffee. 'I don't know . . . ages, I suppose. Can't remember.'

'Oh, right,' Henry said, feeling dithery and nervous. He nodded sagely, wondering whether to pounce or play. 'Where did you get to about three o'clock yesterday afternoon, Pete?'

'What do you mean?'

'You know . . . when I went out to deliver that death message from Gran Canaria, where were you?'

'Here, sorting stuff,' he stated.

Henry pouted, then said, 'No you fucking weren't. You left the MIR after I'd gone up to Shoreside and came back after I returned, then went to the post mortem.'

'Henry, what the hell is this, the Spanish Inquisition? I went to the canteen, grabbed a bite to eat. That OK?'

Henry could sense Woodcock's panic beginning to escalate.

'Right, Pete, let's just start this again: where . . . were . . . you? Simple.'

'What? What is this? I went for a sandwich.' His hand gestures were starting to betray his worry and uncertainty.

'Try again,' Henry said, breathing down his nose. 'I'm very patient – up to a point.'

'I don't know what you want me to say. Sorry, I was out of the office getting a butty, mate.'

A shimmer of cold steel ran down Henry's spine. 'Don't call me mate,' he said chillingly.

'OK, sorry . . . boss, then. Look, what is this? Do I need my solicitor?' He laughed at his feeble joke.

'I've done a bit of checking through this year's custody records – you know, the actual paper ones that go into the binders, the ones that get actually written on, that say what happens to prisoners in custody.'

'And?'

'Roland Barclay has been arrested three times this year . . .'

'Not by me!'

'No, you're right there, but on all three occasions he was interviewed by you, wasn't he? And then released without charge. I haven't had time to listen to any tapes, but I imagine they won't tell me very much.'

'Fuck, you must have got in early, Henry. Did you wet the bed?'

'Actually, don't call me Henry, call me sir.'

Woodcock leaned back in his chair, his face a stony mask now.

'When I say so, and not before, I want you to turn round and look at the wall behind you and the photographs on it. Now, go on, look.'

Woodcock eyed Henry, then turned slowly and took in the six A4 size photographs Blu-tacked to the wall. Each one downloaded from a CCTV camera and each one showing a slightly different frame of Woodcock and Barclay in conversation on a Blackpool street. His eyes widened and Henry said, 'Taken yesterday, just minutes before you supposedly spotted Hawke on the street and gave chase on foot.'

'I did chase him.' He spun back, furious. 'What the hell is this?'

'Fuck the chase,' Henry said. 'You saw and spoke to Roland Barclay yesterday, didn't you? Don't even think about lying.'

'Well OK, so what? He's a local toe rag. It's what detectives do, talk to scrotes like him on the street.'

'D'you want to tell me where you were when I went out yesterday to deliver those death messages? And don't say "the canteen" again.'

'It's all I can say.'

'All right, make yourself look a dick. I saw you pulling out of Severn Road in your car when I was being driven past in Karl's Jeep – then you came in after me.'

'What were you doing near Severn Road? I thought you were up on Shoreside.'

'One of the death messages was at a house in South Shore.'

Woodcock looked slightly nauseous.

Henry sniggered and said, 'Right, let me have a punt at this. Barclay is a seasoned distraction burglar. He cons old people into letting him and others into their houses and steals from them and if it goes wrong, he assaults them. He has convictions for this, as you know.'

Woodcock watched Henry as blandly as he could.

'He was arrested earlier this year for committing offences like this, purporting to be from the council. You interviewed him and he walked every time without charge. What did he say to you to get out? What relationship did you form with him? Was he the one who knew an old bloke who had shed-loads of diamonds in his house, but also a shotgun? Who only let in people he knew – and cops?'

'Pure speculation,' Woodcock said, shaking his head. 'There just wasn't evidence to charge him.'

'But you were intrigued, weren't you? A bit of research on your part, find out he was talking about Archie, who had previously been hit by bogus officials, and as you look through the crime reports – as I did at three this morning – you learn the old guy suffers from Alzheimer's disease and has a memory like a goldfish. Which means, bless him, he's a rubbish witness. And it also means you can waltz in there, flash your ID, spin the poor guy a yarn and then dump him on Pointer Island in Lancaster while your new friend steals his diamonds. How does that sound?'

'Preposterous.'

'You know, I like it when suspects move from outright denial to using words like "pure speculation" and "preposterous".'

'I bumped into him in town, yeah, I'll have that – but the rest, nonsense.'

'"Nonsense" – another good word. And yet you didn't bother to tell me you'd seen him earlier when we were both looking at his dead body. Why was that?'

Woodcock shrugged.

'But you went to his house earlier, didn't you? When I saw your car coming out of Severn Road . . . bearing in mind that Severn Road is covered by CCTV cameras.' Henry smiled thinly. 'He was already dead then, wasn't he?'

'How could you possibly know that?'

'I went to his post mortem at three thirty this morning. It's the pathologist's best guess that Barclay died sometime between being shot and about two p.m. yesterday. One of the shotgun pellets severed an artery in his leg. He managed to get home and probably died as soon as he got there.'

'You've been busy.'

'I still am, Peter. You know I like opening oysters.' Henry made a show of checking his watch. 'A support unit team with two detectives will be waking up your wife, just about now.'

'You bastard!' Woodcock lurched forward threateningly.

'Is she lying there adorned in diamonds?'

'You leave her out of this.' Woodcock then threw himself across the desk and his outstretched hands went for Henry's throat. Henry rocked sideways, half-expecting the assault. Woodcock missed and slid across the desk, scattering all the paperwork as Henry shot out of his seat, twisted and grabbed the back of Woodcock's jacket and, using his momentum, hauled him over the desk and flattened him on the floor. He dropped onto his back and pinned his head to the floor with his hands.

'Archie had flashes of clarity, didn't he? Sometimes everything was there for him, wasn't it?' Henry demanded through grinding teeth. 'He clocked you, didn't he, when you went to see him, because you were the one who dumped and robbed him, weren't you? And all this bollocks about chasing Hawke was just that, wasn't it – bollocks? You made all that up because you couldn't risk me going round to see Archie again and him fingering you, so while we chased fucking shadows around Blackpool, Barclay paid Archie a visit and beat him to death – unfortunately for him, he got shot too.' Henry slavered as he spoke these words whilst holding Woodcock pinned to the ground. 'I can't believe I called you mate. You're a disgrace, and all I've said is right, isn't it?'

Tears formed in Woodcock's eyes. He crumbled. 'Yeah, yeah.' This was much to Henry's relief because a lot of it had been conjecture as much as anything, although it was also based on reasonable suspicion and he knew he could justify putting the allegation to

Woodcock if necessary. All it needed was wheedling out . . . prying the oyster open.

Shaking with fury, Henry rose off him, out of breath from the brief but intense moment of exertion. He pulled Woodcock to his feet just as a whole bunch of faces crammed into the office doorway – Jerry Tope, Marion Lang, Karl Donaldson, a detective superintendent from FMIT and the chief superintendent of the division. They had all been waiting nearby and listening to an audio link that had been quickly fitted to Henry's office and piped through to another office.

'You OK, Henry?' Donaldson asked.

'Yeah, yeah,' he breathed. 'Can someone drag this disgrace of a cop over to the cells?' Henry addressed Woodcock. 'I'm arresting you on suspicion of the murder of Archie Astley-Barnes, also the theft of property from him.' He cautioned him and then said, 'Will I need to arrest your wife, too?'

Woodcock shook his head. 'It's all me.'

'OK.' Two uniformed PCs came in and took Woodcock away.

Henry exhaled a long, stuttering sigh, and perched on the edge of the desk. His eyes searched out Marion, with whom he had – professionally – just spent the night. She smiled shyly at him and he gave her a nod of acknowledgement. She backed away as the others crowded into the office

'Well done, Henry . . . always like to weed out the bad apples,' the chief super said and patted him on the shoulder.

'Cheers, boss.'

'Let me know how it goes . . . in the meantime I'll bring the chief up to speed and contact the IPCC.' He then left.

The other detective superintendent, by the name of Alan Mercer, one of Henry's FMIT colleagues, said, 'I'll take it from here, H.' He slapped Henry on the shoulder and left. It would be his job to see this through and Henry knew him well enough to trust he would do a brilliant job.

'Tough one,' Donaldson said.

'Bit of a tester,' Henry agreed.

Jerry Tope had also been up all night, having been roused by Henry at an ungodly hour to assist with the research. He looked curiously at Henry.

'What?'

'Severn Road doesn't have CCTV.'

'I know that, but he doesn't have to know, does he?'

Tope shrugged unsurely.

'There are other cameras in the area that will have picked up his car about the time I saw it . . . it's sortable if it becomes an issue, which it won't.' He smiled tiredly, then said, 'I'd better get across to the nick and book him in, then give Al everything I've got.'

Flynn was also up early wanting to catch Eduardo down at Puerto Base; he had said he would be having breakfast at a café on the waterfront. He had told Flynn to see him there early because he had to take a fishing party out at eight and would not be back until six.

Flynn found him dunking churros into thick hot chocolate, sitting at a table outside a tiny café, so small that it was easy to miss. Flynn ordered the same and sat next to the old guy and began dunking and consuming what could only be described as an awesome breakfast.

After his first mouthful, Flynn said, 'La información?'

Henry returned to the MIR two hours later and sat at his desk, after putting back everything that had gone flying when Woodcock had lunged at him. He was thankful that he had a skeleton because his whole body wanted to drain away and it was only his bones keeping him from becoming a gooey liquid.

'You might want this, boss.' Marion Lang came through the door, bearing a steaming mug of coffee and a sandwich crammed with crispy bacon.

'Wow. I am very grateful.' He sipped the coffee.

'Sorry to have ruined your night,' she said meekly.

'Yeah – don't do it again,' he joked. Then, 'Look, well done. Following your instinct is usually a good thing and it took guts. Hey, you should come to the Tawny Owl one night soon, have a proper night there – on the house. Bring your boyfriend, or whoever.'

'Really?'

'Absolutely. I'll fix it up.' He glanced past her shoulder. 'And the queue begins.'

Tope and Donaldson were at the door, Tope armed with a manila folder, his weapon of choice.

Marion gave Henry a nice smile and left, the two men coming

in and closing the door. Tope laid the file reverently on Henry's desk.

'William – Liam – Costain,' he announced.

'Hit me,' Henry said.

Tope and Donaldson took seats. Tope began. 'Ex-IRA enforcer, suspected of many killings in the bad old days of the Provos. Moved into organized crime when the peace treaties were signed and the IRA crumbled like the Berlin Wall. Now into protection rackets, prostitution. Suspected of people trafficking and drug smuggling. The Northern Ireland police were hot on his wheels, so to speak –' Tope grinned at his joke – 'which may be why he's shifted over here. He has US connections from way back when various factions and people over there supplied the Republicans with money and weapons.'

'Nice fella. Presumably all directed from a wheelchair?'

'For the last fifteen years, yes. Took a bullet in the spine after a big falling out between gangs, and was paralysed from the waist down.'

'So, too much heat over there, comes over here and, what? Starts to direct Costain family operations?'

'Could be,' Tope said.

'And marries Cherry? She'd kill him if she mounted him, if there is anything to mount.'

'Anyway, that's him in a nutshell and maybe that doesn't help anything as such, but this might. As you know I've been checking on Percy's recent trips abroad, to the Canaries and Florida.'

'And we know that in Florida Percy spent time on a fishing boat belonging to Giancarlo Fioretti, who I've also been researching further,' Donaldson said.

'Go on,' Henry urged him.

'His history is linked to gun running for the IRA and money laundering, but many years ago. He's suspected of being Costain's main US connection back then, a relationship that probably survives to this day, *and* Fioretti is suspected of people trafficking. And Jason Hawke, of course, is one of his enforcers, has been for over ten years.'

Tope and Donaldson exchanged glances. Henry said, 'There's more?'

'Like I said,' Tope explained, 'I've been looking into Percy's travel arrangements. As regards the Canaries I couldn't get much, except that he stayed in Puerto Rico at one of the big, posh hotels. Florida, though . . . I unearthed Percy's and Lottie's travel visas and also looked at the passenger manifest for the flights they took. A Virgin flight from Manchester direct to Miami. On the visa application they were required to state where they were staying and they gave the address of a villa in Key West.' Tope looked at Donaldson.

'Which belongs to Fioretti, who, as you know, also owns *Silverfin*, the sportfishing boat.'

'Brilliant,' Henry said.

'There's more,' Tope said. 'The passenger lists – which, incidentally, I *haven't* seen, if you get my drift.'

'You hacked into Virgin Atlantic's website?'

'Merely paid it a flying visit. Anyway, flight out, flight back.' He took two sheets of paper from the manila file and slid them over to Henry, who spun them round. They were simple lists, about two hundred and fifty names on each in alphabetical order, with the flight numbers at the top.

Two names were highlighted quite close to the top of each list: Astley-Barnes, Percival Aldous and Bowers, Charlotte. Henry nodded. 'And?'

'Start reading,' Tope encouraged him.

'These are two very long lists,' Henry whined.

'I had to read them,' Tope muttered. 'Anyway, you don't have to read too far.'

And he didn't.

Running his finger down the first list, the flight out, he stopped abruptly under the letter 'C'. Quickly looking at the return flight, he also stopped at 'C'.

'Costain, William Sean.' He raised his head. 'Our Liam?'

Tope nodded. 'I also cross-checked to the passports, which are scanned on departure and arrival. It's him. I found his visa application, too.'

'Where, exactly,' Henry said, 'did you find these documents?'

'Erm . . .' Tope hesitated and glanced guiltily at the FBI employee sitting alongside him. 'Probably best not to know at this stage – but don't worry, I covered my tracks as ever.'

Henry scowled and Tope went on quickly, 'The address on Costain's visa application was the same one that Percy and Lottie stayed at, in Key West. Fioretti's.'

Henry held up a finger. 'Let me get this straight – Percy and

Lottie go to and from Florida on the same flight as Costain. They stay at the same address, which is owned by a Florida gangster, and now they're both dead, killed by a hit man working for that gangster. On top of that, Liam Costain has bought diamond jewellery from Percy's shops?'

'So it would seem.'

'And then, Percy and Lottie also visited Gran Canaria, where Scott Costain came to a sticky end – although they were both here, and dead, when that happened.'

Tope nodded.

'And Steve Flynn gets locked up for that murder and his ex-partner Jack Hoyle is also tied in somehow, because he's in one of Lottie's photographs.'

'Except that I know Flynn has been released without charge. He texted me,' Tope said.

Henry took this in and said, 'Whatever. But for some reason Percy had got himself involved with some very scary people. Looks like he got the heebie-jeebies, maybe chickened out, then got whacked.' Then something struck him. 'Hang on,' he said. He snatched up Lottie's digital camera and found the photograph with Jack Hoyle in the background. There had been something in the bottom corner of the picture that Henry could not quite work out before – but now he knew what he was looking at. He zoomed in on that section where he had seen something that had resembled part of a bicycle wheel.

He turned the camera outwards to Tope and Donaldson. They leaned to peer at it and the expression on both their faces changed at exactly the same time.

'Part of the wheel of a wheelchair,' Henry said. 'I know it's not proof of anything but I think it's time to visit our ex-IRA man and wheel him in for a long chat and if he won't talk, I baggsie leaving him on the beach at low tide.'

NINETEEN

'Let's just keep it as low key as we can,' Henry said. They were in Donaldson's Jeep making towards Shoreside, the American at the wheel, Henry alongside and Tope in the back seat. Henry was half-turned, speaking to Tope over his shoulder. They had left the major incident suite, but instead of threading through the streets Henry directed Donaldson on to Yeadon Way and they were travelling out of the resort on the two mile stretch of road that linked the centre of Blackpool directly to the M55 motorway. Built on the former Blackpool to Kirkham railway line, it is a tight stretch of road, funnelling in motorway traffic on to a single carriageway road, one lane either way. For much of its length there is no way for vehicles to escape or swerve sideways because of the concrete walls on each side of the road. Henry thought that it would be just as quick to get to Shoreside by nipping down Yeadon Way and coming off at the first motorway junction – Marton Circle – getting on to the estate from there. 'There's a section van on standby at Tesco,' Henry went on, 'so when we're ready, I'll call it in and we can lift Costain into the back and whizz him down to the nick.'

'It's a definite arrest then?' Tope asked.

'Oh yeah,' Henry said with certainty.

'Gotcha, boss,' Tope said, then made Henry jump by pointing past him through the front window of the Jeep. 'Speak of the devil.'

Henry spun forward and immediately saw the black Mercedes-Benz Viano with the blacked out rear windows that had been parked outside Costain's house on Shoreside on their previous visit. The vehicle whizzed by in the opposite direction, towards the resort, Cherry at the wheel, no one in the front alongside her. It was impossible to see if anyone else was in the back.

'Bugger – think she saw us?'

'Dunno,' Donaldson said.

'Follow her. If Liam's in the back it'll save us putting him in a police vehicle.'

They were about halfway along Yeadon Way, concrete walls either side. Because of traffic flow there was no way of spinning the big car around, except dangerously. Donaldson indicated their position.

'Up to the roundabout and come back,' Henry said.

Donaldson nodded, floored the accelerator and the three litre engine growled with power. At the roundabout with the stainless steel sculptures in the centre of it he went all the way around, the car swaying on its soft suspension, then he put his foot down again.

There was no sign of Cherry and the Merc. Henry told Donaldson to come off at the junction with Waterloo Road, which was in South Shore.

'Wonder where she's headed?' Donaldson mused.

'Unless she's taking him shopping, they might've gone to the club,' Henry speculated. This was the one in South Shore where Runcie Costain, Liam's son, had been murdered. It was the only place Henry could think of.

'Why would she do that?' Tope asked.

'I don't know, do I? Just guessing. If they're not there, we'll get a patrol to sit on the house until they get back.'

Henry turned to Donaldson. 'It's the place that belonged to John Rider – remember?'

'Do I?' Donaldson said with emphasis, pursing his lips. He knew the place because he and Henry had uncovered a gun running racket operating from the place many years before that had ended up very unpleasantly indeed. The 'John Rider' Henry referred to had been killed in a shoot-out in the pub.

'Runcie Costain took it over a while back,' Henry explained, 'but when he came to grief it never reopened . . . at least I don't think it did, unless it's under the radar. Let's just check it anyway. No harm done now. Remember where it is?'

'Think so,' Donaldson said. He swung the Jeep over the railway bridge at Waterloo Road, then dropped on to Lytham Road, turned left, then third on the right – not too far from Severn Road – on to Station Road, leading on to Withnell Road where the club was situated.

Turning into it, there was no sign of the Merc. Donaldson drove down the road towards the promenade, past the club, a huge building set amongst the terraced houses. Way back it had once been a casino; it had always remained licensed premises of sorts since and had not suffered the ignominy of being converted to flats like so many other buildings in Blackpool had.

'Go to the bottom, turn left, left again,' Henry told Donaldson, who complied, driving back up Osborne Road and glancing down the alley that ran at the back of the club. That was where they spotted the Mercedes, which was effectively blocking the alley, parked at the back gates of the club.

Donaldson pulled in to the kerb a little further on and said, 'What now, boss?'

'Let's go and say hello.'

Donaldson nodded, as did Tope – but with far less enthusiasm.

Henry dropped out of the Jeep, the other two behind him, and walked into the alley.

Henry stopped abruptly. His right arm shot out, stopping Donaldson and Tope, then he herded them into a doorway at the back of a yard.

He had seen Cherry slide open the rear passenger door of the Merc and look inside, not having seen the cops. She then pulled out and extended a metal ramp from the open door and Costain appeared in his wheelchair, rolled down the ramp and through the double gates into the yard at the rear of the club.

Cherry was still leaning into the Mercedes, saying something to someone inside, although it was impossible for Henry to hear her words or see who they were directed at because of the darkened glass.

He remained tense, hoping Cherry wouldn't glance his way, but he knew his luck couldn't hold.

Cherry gestured to whoever was in the car to get a move on. Her body language showed irritation and annoyance. Then she reached in and hauled out a slim young Asian female, who was trying to pull her arm away from Cherry's grip, but without success. Cherry dragged her out of the car and into the back yard, but just before she went out of sight she had a quick look around and saw the three men.

Her face registered dismay.

Henry set off at a run, not remotely liking anything he was witnessing here. Something terribly wrong was happening and even as he started his run his mind was telling him, *trafficking*.

He heard Cherry yell something – a warning – and Henry ran faster, spinning into the yard to see Cherry forcing the girl through the back door of the club, screaming at her to get in and pushing past Costain who, in his wheelchair, was obstructing the door.

Cherry shouted, 'There!' She turned and pointed at Henry, then stumbled past Costain with the young girl.

Costain seemed to panic, grinding the joystick control of his wheelchair around as though he was mixing food with a pestle and mortar. The wheelchair jerked backwards, then jumped forwards, the front wheel spinning, then back again and the whole contraption became jammed in the doorway, the electric motor whirring frantically, and smoke began to rise from somewhere underneath the chair, near to the battery. A flame licked up through the spokes of the rear wheels and Costain started jerking around like a marionette in a panic.

'Get me out of this,' he screamed, 'get me out of this.'

Henry slowed to a deliberate walk, a smile on his face, Donaldson and Tope behind him.

Costain saw what was happening. 'You bastards – get me out of this feckin' contraption.' He tried to heave himself up with his arms and throw himself out of his chair, a cloud of black smoke surrounding him, a thin flame licking up between his useless legs.

Henry gestured for Donaldson and Tope to help the old man out. They grabbed his upper arms and lifted him out between the two of them, light as a tailor's dummy. As they raised his bottom from the seat, something clattered to the floor between the chair and the footrest.

Henry picked up the little pistol Costain had had hidden under his legs and looked at it closely as Donaldson and Tope held the withered old man up between them. The weapon was definitely for real, small though it was, probably a .22, Henry guessed, his knowledge of firearms a little hazy these days.

He waved it in front of Costain's face and said, 'What's in the club?'

Costain, suspended between the two men like a onesie on a washing line, pulled his lips back into a snarl and then spat at Henry, the globule of drooling spittle hitting him on the chest. The expression on Costain's face turned to one of victory at this.

'Nice man,' Henry said. 'What am I going to find in there?' he asked Costain, gesturing with the gun to the club.

Costain's eyes then bore into Henry's as though he had the devil behind him. 'Hell on earth,' he growled.

'What shall we do with him?' Tope said.

'Hold him here and call the van . . . I'll go and see what delights await.' He turned.

The wheelchair was well alight now, flame and smoke filling the doorway to the club. Henry went towards it and hitched his toe under the footrest and tried to drag it out whilst leaning backwards at an angle and wafting the smoke away with the gun. He managed to edge it forward enough to give him a gap through which he could sidestep inside.

The club that had once belonged to John Rider and had fallen, via a series of sales, into the nefarious hands of the Costain family had indeed not suffered the indignity of being converted into flats for out of work people. Instead it had become something much more dark, brutal and squalid. On the first floor, a series of fifteen small rooms no bigger than police cells had been created by inserting thin dividing walls lower than ceiling height, and furnishing them with grubby beds and cheap canvas wardrobes. More sinister, steel securing rings had been drilled into the walls, to which chains and manacles were attached.

Two days later, Henry could still hardly believe what he had stumbled on. The end result of a people trafficking operation in which thirteen young women from various backgrounds and countries worldwide had ended up, via William Costain, as prostitutes in Blackpool. Some had been chained to their beds, some not. All were drug users, having had addiction thrust on to them, living a life of sheer, brutal purgatory less than two miles from the house he owned on the edge of Blackpool. It was something like a horror film, thirteen women raped and abused many times, every single day, by people who lived in Blackpool or visited the resort for just that purpose.

At least Henry had freed them from this terrible existence.

But he knew this was only the present batch. Many others had been before, used, abused, then sent on to other locations. Hundreds, Henry believed, had been through this system, the destruction of which had now become the focus of his life. It was a business worth thousands of pounds a week, millions a year.

And the investigation – which had caused an international media frenzy – had only just reached the point where Henry, as he sat down to interview Cherry for the sixth time, was able to say, 'Tell me about Percy Astley-Barnes.'

Of the two prisoners, Cherry was the only one talking. Liam Costain said nothing at all and hid behind a wall of solicitors and complaints of police brutality.

Cherry was a different kettle of fish and sometimes she was so garrulous it was hard to shut her up, but she was fighting for her freedom, and although she claimed her only role in proceedings was just to look after the girls, Henry suspected it went much deeper than that. He would play her and eventually find out the truth.

'What about him?' she said.

The tape was running, recording everything.

'Everything,' Henry said.

Cherry sniffed up. 'He had nothing to do with all this,' she said. 'He came to Liam with some half-baked information about diamonds and Liam, being who he was, couldn't resist a sparkle.'

'What information?' Henry asked.

'Percy's in the diamond business, yeah? He hears stuff and there's a rumour that a shedload of blood diamonds on a boat bound for some dealer in Amsterdam got wrecked off the coast of Gran Canaria in a storm. Percy reckoned he'd done his research, knew where the boat had gone down but needed a backer to finance a dive to find it . . . it was believed that the diamonds were in a security box and could have survived the accident.'

'Blood diamonds?' Henry said.

'Conflict diamonds or whatever. I didn't even know what the fuck that meant really . . . apparently they're from West African diamond mines, used to finance terrorism or wars by being sold through legit markets in the West . . . I dunno . . . anyway, Percy thought he knew where they were, hooked Liam with the story . . . but then, fuckin' stupid Liam, being Liam, did a shitty thing.'

'Which was?'

'Got Percy drugged up, then videoed him screwing one of the Asian girls, thinking it would make him loyal, give him power over him . . . instead it put the shits up Percy, who panicked and threatened to blow the whole trafficking thing out of the water. He said some things he shouldn't, Liam got mad and – bang!'

'A hired killer does the rest?'

'Something like that.' She shifted uncomfortably. 'Liam couldn't afford that to happen.'

'Why did Percy go to Florida with Liam?'

Cherry looked quickly at Henry. 'You know about that?'

Henry tipped his head. 'I'm presuming that was before Liam's shitty thing?'

She nodded. 'I didn't go, but I know they visited Liam's contact over there, some Italian guy called Fioretti. I've never met him. He's the one Liam's in the people business with, been in business with him for ages, right back to his IRA days when he was gun running for the republicans. He was going to put up the finance for the dive on the wreck – well, him and Liam were.'

'That would have cost a lot.'

'Not in comparison to the possible end result . . . Percy thought there would be about four million pounds' worth of diamonds down in the drink . . . twenty, thirty grand upfront to dive on it is nothing. There'd be enough for everyone, and Percy was planning to put his share back into his business – which, if you're interested, is going tits up – and he was going to sell the rest of the diamonds on the market for the other two. Truth is Percy wouldn't have got anything anyway. If the diamonds were there, Percy would have ended up with a bullet in the skull anyway, I reckon. People like Liam and Fioretti do not share, certainly not with people like Percy, and Percy hadn't got a clue what he was getting himself into. Naive idiot.'

'OK . . . and this killer, Hawke? He works for Fioretti?'

Cherry nodded and Henry said, 'For the purposes of the tape, the interviewee has just nodded.' He didn't really need to say it because it was being videoed as well.

'And Hawke was brought over from America especially to kill Percy?'

'Yes. We don't have any contract killers on our books,' she laughed, then stopped sharply on Henry's hard look.

'And poor Lottie, Percy's girlfriend . . . ?'

'Collateral damage?' Cherry ventured.

Just like he would have been. 'Where is Hawke now?'

'I don't know and telling you would be nuts, even if I did.'

Henry squinted, trying to work it all out. 'So what was Scott Costain doing out in the Canaries and is his death connected to all this?'

'Oh yeah. He went out for a recce . . . but someone was there already, diving where the wreck is supposed to be. Whoever it was musta whacked him and Trish.'

'Who do you think that was?'

'Not sure, but Liam's been putting all this together and he thinks someone overheard him and Fioretti planning when they were out in Florida and decided to go for the diamonds first. He reckons the only time that could have happened was when they went out on a fishing boat owned by Fioretti and maybe one of the crew members was working for someone else and passed the info on . . . nobody's sure.'

Henry visualized the face of Jack Hoyle in the background of Lottie's photograph, wondering if it was him and what his connections were with organized crime in Florida. Interesting ones, he thought. But where the hell was Hoyle? So far, with Karl Donaldson's help, the FBI in Florida had been trying to trace him but no one had seen him in Key West for a few weeks and certainly not on the *Silverfin*. Rumour was that Hoyle was double-crossing Fioretti by acting as a double agent for some other nameless hood out there and feeding that person any information he could glean from conversations overheard on board the boat which, it seems, Fioretti often used for planning criminal activities, well away from snooping Feds. Instead, it was his own staff snitching on him.

'Who's Jack Hoyle?' Henry asked.

Cherry stared blankly. 'No idea.' Henry believed her.

Henry took all this in, the first real interview about Percy's death, knowing there was much more to learn and that he would get to the bottom of it and would finally destroy the criminal enterprise that was the Costains. If it was the last thing he did before retirement.

'So why did Liam come over here from Ireland?' he asked Cherry towards the end of this particular interview.

'Too much heat over there, wanted to whip the Costains into shape over here. Big plans to turn them into something international . . . would've succeeded if you hadn't turned up when you did.'

'I doubt it,' Henry said. 'And why did you marry him, Cherry?'

Cherry gave a long, deep sigh, rested her head sideways on the palm of her hand and said wistfully, 'Fucked if I know.'

The interview went on for much, much longer but in the end there had to be a break and, as Cherry was taken back down to the cells, Henry's head was swimming with it all. In his jacket pocket, he felt his mobile phone vibrate. He took it out and saw the caller was unidentified. He half-thought of not answering, but did.

'Henry Christie,' he said.

'Henry Christie,' came a voice he knew well. 'How the hell are you?'

'What do you want?'

'You still interested in Jack Hoyle?'

'Why?'

'Because at this very moment in time,' Steve Flynn said, 'I'm looking right at him but, get this, he has no idea that I'm here.'

TWENTY

H

e had been watching for three days and nights from the second floor apartment in which he'd been ensconced with Karen.

The information from Eduardo, the old sailor, had been correct. *Destiny* was moored in Puerto de Mogán, almost under Flynn's nose, as Mogán was the next port along the coast from Puerto Rico. Eduardo had told Flynn the boat had sailed in from Lisbon seven days before and was registered to a boat hire company in Lagos, on the Algarve. That was all the old man knew, but it was enough for Flynn. He'd found the boat.

After Eduardo had passed Flynn the information, he and Karen drove over to Mogán and, after checking out the marina and finding that *Destiny* wasn't in, they spent the day mooching arm in arm like real tourists and lovers through the market lining the fisherman's quay, and eating and drinking at a few of the bars and restaurants that lined the port.

Destiny motored in smoothly at five that evening. Flynn and Karen had been able to watch her tie up from the cover of one of the restaurants, sitting at the back of the terrace behind multi-coloured bougainvillea and trailing geraniums. From that position, though, they had only been able to watch the boat's activity from a discreet distance but they saw two divers cleaning their equipment, then leaving the boat in a battered four wheel drive.

'Hired help,' Flynn said to Karen.

That left two people on board and Flynn, who could now see properly through one recovering eye and one good eye, recognized Jack Hoyle and one other man, unless there were others who had not shown themselves.

Flynn and Karen dawdled in the restaurant for another hour, happy in each other's company but tense from the situation, particularly when Hoyle and the other man, looking as if they had showered and changed, hopped over the side of the boat and began walking towards them. Flynn flipped the cost of the meal on to the table and he and Karen exited via the back of the restaurant, on to the tight, pretty streets of the port, which was known as Little Venice.

'What are you going to do?' she asked him.

'Kill him?' Flynn suggested.

At that, Karen stopped him dead and swung him around to face her. 'Flynn!' she admonished him with one syllable and the look in her eye.

'OK, I won't kill him, even though I want to. But I want to know what he's up to.'

'So keep an eye on him?'

'How, exactly?'

'Just above the restaurant is an apartment for rent. That would give you a good view of the marina . . . maybe?'

And for the next three days and nights, Flynn had been sitting just inside the sultry apartment watching the comings and goings of *Destiny*.

Jack Hoyle and the other man were staying on board and the two divers arrived at nine each morning. They sailed at ten – Hoyle at the helm – and were gone until five each day. Flynn guessed that they were out on the water near GuiGui where he had first encountered them, searching for whatever it was they believed to be down there.

He wasn't certain what he should do for the best, apart from wanting to come face to face with Hoyle again. Problem was, Flynn was intrigued by what was going on, wanted to know what they were searching for, and he knew that the best policy – instead of running at the problem like a bull – was to chill back and watch for any change in behaviour when they returned to port that might indicate a 'find'.

On the third day, Karen – despite having enjoyed spending time with Flynn – said, 'Enough's enough, Steve. We both have to get back to the real world so can't we just let this be, now? Adam's constantly texting me and he's getting frantic for *Faye* to be available, even though it's pretty quiet.'

Flynn took his time considering her words, knowing they were sensible.

It was just after five p.m. and both were on the balcony of the apartment when *Destiny* smoothly entered the marina from her day at sea. They watched her moor, the boat controlled expertly by Hoyle, the divers acting as crew. They went through the usual rigmarole, cleaning the diving gear, then the two divers leaving for the night. Flynn had discovered they were staying in an apartment in Puerto Rico, so they definitely were hired help.

When they had gone, Hoyle sat on the deck of *Destiny*, relaxing in the declining heat of the day, his head tilted back. Flynn wondered if he had killed Costain and the girl – and was pretty sure that was the case.

Karen was watching Flynn carefully, still waiting for his response, hoping he would see sense and back off.

Instead, he picked up his mobile phone and called Henry Christie.

Henry could not quite keep the look of disbelief off his face as he listened to Steve Flynn recount the story of his last week on earth. Flynn had only agreed to tell Henry (almost) everything on the understanding that it was all off the record and if Henry repeated any of it, he would simply deny ever saying a word.

'So what it boils down to is that you were picked out of the blue by Scott Costain to take him on a trip where you then bumped into a boat full of people who took pot shots at you; then you were kidnapped by Jack Hoyle and escaped somehow,' Henry said dubiously, 'and then just happened to walk into a double murder scene.'

'Nutshell,' Flynn said. Then, to lighten the moment, and poke a shitty stick at Henry, he said, 'And how is the lovely Alison?'

He enjoyed seeing Henry's face scrunch into annoyance. Henry knew Flynn had a bit of a thing for Alison and suspected the pair of them shared a secret that, in some way, would bond them for the rest of their lives.

'Let's just keep on target, eh? You've dragged me all the way out here, told me this pretty silly tale and, pleasant as it is to sit here, I don't see Jack Hoyle.'

On receiving the call from Flynn the day before, Henry had taken a chance and booked a flight to Gran Canaria due to leave Liverpool at six the next morning, with a return flight for the day after that. Not finishing work until after ten, Henry had hurtled up to Kendleton, where the Wild Geese were providing a disintegrating level of protection for Alison, but two of them who were not drunk promised to stay overnight. Henry threw some items into a rucksack, then drove down to Liverpool airport, arriving there at two, and crashed out until he stumbled tiredly on to the plane, where he fell asleep again with his chin on his chest.

He landed at Las Palmas at ten thirty a.m.; there he was picked up by Flynn in Karen's Fiat Panda and driven to Puerto de Mogán. In spite of the weather, the drive was frosty right from Henry's first comment, which had been, 'This better be good.'

Henry's mind had been swimming with exhaustion and, as nothing was spoiling, Flynn had shown him to the spare bedroom in the apartment where Henry stripped off, climbed into the slightly musty bed and fell asleep.

Just before five that afternoon, having had a boccadillo and a long cold beer, Henry was sitting with Flynn and Karen on the balcony, looking towards *Destiny*'s mooring. Flynn had explained how this point had been reached.

'He'll be here soon,' Flynn said confidently, 'and when he does turn up, what are you going to do?'

'Make sure it is him first, then tell the police and have him arrested.'

'On what grounds? I'm only surmising that he had something to do with Costain's death.'

'I have an arrest warrant with me,' Henry revealed, 'just in case. Suspicion of theft of a million pounds. Got it signed by a tame magistrate last night. You reckon he took that drug dealer's money, so let me speak to him properly about it. Anything else can be addressed when he's locked up . . . such as murder. Will that do?' Henry did not wish to expand on this and tell Flynn anything about Hoyle being photographed on the same boat as two murder victims, or about four million pounds' worth of diamonds that could be in a chest in a wreck off the Gran Canarian coast. That wasn't his business to know.

Flynn's face creased with a smile of pleasure. 'Nicely.'

'Now all we have to do is wait for him to show up.'

'He'll come. We saw him sail out this morning.'

Destiny did not return to port at the usual time. This made Flynn start to fidget and exchange glances with Karen, who tried to give him reassuring looks. Nor was the boat there at six p.m., or seven p.m.

'Talk about wild geese,' Henry muttered at one stage.

They ate a meal of spaghetti bolognese, accompanied by chilled water, at the restaurant below the apartment, little conversation passing between the men.

'She's here!' Karen said at last, breaking the tension and pointing to *Destiny* as she entered the marina and was manoeuvred gently into place by the jetty. Although darkness had fallen, she was clear to see under the bright lighting of the port.

The first thing that struck Flynn was that it was the man who had been with Hoyle, rather than the two divers, who dealt with securing the mooring ropes. Previously it had been the divers who had done all the hard work required when bringing a boat in, but this time Flynn couldn't even see them. He knew they had gone out on the boat with Hoyle that morning.

'Odd,' he said quietly.

When the boat was moored, he expected to see the divers cleaning off their equipment with the hoses as they had done on every other night. There was no sign of them at all.

Karen had noticed this change too. She exchanged a glance with Flynn and said, 'I don't like this.'

Henry looked at them both. 'Like what?'

'Divers this morning, no divers tonight,' Flynn said. He stood up and walked a short way down the road and peered into the car park behind the block, then returned and sat down. 'Their car is still parked up,' he said, then, 'There's Hoyle.'

Henry looked and saw a man on the deck of *Destiny*, leaning over and looking at the water for some reason. The man then looked in their direction, put his hand over his eyes to shade them, then turned away and went into the boat.

'That's him,' Henry confirmed. 'He's still got a plaster over his nose.'

'Oh yeah,' Flynn said, recalling the head-butt.

'I wonder where the divers are,' Karen said. 'I think I'll walk to the end of jetty and have a look, tourist style,' Without giving either of the men time to disagree, she stood up and sauntered along the crowded jetty, past *Destiny*, stopped at the end and looked into the water like many of the other tourists did, then strolled nonchalantly back and sat down. 'No sign of any diving gear,' she said.

'It was there this morning. Shit,' Flynn said. 'Something not right here.' He looked at Henry. 'D'you want to pay him a visit?'

'Only after I've briefed the local cops.'

'What?' It was Flynn's turn to scrunch up his face.

'I don't want to screw anything up procedurally,' Henry bleated, 'otherwise he could walk. You're jumping to conclusions here, thinking something bad has happened. Maybe he's dropped the divers off somewhere else.'

'Tell you what, Henry,' Flynn said, rising from his seat. 'I'm going to have my moment with that bastard now. Know why? Because I counted four out and only two have come back and that tells me something.'

'What?'

'They've found what they're looking for and they've killed any witnesses.'

He pushed away the table. Henry shot up. 'That's a hell of a conclusion . . . let's get the Spanish cops here, then go in,' he said.

Flynn had a think about it, then shook his head. 'Nah.' He turned to go just as a long limousine drew up across the road and the back door opened. A short, very dark-skinned man dressed in a silk shirt, black silk trousers and Gucci loafers climbed out, said something to the driver of the limousine, then started to walk along the jetty.

Henry took hold of Flynn's arm and pulled him back behind the bougainvillea, then spun quickly around himself when a big hand clamped down on his shoulder. Karl Donaldson and another man were standing behind him.

'Siddown, guys,' Donaldson said to Henry and Flynn. Both men complied, Flynn doing so without hesitation. He knew Donaldson, had met him on a few occasions and knew his match when he saw it. All the men and Karen sat back at the table.

'What're you doing here, Karl?' Henry said. He hadn't seen or heard from his friend for a couple of days but knew he'd been working on the American connections from his office in London.

'That,' he said, pointing to the man walking confidently along the jetty towards Hoyle, 'is Ronnie Brinscoe, and he is the man who we believe owns Jack Hoyle, the one financing the parallel deal to bring up the diamonds, hence *Destiny* and the divers.'

'Diamonds!' Flynn blurted, and shot an accusatory look at Henry. 'They're after diamonds? What diamonds?' His eyes narrowed. 'Did you know this?' he demanded. Henry just opened the palms of his hands in a gesture that said, *yep*.

'How did you find this out?' Henry asked Donaldson, not caring too much about Flynn's feelings.

'By field agents talking to people, being detectives . . . it happens, y'know?' Donaldson explained. '*And* we have a guy in Brinscoe's organization, which helps. Brinscoe and Fioretti are at loggerheads over every single piece of turf from Fort Lauderdale to Key West. Seems Hoyle is Brinscoe's man in Fioretti's set-up. He overheard

Costain and Fioretti talking while out fishing and pitched the whole thing to Brinscoe, who let Hoyle run with it, hoping to find the diamonds first.'

'Why is Brinscoe here?' asked Henry.

'To oversee things? We're not sure, but we couldn't get an agent to follow him from the US, so I hopped on a plane this morning from Gatwick, teamed up with this guy here –' he jerked a thumb at his companion – 'Jamie, down from the FBI Madrid office.' Henry nodded at him. 'Heard you'd headed south and I guessed our paths might just cross.' He raised his eyebrows, smiled, then turned to Karen and said, 'Ma'am,' very courteously. She just stared back at the very good looking man with her eyes all a-goggle.

'We think something may have happened today,' Henry started, seeing Flynn roll his eyes in disgust and mouth the word '*we*?' Henry ignored him and continued, telling Donaldson about the divers – or lack of them – concluding, 'It looks odd, according to Flynn. Their car is still here.'

Donaldson took it all in, said, 'It would be very nice to pay these guys a visit while they're on board.' He looked at his colleague. 'What are the chances of getting a Spanish team together qui—'

His words were interrupted by the sound of six gunshots from the far end of the jetty. Three double taps.

Sometimes, Hawke thought, you had to take the chances that were presented to you. Especially when served up on a plate.

He knew all about the diamonds and their possible value if they were ever found at the bottom of the ocean (which he doubted), and that his boss Fioretti would love to get his hands on them and let them sprinkle through his fingers. His boss would absolutely love that . . . but he knew something else he would love even more: the brutal death of his main rival, Ronnie Brinscoe, a guy Fioretti hated with a vengeance. And if he could get the diamonds as well, even better, but getting diamonds from the sea bed was not his job. His job was to kill people on his boss's orders – which is why he had come to Gran Canaria after leaving the UK on a false passport.

His job here was to hunt down the people who had killed Scott Costain and his girlfriend, and also the people employed by Brinscoe who had already started searching for the diamonds. Hawke knew they were one and the same and were using a motor cruiser called *Destiny* – information that had come from Scott Costain before he was killed – so it was simple for Hawke: find *Destiny* and then everything else would slot into place.

It hadn't taken him long, using the internet, a few phone calls, a chat with a few people, including an old salt in the marina in Puerto Rico who, for a few drinks and a handful of euros, had happily told him that *Destiny* was moored in Puerto de Mogán. The only downside to that particular conversation was that the old man admitted someone else had asked him the same thing, but then claimed he didn't know who that guy was and that he hadn't told him anyway. Hawke didn't have the time to follow that up.

Hawke had been in Mogán for two days now, having booked into a hotel some way back from the waterfront, but he had seen *Destiny* arrive back on that first evening whilst eating a nice meal at a restaurant that looked directly down the jetty where she moored.

He'd watched the divers leave *Destiny* and then, later, two other men – one of whom Hawke instantly recognized as Jack Hoyle, the English guy who basically ran Fioretti's sportfishing boat out of Key West.

Hawke kept his face down over his food as Hoyle and the other man walked past within feet, and up into the resort. Hawke followed them and watched them walk into a restaurant to eat. He later followed them back to the boat, where they bedded down for the night.

Next morning he watched the divers arrive and climb aboard *Destiny* and sail out of harbour. He killed the day by driving up to Las Palmas where, in the back streets, he easily sourced a 9mm handgun and twelve rounds of ammunition, which would have to be his weapon for this particular job. He'd had to leave his kit back in the UK, where, he'd learned, things had really gone badly for old man Costain and his girlfriend when the cops busted them. Hawke only hoped there wouldn't be a backfire into his boss's operation in Florida, as the two were closely linked.

Not his problem.

That evening he chose a different restaurant to eat at on the waterfront, which had a slightly different view of *Destiny*'s mooring. But the boat did not arrive until late, and without the divers, a fact that put a cynical grin on Hawke's face. Instinctively he knew they were dead divers.

He waited for Hoyle and the other man to leave the boat, because he'd decided that he would take them both out just as they waited for their table at whatever restaurant they decided to eat at. His car was only a dash away and he would be gone. Just keep it simple and fast.

The arrival of the limo threw that plan into disarray, especially when he saw who stepped out of it. None other than Ronnie Brinscoe. Hawke had to make himself breathe normally at the sight of the guy in his silks and slippers. A new plan – if it could be called a plan – formulated instantly in his brain and he was up, walking towards the jetty, shouldering his way through the strolling tourists who, unwittingly, would be his cover.

He was working it through as he stepped on to the jetty.

He needed to time it so that he was right behind Brinscoe at the moment he was alongside *Destiny*. The time when his back would be visible to Hawke. Hopefully the other two, Hoyle and the other guy, would be facing him. Like a little trio. Hawke was working it out – Brinscoe first, two to the back of the head. Double tap. Bang, bang. Then even before he fell, instantly taking out the others, head shots, still from a close distance. And that would be it, over in two, maybe three seconds. Turn, then walk – not run – through the tourists, head low, toss the gun sideways into the water, use the cover of the shock and chaos. Kill and go.

He should never have raised his eyes, even once. But he did, and as Henry scrambled through the tourists, following Donaldson, Flynn and the other FBI guy towards the sound of the gunshots, some rushing towards him to escape whatever had happened, others rushing towards it, he saw the one man walking away who didn't quite fit, the one with his head down, the one not panicking or excited and, maybe because there was some almost spiritual connection between the two of them, this man and Henry looked into each other's eyes across the jetty and neither one of them could disguise the instant recognition.

Hawke hadn't disposed of the gun. It was still tucked down the waistband of his pants at his lower back, his hand still gripping it as he walked away from the scene of death. He drew it and pivoted towards Henry, dropping into a combat stance, but was buffeted by a female tourist who saw the gun and screamed. Hawke smashed the gun across her face, knocking her brutally out of the way, brought the weapon back to aim again at Henry – but all he saw was a blur of speed, Henry charging low across the jetty, moving faster than he had ever done since he had played rugby for the county.

Hawke couldn't re-aim in time and Henry powered low into him, his bad shoulder connecting with Hawke's gut, sending the air out of his lungs, then driving the both of them, locked together, over the side of the jetty into the icy embrace of the water below, hitting the surface hard, grappling as they went under. The gun flew from Hawke's grip.

They fought violently in what was immediately pitch blackness beneath the surface, each scratching the other, each trying to grip the other, and then they shot up, wheezing for breath. Henry knew then that he was going to struggle badly here. They broke apart for a moment, but then Hawke went for him and took him under, managing to get his right forearm around Henry's neck and pull him down, at the same time crashing his forehead into Henry's temple, curling his legs around Henry's hips and clinging to him like a monkey, using the strokes of his left arm to take them both under again.

And of course he didn't have to strangle Henry – that would have been counter-productive, actually to constrict his throat. He wanted to drown him, so he gripped on just tight enough so that Henry's mouth was open and the cold Atlantic water, tinged with diesel from the boats, went down his gullet.

Henry fought, squirming manically, unable to get free, feeling his strength sapping from him, trying to prise Hawke's arm from around his throat, but it wasn't happening, his lungs involuntarily sucking in sea water, which started to saturate them.

He knew he was going to die here and had almost accepted that fact when, for the second time, he shot up to the surface, free from Hawke's grasp, splashing madly with his arms, coughing and choking horribly as he retched and breathed at the same time.

He reached out and wrapped his arms around a stanchion under the jetty, then looked around and saw Steve Flynn's head bob to the surface about a dozen feet from him. Alongside him was Hawke. Flynn was holding Hawke's shirt by the collar, but Hawke wasn't moving. His face was still in the water, his body lifeless.

Using the lifesaving stroke, Flynn paddled across to Henry dragging Hawke in his wake.

'You OK, mate?' Flynn asked Henry, who still had water cascading up his throat and down his nostrils.

Henry made a snotty gurgling noise that meant *yes. Thank you.*

*   *   *

Henry looked up as Flynn sat down at the restaurant table and the two men eyed each other warily for a few seconds.

It was one hour later. In front of them, the jetty had been cordoned off and beyond the barriers there was a lot of intensive police activity, but not much to see now, as several screens had also been erected to hide the horror that had taken place from prying eyes.

None of the bodies had been moved, even Hawke's, which lay where it had been dragged on to the jetty like a huge fish. Further down there were three more bodies, all killed by gunshots to the head. Somewhere in amongst the police activity were Donaldson and his FBI colleague, and a Spanish detective called Romero, who was in charge of proceedings.

'Thanks again,' Henry said.

Flynn held up his hand. 'Enough. I just leapt in and dragged him off you and then he went for me, so I just held on tight.' He shrugged and smiled. Henry nodded. 'So, Henry, you going to tell me what all this has been about?'

Henry was about to speak when they saw Karl Donaldson duck under the cordon tape and walk towards them, accompanied by a Spanish cop and carrying a box of some sort.

He came up to them and placed the box on the table. Henry looked at it. It reminded him of an old-fashioned biscuit tin, but instead of jolly Victorian street scenes on it, the metal was rusted and discoloured.

Donaldson said nothing, but prised the lid off to reveal its contents.

'These,' Henry said, 'are what this is all about, and they have cost far too many lives . . . may I?' he asked Donaldson, who nodded. Henry dipped his hand into the tin and picked up a handful of raw, uncut diamonds which he then allowed to dribble through his fingers.